Don't Dare a Dame

Maggie Sullivan mystery #3

M. Ruth Myers

Published by Tuesday House

ISBN:0615965075
ISBN-13:978-0615965079

This book is a work of fiction. Names, characters and incidents are products of the author's imagination or are used fictitiously. Any resemblance to actual events or persons, living or dead, is entirely coincidental.

Cover design by Alan Raney

ALSO BY M. RUTH MYERS

– Maggie Sullivan mysteries –

No Game for a Dame
Tough Cookie

– Other novels –

The Whiskey Tide
A Touch of Magic
A Journey to Cuzco
Costly Pleasures
Friday's Daughter
Captain's Pleasure
Love Unspoken
An Officer and a Lady
Insights
A Private Matter

ACKNOWLEDGMENT

I would like to thank Jack Barstow
for generously sharing family photographs
and memories
of his grandfather, Rudolph F. Wurstner.
Chief Wurstner served as Dayton's chief of police
throughout the Maggie Sullivan era
and was the nation's longest serving
chief of police.
He was an innovator
and an amazing individual.
He's also the only "real" person
to appear in the Maggie Sullivan mysteries.

ONE

Two old maids who wanted to hire me had asked me to tea, so I'd treated my nails to a fresh coat of raspberry pink and put on a hat that matched and a Smith & Wesson that didn't.

Usually clients came to my office, but this afternoon I was glad to escape downtown Dayton. People had gone nuts over the 1939 World Series, crowding around the *Daily News* building to wait for the wire service boys to lower a sheet displaying the latest score out a window. Ten minutes away, the tree-lined street where I'd parked my DeSoto was lazy with autumn. I went up the steps to a square red brick house and turned the doorbell.

"Listen, you dope, you need to come back later," the woman who yanked the door open said in a rush.

"Gee, people usually get to know me before they call me a dope."

Her hand went to her throat. Her cheeks blossomed. She was tall, maybe five-foot-eight, with black hair cut in a bob. I'd seen nuns gussied up more.

"Oh! I'm so—. You must be the - the private investigator. Miss Sullivan."

"Maggie. Please."

"I do apologize. There's... a neighbor boy who's a pest. Won't you come in? I'm Corrine Vanhorn."

The tension in her manner seemed excessive for a pesky kid, and her gaze was fixed beyond my right shoulder. As I stepped inside I took a quick glance back. All I saw was a street so quiet I caught the thump of a black walnut falling.

Inside, a shorter woman with permed brown hair hurried to meet us with hand outstretched.

"Miss Sullivan, do forgive me. I had a phone call. Work. I'm Isobel, the one who spoke to you this morning."

The parlor she ushered me into made it obvious the Vanhorn sisters didn't have to pinch pennies. It didn't shout wealth, but it conveyed substantiality. An upright piano in one corner glowed with polish. In front of a spotless fireplace, matching needlepoint sofas and a couple of chairs surrounded a low table. The other furnishings were arranged somewhat severely around the perimeter. To my way of thinking, it made the room feel uncomfortably large. Then again, I lived in a rented room and the only stick of furniture I owned was my dad's armchair.

By the time I'd settled on one of the needlepoint couches and Isobel on the other, Corrine returned with a large silver tea tray. I was struck by the gracefulness of her movements. It wasn't just the ease with which she carried the heavy load. She seemed to glide, back straight and head aloft, without glancing left or right. As she set the tray on the table between us, it was clear she owned this room. This was her domain. Like other pairs of spinsters, she was the sister who stayed home and kept house while the other one went out to work.

This pair was younger than I'd expected. Corrine was probably nearing forty and Isobel looked several years younger. When Isobel contacted me, she'd told me she kept the books at a furniture store where she got off at noon on Thursdays, but I doubted they'd come by a place like this on a bookkeeper's salary.

"You may think it a bit odd, what we want you to do for us," Isobel began hesitantly. "Some may even think harshly—"

The doorbell rang. The sisters looked at each other.

"You *know* who it must be," Corrine said, struggling to hide her displeasure.

"You didn't reschedule a student—?"

"Of course not."

"Well, I'll get rid of him." Isobel sprang up.

Corrine set down a teacup she'd been about to fill. From the hall came the sound of an opening door, then Isobel's voice, filled with irritation.

"What are you doing here? We told you this afternoon wasn't convenient."

"Convenient or not, I'm here to get Alf's things. It's bad enough you two threw him out of his own home—"

"His *home?* This place wasn't fine enough for him, remember? He had to build that big monstrosity. Don't expect me to feel sorry now that he's lost it with more of his bad investments. We're busy—"

"Too bad."

"We have a guest. Neal, you can't come in now! Let go of me!"

Corrine sprang to her feet. I was ahead of her. When we reached the hall, a struggling Isobel was kicking ineffectually at a good-sized man who held her by both wrists. She appeared more angry than scared, but she was a little of both.

"The lady asked you to clear out," I said sharply. "I think you should."

The man's head jerked up. He was in his early forties with thin features. His eyes ran over me. They lingered more than they needed to in places.

"Yeah? Who's going to make me?"

"Me, if I need to."

"She's a private investigator, Neal. A detective."

Isobel fired the words with satisfaction. She used his stunned immobility to yank herself free. I watched comprehension seep into his eyes, followed by anger.

"You spiteful little harpies! You really did it." He rounded on Corrine, who was moving protectively toward her sister. "This is your doing, filling her head with nonsense all her life — all because you couldn't be Daddy's spoiled little favorite any more, you pathetic old hag!"

Her mouth crumpled once at his final words, but her chin lifted.

"Get out, Neal. You can come back anytime this weekend to get Alf's things. Or he can come himself."

"I'm here now — and I'm sick of your run-arounds."

He started toward the stairs that rose along the left wall of the hall. I stepped in front of him.

"The ladies asked you to leave."

Lots of men sneered inwardly at the idea of a woman who stood five-foot-two posing any kind of threat. Neal was more open.

"Keep your nose out, toots, or it might get hurt."

I hated to persuade him, but Neal seemed like one of those guys who needed taking down a peg or two. I gave him a quick little kitten jab in the snoot. Not enough to break it, just enough to start blood gushing down to his chin and get his attention. He howled like I'd attacked the family jewels, and clutched his nose.

I balanced on my toes in case I hadn't convinced him.

"Don't drip on the rug on your way out," I said.

Neal decided not to test whether I could punch any harder. With a furious look he called me a name that wasn't polite and sulked out, slamming the door.

TWO

The corners of Corrine's mouth gave an odd upward jerk that suggested delight.

"That was magnificent!" she said.

"He wouldn't have hurt us." Isobel's voice wavered. "Neal's our brother."

Both Vanhorn sisters looked white as skimmed milk.

"Why don't we go sit down so you can explain why you asked me here," I suggested.

Corrine poured tea and we sipped it in silence. She moved a stack of small china plates from the tray to the table.

"It - it has to do with when we were children," Isobel resumed. "Corrine was twelve and I was eight."

I nodded and waited. The Vanhorn sisters needed time to recover. Corrine began to slice a fancy little cake she'd brought in with the tea, pivoting her knife at the center to make each piece precise.

"As I'd started to say when Neal interrupted, others may think our interest odd, or - or wrong. But it matters a great deal to us."

Her sister handed the cake around on the china plates.

"What Isobel is trying to tell you is, we want you to investigate our father's disappearance. It was during the flood. We think — we've believed for a long time — that he was murdered."

"The flood?" I couldn't remember anything that qualified as a flood. Then it registered. "The flood of *1913*?"

I set aside the plate I'd just received, too stunned for politeness.

"By the man who became our stepfather," said Isobel. "Alf Maguire."

My mind staggered. The Great Dayton Flood of 1913 had happened the year before I was born. I didn't even qualify as one of the 'flood babies' born nine months later. These two women were talking to me about looking into something that had happened a quarter of a century ago. Moreover, they believed a man who apparently had lived in this house until recently was somehow involved.

"You say he disappeared?" I was struggling to process it. "From what I've heard, a lot of people disappeared, swept away by the waters."

"We're aware of that," Corrine said primly.

I drank some tea.

"You realize odds of finding out what happened to someone that long ago would be low, even under the best conditions."

"Yes, of course."

"And those weren't the best of conditions."

"No."

"We didn't feel we could ask anyone to look into it while our mother was alive. It would have upset her," explained Isobel. "She died last year. It's taken a while to - to sort out—"

"Our stepfather challenged her will," Corrine said bluntly. "Two weeks ago the court finally ruled in our favor."

"It was nothing but spite, Alf wanting this house. Mama left him almost everything else. The business our father owned, investments, a much bigger house. She left modest bequests to Neal and Corrine and me. And she left Corrine this house. Where we grew up."

"She wanted to make sure I was provided for," Corrine said. She sat erect and determined. "I earn a small income giving voice and piano lessons, which I couldn't do if I had to rent rooms somewhere. And Mama knew that even apart from my age, few men would be interested in a blind wife."

It robbed me of speech even more than their request to investigate something that happened during the Great Flood.

"Miss Vanhorn — Corrine — are you saying that you're...?"

"Blind. Yes." She looked proud I'd needed to confirm it. "I had measles when I was four."

Her blindness explained why most of the furniture was placed around the edge of the room. I thought of how gracefully she moved. How confidently she'd managed the heavy tea tray. I realized, too, that she hadn't been looking at something behind me when I arrived. Even now her unseeing eyes were fixed not on me, but a spot just beyond me.

"You sure fooled me," I said awkwardly.

In part to recover, I moved to questions I needed answered to help me determine if there was any good reason to start poking around on the sisters' behalf. As impressed as I was with Corrine, everything I'd learned so far made me suspect this was family grievances turned to imaginings, rather than anything involving an actual crime.

"Let's forget the tussle over this house for a minute," I said. "What makes you think your father didn't get swept up in the water and drown? There were plenty who did. I'm pretty sure some were never accounted for."

The sisters looked at each other. Except now I knew that Corrine couldn't actually see her sister. It didn't matter. Some invisible link connected them, communicating thoughts. *Who's going to tell it?* this one asked.

"A year or so before Papa disappeared, Alf started hanging around and flirting with Mama," said Isobel. "Making her laugh. Saying she looked pretty. He even brought her flowers a time or two, and sweets."

"Your father didn't object?"

"He and Alf were second cousins or something like that. I don't think Papa cared much for Alf, but you know how it is when relatives drop in."

I didn't, actually. Both my parents had left kith and kin behind in Ireland.

"Sometimes, though, Alf would stop by when Papa wasn't around." Corrine put in. "One summer — we think it was the summer before Papa disappeared — we were playing in the yard after supper. Neal was off somewhere, so it was just the two of us and our little brother Jem. No sooner was Papa out of sight than here came Alf sauntering down the street like – like he'd been watching!"

So far I hadn't heard anything to suggest murder. To buy me time to think what to say, I ate a bite of cake.

"A couple of years after Alf and Mama were married — it was summer again — Alf and this great pal of his who'd stopped in that evening came out in the back yard," resumed Isobel. "Neal and our stepbrothers George and Franklin had built a big tree house. For days they'd been lording it over us, bragging how it was just for boys and not letting us in it. Corrie had hatched a plan how when everyone else was in bed, we'd climb down the trellis and spend the night in the tree house. We'd have a good laugh at them when they came out and found us there the next morning."

"And you were up in the tree house?" I pictured a blind girl picking her way down a trellis, then climbing a tree.

Both women nodded.

"It must have been nearly midnight. We'd waited until we were sure everyone was asleep," said Corrine. "Alf and his friend must have been here in the parlor, talking and drinking. They had a bottle when they came out, and they sounded a bit slurred."

"We think they were discussing whether to make some sort of investment." Isobel swallowed. "All at once we heard Alf's pal saying 'You didn't mind taking a risk when we saw a chance to feather our nests or to make a widow of the woman you wanted.' Alf told him to shut up, what if the neighbors heard."

Corrine leaned forward, her cheeks aflame with excitement.

"The other man laughed. He said so what? There was no evidence; it had all washed away a long time ago."

"That got us remembering," Isobel said. "The night Papa went out and didn't come back. We remembered how scared we were because he'd been gone for hours, and we didn't know how high the water was going to get here. If it would come into the house. If we'd have to get on the roof. We wouldn't leave Mama's side, and all at once there was this pounding. It was Alf, and he was wild-eyed and – and almost chipper at the same time."

"Talking too fast."

"Yes. Asking were we all okay, did we need anything? Acting odd, almost like—"

Something crashed somewhere in the house. Something that shattered. The women across from me froze.

"The kitchen." Corrine jumped to her feet. "Someone's in the kitchen!"

Her familiarity with her surroundings still was no match for sight. Isobel, who had both, shot out of the room with me at her heels.

Running into the kitchen we both nearly stumbled on chunks from a thick white pitcher that matched dishes on a utility table next to the door we'd come through. Like the parlor furnishings, the table was flush to the wall. I flung my arms out to block Corrine as she caught up.

"Broken china all over the floor," I warned quickly. The back door stood open. I headed out.

A wooden fence surrounded the back yard. At the far end, on the other side of the fence, a man in a hat was running away. I made for the gate. The lift-latch was oiled, with no trace of rust, but when I flipped it up and pushed, the gate didn't budge. I put some muscle into the effort. No dice. Either the man had pulled something up to block the gate on the other side — a trash can, probably — or he'd come over the fence. Swearing mentally at the prospect of ruining my stockings, I hiked up my skirt and prepared to climb. A blood-curdling scream behind me froze me in place.

I spun back toward the house. Somewhere along the way I'd drawn my Smith & Wesson. As I got closer, I saw Corrine kneeling in the grass beside some bushes.

"It's Giles!" she shrieked. "Merciful lord, someone's killed him! *Murdered* him! He's dead! Sweet little Giles is dead!"

THREE

She cradled a big yellow dog in her lap, a Labrador maybe. Its coat was matted with blood from the slash to the throat that had almost severed its head. Tears drenched her face. Aimless and wild and glistening with red, her hands moved from her mouth to the dog, up to clutch at her head in despair, then back to stroke the shape in front of her.

From inside I caught snatches of Isobel phoning the cops.

"Please hurry... intruder...."

"He's dead! Someone's killed him! Oh, there's so much blood...." Corrine wailed.

She shook uncontrollably. All at once her arms thrust out. They groped. They hunted frantically.

"Isobel? Isobel?" she cried in panic.

I'd seen worse gore. I'd seen worse loss. Yet witnessing such frightened helplessness in a woman who moments before and against daunting odds had been in control of herself and her world hit me in the gut.

"Isobel's inside," I said.

Corrine shrank away from the sound of my voice.

"It's Maggie," I soothed. "Maggie Sullivan. I'd come to see you, remember?"

She lapsed into sobs and petted her dead dog while my thoughts raced trying to sort it all out. Someone had been listening when the two sisters told me about their suspicions concerning their stepfather. Whoever that was must have killed the dog on the way in, presumably to make sure it didn't sound an alarm. But how had they managed to get that close? I wondered if it could have been brother Neal.

Isobel hurried out of the house.

"The police said they'd have someone here as soon as they could," she said, more to me than to Corrine. She'd had the presence of mind to grab some flour sack towels. "I'm so sorry, dearest," she murmured as she began to wipe the worst of the gore from her sister.

"I'll have a look around, see what I can find," I said.

Isobel nodded.

If anything caught my eye, I'd leave it undisturbed for the cops, but I wanted to make sure I saw it too. Whether this had to do with a man disappearing twenty-six years ago or the recent dispute over property, I had a feeling the Vanhorn sisters needed some help right now. The unnecessary viciousness with which the dog's throat had been cut bothered me.

I'd been catching glimpses of bright blue beyond some old quince bushes that blocked the view on one side of the fence. I moseyed toward it.

A head tied up in a kerchief for cleaning bobbed up to greet me.

"Is everything all right?" asked the middle-aged woman standing on tiptoe. She sounded concerned rather than nosy. One hand held a wet rag.

"Someone killed their dog," I said. That was enough information for now. "I was here visiting."

"Oh, dear!" said the neighbor. "Poor Corrine! I thought I heard someone screaming. Giles was one of those special dogs, you know. For blind people. She went away for weeks and trained somewhere when she got him. He took her everywhere. On the streetcar.... Who would do such a thing?"

"I don't suppose you saw anyone back here? Or heard anything?"

"Sorry, I was inside. Washing windows. I saw Neal come out and drive away when I was doing one of the front bedrooms, but that was quite some time ago."

From the way she said it, she didn't appear to think Neal might have been involved. We kept on chatting until I heard car doors slam. The cops were here. I headed inside.

***

What I encountered in the parlor made my jaw clench.

Corrine sat on one of the needlepoint sofas, pale and trembling. There was still a smudge of blood on her chin and the front of her dress was stained. Her hands were kneading a lace-trimmed hanky, tugging so hard the lace, if not the fabric, was likely to rip. Isobel stood protectively at her side with a hand on her shoulder.

Two detectives in cheap suits stood nearby. At least one of them was a detective, a blond cop named Boike.

The other was the north end of a southbound horse that answered to Fuller. The last I'd heard, he'd been in uniform. He stood spraddled with fists on his hips looking cocky as all get out. The jerk was yelling.

"Lady, we're a homicide unit!" he scolded Isobel. "You got us out here under false pretenses. Claiming there'd been a murder—"

"I never said—"

"Screaming about all the blood."

"I said we'd had an intruder! And that someone had killed our dog."

Corrine had a dazed look about her. She didn't seem to be hearing.

"There's a law against wasting police time, you know."

"But—"

"We come out when people are killed. *People,* understand? Not mutts."

Corrine sprang like a tiger, striking his chest with her open palms.

"He wasn't a mutt! He was pure-bred, and he was highly trained. Anyway, why does it matter what kind he was? He was my *friend!* He made me feel safe. And someone killed him, do you understand that? *Someone killed him!*"

She hit his chest again. Not hard, just frustrated smacks. Her fine aim at someone she couldn't see impressed me.

Fuller went six shades of red. He retreated half a step and stabbed a finger at her.

"You just bought yourself a charge of assaulting a policeman, missy."

Boike cleared his throat. He was a placid man who ordinarily trailed his boss, the homicide chief, and didn't get much chance to speak. "Officer Fuller—"

"Back off from her or I'll show you assault," I said stepping forward.

The little tableau noticed me for the first time. Fuller snarled.

Once at a party Fuller had waylaid me as I returned from the loo. I'd had to apply my knee where it counted to convince him I didn't like his attentions. Right now my knee was itching to pop up again.

"Hope you've had your rabies shot, Boike, the way this boyo's acting. You're a disgrace to the department, Fuller. Can't you see these women are terrified? They don't need you adding to it by being a bully. I don't know why you two got sent here, but I heard Isobel making the call. She may have said their dog was dead, but she never reported a homicide. Since you're already here, instead of complaining maybe you could trouble yourself to go out back and have a look."

I was mostly hoping Boike would take the suggestion. He did.

"Officer Fuller, you call dispatch and ask them to send someone from burglary. My apologies for the confusion, ladies." Boike tipped his hat and made for the hall like he was relieved to escape.

"I'll show them the way," I said to Isobel. "You stay with your sister."

I pointed Fuller toward the telephone on a little table in an alcove under the stairs. He was capable of walking right past it. Of all the cops on the force, he was the only one I had a beef with, not only because we'd tangled a couple of times, or because he'd once tried to frame me for murder, but because he did sloppy work.

"Those have been kicked around," I said indicating the chunks of broken ironstone as Boike and I reached the kitchen. "Looked like the pitcher they came from set on that table. The three of us were in the other room and heard the crash."

Boike nodded. He went out the back door.

"Vicious," he said squatting to study the dead dog. "Way the head's almost severed makes it look like a grudge."

"Same thing occurred to me. I got a glimpse of a guy running, other side of the fence." I pointed. "By the time I got there he was gone. Then I heard Corrine scream and turned back."

"I don't suppose you got a good enough look to describe him."

"Just saw him from the shoulders up. Had on a fedora."

Boike was eyeing the fence. "That looks like about five feet, so if you saw his shoulders, he'd be somewhere around five-ten. But as Fuller pointed out with such tact, it's not a situation where we'll be involved."

He circled the dog again, frowning.

"Where's Lt. Freeze?" I should get back inside before Fuller did any more mischief, but I was too curious. I thought I heard Boike sigh.

"Had to be somewhere else. And Graves quit, went to be chief of police in some podunk place near Columbus. So we're making do with a couple of men who might be in line for detective — him included." He jerked his thumb.

Shite. Mick Connelly wanted to make detective too, and he was as smart as they came. He worked three times as hard as Fuller. He was possibly even good-looking once you got past the reddish cast of his brown hair, but I wasn't inclined to explore that particular question.

"Fuller couldn't find his important body parts with both hands," I said.

"I know," agreed Boike glumly.

***

A team from the burglary unit showed up. They were as courteous as Fuller was rude.

"Please — won't you stay?" Isobel caught at my sleeve as I started to leave. "You may be better remembering details than we are."

Corrine looked utterly drained now. Isobel was out of her depth and upset. After what the two had just been through, it seemed like sticking around for them was the least I could do.

The burglary boys asked their usual questions, but I knew as well as the cops did that chances of anything coming of it were low. As nearly as Isobel could determine, nothing had been stolen. The women themselves hadn't been attacked. There was probably a law against killing dogs, but as undermanned as the Dayton department was, that sort of crime wasn't likely to be a priority.

I added the details concerning the man I'd seen running. As soon as Isobel got back from ushering the second batch of cops out the door, I gathered my handbag and stood.

"I think Corrie and I are too worn out to talk any more just now," apologized Isobel. "But please—will you come back tomorrow?"

I hesitated.

"Are you saying you still want to hire me?"

Isobel looked at her sister. Through that telepathy they seemed to possess, Corrine sensed it. She nodded listlessly.

"Yes."

"To look into your father's disappearance."

"Yes," they answered as one.

"I would have to bill you, even if I learned nothing at all."

"We understand. We'll pay in advance, if you wish," said Isobel.

I thought for a minute. About the dog, for one thing. Like Boike, I saw something significant in the violence with which the animal had been killed. A quick, shallow slash of the knife would have silenced it just as thoroughly. For that matter, how would a stranger know there was a dog to be silenced until it started to bark an alarm?

The direction those thoughts led disturbed me. I couldn't begin to guess what was going on, but I had no doubts that right now these two somewhat sheltered women needed someone looking out for them.

FOUR

The business with the Vanhorn sisters got to me. It wasn't just the savagery of the attack on the dog. It was also the idea someone would deprive a blind woman of an animal so crucial to her functioning.

That morning I'd dropped off a bundle of clothes at Spotts' Laundry, as I did every Thursday. On the way back to my office, I stopped to retrieve it, hoping the familiar routine and yakking with the counter girl would lift my spirits. It didn't. Since Finn's was a good place to brood, and to find the man who could maybe fill me in on a thing or two about the flood that had become a cornerstone of the city's history, I headed there.

I'd been eighteen when my dad died. Two days later, bawling so I couldn't see, I'd said good-by to the house where I'd grown up. Unknown to him, I'd had to sell it to cover the bills from his long illness. I'd walked to Finn's where an old school chum who knew the score had given me an awkward hug. Finn, the owner, had drawn me a half pint of Guinness from a barrel marked Root Beer, repeal of Prohibition still being one year away. The pub had been the nearest thing I had to a home ever since.

"Hey, Maggie," called a man at the bar that ran along the right wall as you came through the door. He drained the last of his stout. "Wee Willie here's claiming he kissed you out on the playground when you two was in the fifth grade."

"The only one likely to kiss Wee Willie in fifth grade was one of the nuns. He was their little darling."

Hoots erupted. The man with the empty glass gave Wee Willie a thump on the back that almost knocked him from his stool. Willie Ryan, who'd gotten his nickname because of his tiny stature, waggled a finger at me. We'd been slagging each other since we were old enough to tie our shoes. We'd still be doing it until one of us died. Maybe longer.

After I'd yakked with Finn and he'd pulled me a pint and then let it rest until he could give it a perfect head, I carried it to one of the tables with mismatched chairs that occupied the rest of the place. It was the time of day when regulars drifted in after work, among them numerous cops with collars undone to show they'd come off duty. I'd gone to a Swedish massage place once and come away feeling like I'd been beaten up in an alley. Sitting here while a rhythm as predictable as my own pulse seeped into me and voices I knew engaged in arguments I'd heard a thousand times relaxed me a lot better.

Maybe I didn't want to brood as much as I wanted to think. Somebody had it in for the

Vanhorn sisters. Somebody well enough known to them that their dog hadn't sounded an immediate alarm. Their brother Neal would be my pick. He didn't appear to care what happened to anyone else, just what suited him.

Then again, couldn't the same be said of my own brother?

I'd been ten and he was four years older when he took off. He'd known it would leave me to bear the brunt of our mother's scalding resentment. Not that she didn't lash Ger with the same criticism she poured on me. Occasionally, though, she'd managed a word of approval for Ger.

Maybe it was the shattered crockery in the Vanhorn kitchen that had shoved the past into my thoughts. Our small frame house. A smaller kitchen. A note wedged under the sugar bowl when the rest of us came out that morning. My father had spotted it first and picked it up. His stricken expression filled me with terror that he was having a heart seizure. Seeing it, my mother ran to him, and he held the note out. It was one of the few times I saw the two of them interact normally.

As she read it, my mother let out a scream. Dad put a protective arm around her shoulders. She shoved him away. With small, whimpering sobs she fled to the bedroom. My father's eyes were flooding with tears. When he turned to dash them away, I picked up the note that had fluttered from Ma's nerveless fingers. My brother's words scrawled over the page.

I can't stomach any more of this hell hole.
Sorry, Sis. Don't try to find me.

We had tried, of course.

I took a swallow of Guiness. It was halfway down when I felt the same current that charges the air before lightening strikes.

"I've seen happier faces at wakes," said a voice.

I looked up into steel blue eyes.

"Hiya, Connelly."

I was hoping he wouldn't sit, but he did. Mick Connelly had gotten it into his head that he was going to wear me down until I fell for him. I had to stay on my toes to make sure he didn't. It was harder at close range.

Tossing his uniform hat in a chair, he savored a deep drink of stout. His gaze was like a camera lens, capturing every detail in an instant. Right now it was focused on me.

"Bad day, was it?" With a fingertip he pressed gently on the back of my hand to survey the bruise on my middle knuckle from punching Neal.

Under pretext of lifting my glass, I freed myself as casually as I could.

"Not as bad as it was for the guy on the other end." I searched the length of the bar, though I already knew the answer. "Seamus didn't come with you?"

"Billy shanghaied him into buying a ticket to some dinner Kate's helping with at the parish. Seamus claimed the food would be worth the long-winded speaker, but I wasn't tempted."

I smiled. Officers Seamus Hanlon and Billy Leary were nearing retirement age. They'd been my father's best friends, present in my earliest memories. Billy and Connelly were partners now that a bad knee kept Seamus mostly on desk duty. Seamus and Connelly palled around a lot, though, and as often as not came into Finn's together.

Connelly had tipped his chair back, comfortable as a cat. The tiny cowlick that decorated the front of his reddish-brown hair was asserting itself.

"Is it anything I could help with?" he asked.

"Not unless you were walking a beat here twenty-six years ago."

He chuckled. Connelly probably wasn't past thirty. Not half a dozen years had passed since he'd left Ireland. Since he knew I was aware of it, my answer had stirred his interest.

"This have to do with the scraped knuckle?" he asked curiously.

I nodded. If we were going to be sitting here, talking work was safe turf. I told him about my afternoon with the Vanhorn sisters.

"Christ almighty," he said when I got to the part about the blind woman's dog. He rubbed at his chin. "Anyone know the two of them were expecting you?"

"Not when I was coming," I said slowly. I saw what he was thinking. Nothing had been stolen. It could be because the intruder realized people were home, and searching for valuables would make noise. In that case, though, why not leave? The pitcher that had broken had been next to the exact spot where someone would stand if they were listening, or if they wanted to know why the women had hired a detective.

"What about the brother? Neal, is it?" Connelly asked.

"Making a stink seems to be more his style than running away. Besides, he seemed to have a pretty good idea what they were going to tell me."

I'd already put checking what time Neal had returned to work on my list of things to do the next day. This added a slightly different reason.

"You haven't heard the worst part yet," I said. "Whoever took the call at the station heard Corrine screaming about a killing and sent the homicide unit. Which included Fuller."

Connelly went still as a rock.

"Did you ever put in paperwork saying you want to be considered when a detective slot comes open?" I asked.

He took a slow drink of Guinness before giving a nod. His face betrayed nothing.

"Too early for me be considered much, though. I haven't been on the force long enough, and I've no connections."

His mildness could be deceiving, but it rubbed me the wrong way.

"So you're just going to roll over? Watch that half-witted s.o.b. land a plum slot you're better suited for—"

He sat up so abruptly his knees connected with mine. If I drew back, he'd know the contact affected me. Unfortunately, he probably realized that was how I was playing it. He leaned comfortably over his crossed arms.

"I believe I already told you once, *mavourneen*, I don't give up on things I set my mind on. Ever." His eyes danced with amusement as they held mine.

My pulse beat faster than it should. How the devil could I face down bruisers with guns and then go dry-mouthed around this one man?

"If you're inclined to cheer me after the bad news, though, or to think a bit how we might prevent Fuller from being a fly in the ointment for both of us, I was just about to see if you wanted to get a bite of dinner."

"I can't. I already promised to go with one of the girls."

The advantage to rooming in a house with nine other women was you always sounded plausible if you claimed other plans. It would hardly even qualify as a lie if you found somebody to go with when you got home. That was nearly always possible, but mostly I didn't bother.

Connelly closed one eye and gave me a look.

"That scared, are you?"

"Don't flatter yourself." But I was scared, because he was the first man I knew I could fall for.

He drained his glass and stood. "Tells me that kiss on the Fourth of July affected you more than I realized."

Bursting into a cheery whistle, he turned and walked out, spinning his hat on one finger. He'd gone half a dozen steps before the words sank in enough that I sprang to my feet.

"I did *not* kiss you on the Fourth of July!"

Indignation raised my voice more than was prudent. Several at the bar turned to look. Without so much as a backward glance, still whistling, Connelly strolled out.

FIVE

I got to McCrory's lunch counter early enough the next morning to nab a stool on the end. As far as I was concerned, that was the prime spot. Sitting at the end meant getting cigarette smoke from only one direction.

"Thanks, Izzy," I said as a scrawny little waitress slid a mug of tea in front of me. She set off to get me some oatmeal without even asking. On those rare occasions when I wanted something different, I had to tell her fast.

The rest of the dime store was still roped off, not yet open for business, but footsteps to and from the lunch counter beat a steady tattoo on the wooden floor. The familiar sound soothed me.

Had I kissed Connelly at that rollicking party we'd both attended on the Fourth? Parts toward the end were fuzzy, and the question had kept me tossing and turning all night. Irked that it had resurfaced, I sipped my tea and focused attention on how I intended to approach Alf Maguire.

As shaken as the Vanhorn sisters had been when I left them, I wasn't quite clear on some of the details, but they'd seemed certain their stepfather could be found at a place on Haynes. An apartment, or maybe a duplex. There'd been something about a girlfriend. Whether she'd taken him in or whether he rented the love nest was one of the details that hadn't been clear, but I had the address.

My theory was that Maguire would find it harder to give me the brush-off if I caught him at home with his paramour. He'd talk in front of her rather than face her questions later about why he hadn't. He might lie through his teeth, but even lies yield grains of something useful if you sift them carefully enough. I made short work of my breakfast, eager to start.

As soon as I turned onto Haynes I began to get a bad feeling. I saw two police cars, another that I knew belonged to a hack from the morning paper, and Black Mariah, the city ambulance, which mostly arrived to find its intended passengers had died waiting. Sure enough, all the activity centered around the address I was hunting. I parked far enough back to be out of the way and walked up the street.

"What's the excitement?" I asked a uniform.

"Morning, Miss Sullivan. Looks like some fellow turned on the gas."

"Dead?"

He nodded.

"The guy have a name?"

He shrugged. It might mean he didn't know. It might also mean he had the name but knew enough not to tell anyone.

I didn't figure I'd get inside, but I started up the walk anyway. No harm in trying. The place was a

duplex, light brick. Both front doors stood open.
When I got about halfway there, Boike came out
the door on the left and closed it behind him.
There wasn't much of a stoop to come down, just
four or five steps. He reached the bottom before
he spotted me. For a second or two he hesitated,
gearing himself up before we met

"Alf Maguire, huh?" I said.

From the look he shot the uniformed cop, I knew
I was right.

"Don't worry, your boy at the curb didn't spill
anything. I was coming to see Maguire to ask him
some questions."

"My guess is he's not going to be very chatty."

"Stiffs are like that."

Boike was casting a curious eye at the artificial
flower pinned to my lapel. I didn't usually bother
with such things, but a girl never knows when a
decorative touch may come in handy.

"Questions on what?" he asked.

"This and that."

Before he could press me, the door he'd just
closed opened again, flung back in anger. Two
men clattered down the steps. One was Neal
Vanhorn. His pal was a shorter man of similar age
with a wee pointed chin like a Kewpie doll.

"...no business treating us like...." Neal was
spewing. He broke off as he noticed me. "You!" he
snapped. "You're to blame! It's your fault he's
dead — yours and those self-righteous sisters of
mine. Driving him to despair—"

I slapped aside the finger he'd thrust in my face. Boike was watching intently. Both newcomers seemed unaware of the cop's presence.

Neal's companion was working himself to a question.

"Who are—?"

"She's their private *detective*." Neal managed to squeeze in plenty of scorn. "God knows what my dear sisters are trying to dig up now that they've dragged Alf through court. Infidelity? With his wife dead almost a year?" He laughed unpleasantly.

The eyes of the men looked damp, as though they'd been struggling with tears.

"Are you one of Alf's sons?" I guessed.

"Yeah, he is," Neal cut in. "And you've done enough damage. Clear out. You're not welcome."

"Gee, Neal, do you talk for everybody?" I'd used up what little patience I had sometime yesterday. "Maybe you should be a ventriloquist, get yourself a little Charlie McCarthy doll."

Behind them, Lt. Freeze, the homicide chief, was approaching.

"Miss Sullivan," he said.

As greetings went it was on the chilly side, but it was enough to make Neal spin around.

"If you gentlemen could get to the station without delay, there's an officer waiting to take your statements," he said. Neal and his pal had sense enough not to argue. They took their leave with hands shoved in their pockets. "Boike, get one of the uniforms and start talking to neighbors. We'll meet you downtown," Freeze continued.

I noticed a man trailing him the way his assistants tended to do. Mercifully, it wasn't Fuller. This guy had olive skin and curly black hair.

"I don't suppose you'd care to explain how you happened to turn up at the scene of a death I'm investigating?" Freeze's gaze bored into me.

"Sure," I said. "His step-daughters hired me yesterday. One's the blind woman Fuller pushed around. Their own dad disappeared when they were kids. They wanted me to find out something about him. I was hoping Maguire might give me some names to start with. He and the father were shirttail relatives; spent time together."

It was the last thing he'd expected from me, a straightforward answer. Detailed, too. Freeze frowned suspiciously.

"By you being here, I'm guessing he didn't turn on the gas himself," I said.

"How did—?" His eyes shot toward Boike's retreating figure.

"Not from Boike." I gave my sunniest smile. "I caught a whiff of it."

He probably thought I meant I'd smelled gas. His nose twitched.

"You have five minutes to be on your way, Miss Sullivan."

He hadn't answered my question. He usually didn't. As I sauntered my way toward the curb the hack from *The Journal* nearly sprained an ankle reaching my side.

"What'd he tell you?" he asked. "Two bucks if you know anything useful."

"You have bad breath. Where's my two bucks?"

He didn't cross my outstretched hand with silver as I brushed past him.

***

It wasn't the first time I'd wished cars had phones in them like they did heaters. I needed to call the Vanhorn sisters to tell them Maguire was dead and the cops would most likely come calling. Going back to the office was faster than hunting a pay phone. I played dumb in the face of Isobel's request for details, knowing the women would come off better in the cops' assessment if they were genuinely shocked by anything they were told.

Once I'd hung up, I went across the street to a postage stamp-sized coffee shop just big enough for eight stools at the counter and a table for two at the back. With a mug of joe to make me smarter, I sat at the table and used a fresh page on the tablet I'd brought over to start a list of what I'd learned so far.

The list wasn't long.

– Alf had married a reasonably well-off widow, but to hear her daughters tell it, had lost a big part of her money.

– He'd had designs on the woman when she was still married to someone else.

– Yesterday her daughters had hired me and told me about an overheard conversation which might indicate he had murdered their father.

– Someone had been listening when they told me about that conversation.

– Bright and early today, when I'd gone to see Alf, he already was dead — an apparent suicide.

Was it guilt because he'd been the eavesdropper yesterday? Possibly. One thing seemed inescapable: Yesterday's incident had something to do with his death.

Despite lingering expectations this case would go anywhere, I returned to my office to type up my notes and start a list of things I wanted to check. The office work would allow extra time for the boys in blue to finish talking to Corrine and Isobel. No sense irking Freeze by getting under his feet twice in one day, even though the first time hadn't been my fault. I cranked a carbon set into my Remington and was typing away when the telephone rang.

"Miss Sullivan?" a crisp voice inquired.

"Yes?"

"Please hold for Chief Wurstner."

Before I could even contemplate a reply, the phone on the other end clacked down. I sat and tried to breathe slowly. What had I done to attract the attention of the chief of police?

The next voice I heard was stern. Uncompromising.

"Miss Sullivan? This is Chief Wurstner. You have exactly ten minutes to be in my office and give me very good reasons why I shouldn't cancel your license."

SIX

Private investigators received their author-ization to practice solely at the discretion of the chief of police. If Wurstner cancelled my license, I'd be out of a job. Getting hit in the head with a hammer couldn't have stunned me much more than his phone call.

I scarcely noticed buildings or people as I walked the few, not overly long, blocks from my place to the three-story gingerbread structure known as Market House. It was home to several of the police department's special units as well as the chief's office, and the closer I got, the more baffled I was. Admittedly, I sometimes didn't worry as much as I should about stepping on toes. And yes, when getting evidence or information seemed to warrant it, I'd sometimes opened a lock with a crochet hook instead of a key. Since I didn't remember any toes lately, nor had I indulged in any hanky-panky the law might frown on, the threat from the chief was a bolt from the blue.

Determined to show more confidence than I felt, I hopped up the stairs to the second floor. Wearing what I hoped was a pleasant expression, I

M. Ruth Myers

presented myself in the anteroom to the chief's office.

"I'm Maggie Sullivan. The chief wanted to see me."

"I'll tell him you're here." The man in the anteroom was a civilian, and his voice was just as crisp in person. He rose and tapped on the door behind him, stepping through for just a moment before reappearing. "You can go in."

Chief Rudolph Wurstner was a nice-looking man, trim with deceptively mild eyes and the straightest, firmest mouth I'd ever seen. Its faintly downturned corners suggested forbearance as well as stubbornness. He'd probably needed a good supply of both. He'd been chief since I was ten or so, orchestrating everything from raids on bootleg joints to capture of the notorious John Dillinger. His hands were folded on his desk. He didn't get up. He didn't move so much as a finger.

"Sit down."

It was an order, not an invitation. For once I felt no urge to smart off, whether out of respect for his position or because of something in the man himself. I did as instructed.

"I've heard good things about you, Miss Sullivan. Unfortunately I've also heard you disregard rules at the drop of a hat. Would you care to explain why you've been harassing not only a law-abiding citizen, but his grieving family, less than twelve hours after his death?"

I filed the twelve hours bit away to think about later.

"I have not been harassing anyone," I said carefully. "I'd like very much to know who claims I have."

The hardening of his expression told me he didn't like my answer. When it became clear he wasn't going to tell me who was grousing, I picked my way ahead.

"I'm guessing it's Alf Maguire you're talking about, since he's recently dead and I turned up there. There's not much ground to say I harassed him, though, since we'd never met. I'd never heard of the man until yesterday."

Wurstner frowned. That had caught his attention.

"Nor did I know he was dead," I continued. "I'd come to talk to him. His stepdaughters hired me to look into something involving their late father. Their dad and Maguire were cousins of some sort. I was hoping Maguire could give me names of acquaintances, that kind of thing.

"As to harassing his family, I'd never met his son either, until this morning. His stepson Neal and I had a run-in yesterday because Neal was shoving one of his sisters around. When I ask him to quit, he tried to get tough with me, too. I gave him a bloody nose."

Wurstner unfolded his hands and leaned back. The front of his thin lower lip sucked in a little, which I thought might signal amusement. His manner remained stern.

"If we check thoroughly, I assume we'll fine no discrepancy in what you've told me?" he said after he'd considered the matter.

"You will not."

"And there's nothing you've omitted telling me?"

I almost smiled. It was one of my favorite ploys, though he couldn't be aware of it.

"No."

He frowned to himself.

"I realize people who hire you do so expecting privacy," he said slowly. "Nevertheless, in deaths like this we like to make certain the circumstances were exactly as they appear. Can you tell me, in general terms, what his stepdaughters wanted you to look into? Something to do with their father, you said?"

Despite his casual words, my interest sharpened. I knew very well the force didn't automatically investigate every suicide. And what, if anything, did his question have to do with someone kicking up a stink about me?

"He disappeared back during the flood. His daughters know the odds are against them, but they want me to see if I can learn anything about what happened."

The chief of police stared at me.

"Do you mean the Great Flood?" he asked slowly. "Nineteen-thirteen?"

"Yep."

His head shook slowly.

"Merciful…. A hundred, maybe a hundred twenty, died that we know of. Swept away. Drowned. I saw. I was in the middle of it. God knows there must have been more, unaccounted for. But after all this time—"

"Exactly. I've told them they're most likely wasting their money, but apparently they've got it to spend."

His question about whether I'd omitted anything had come earlier. As I saw it, that meant it only applied to things we'd talked about earlier. Since I'd just now given him details of why I was hired, the possibility of Alf's involvement didn't count. Even if Alf had been involved, why would anyone make a complaint about me now that he was dead?

"That will be all, Miss Sullivan. Thank you for coming in," Wurstner said in dismissal.

I stood.

"So what's my status?" My throat felt tighter than usual.

Already reaching for a folder on his desk, he looked up, irritably.

"What?"

"My license?" I prompted.

"Ah." He didn't fold his hands again, and he didn't look quite as put out as when I'd entered. His mouth made a formidable line. "I don't appreciate people above me pressuring me with no more proof than I've received so far. As far as I'm concerned you're in the clear." His index finger pointed a warning. "Keep your nose clean, Miss Sullivan."

***

"They were very polite this time," said Isobel. "Much nicer than the ones who came yesterday."

"Polite!" Corrine's huff gave her own opinion. "They asked us where we were last night!"

The Vanhorn sisters were seated across from me. We each occupied the exact same spots on the needlepoint sofas where we'd been yesterday. I'd gone to their place as soon as I left Chief Wurstner and picked up my car. I wanted to hear what the police had asked them about while it was still fresh in their minds. Noting down bits of information and sifting as I went along would help me regain my focus as well. I'd been more rattled over the close call about my license than I'd been over anything in a long time.

"It — their asking about last night — made us think they may not believe Alf committed suicide." Isobel swallowed. She looked at me, awaiting confirmation.

"They always ask questions in something like this," I hedged. "It's routine. What did you tell them? About where you were?" I held my breath, braced for them to say they'd been right here. It would mean no alibi if homicide decided to take an interest in this.

"We... went to our music club." Isobel looked embarrassed. "Down at the Y. We go on the first and third Thursdays. There was a guest pianist scheduled — who wasn't very good, as it turned out — and I thought - I thought it might be good for us to get out."

Her cheeks were flaming.

"Do you think we're crackpots?" asked Corrine with a trace of her old assertiveness.

"Not that. But beyond that, I'm not sure what to think," I said slowly. "Your stepfather's death seems awfully convenient, right after you'd told me what you suspected. Who else knew about that? Besides Neal. And who knew you'd hired me?"

"Just - just Neal," said Isobel. "But he never believed... you saw how angry he was that we'd hired you. He idolized Alf. Thought he could do no wrong. He - he ended up acting more like Alf than he did our own father."

Fishing a handkerchief from her pocket, she dabbed at her welling eyes. She'd taken the day off to be with Corrine so her sister wouldn't feel the loss of her dog quite so keenly. Good thing, considering how the morning had gone.

"Neal could have mentioned it to someone," I said as she composed herself. "They could have told someone else."

That might reassure her until I had time to pick my way through the briar patch of what at first glance had appeared a family squabble. Except I wasn't very good at the hand-holding stuff. It made me feel awkward. Nevertheless, Isobel's face brightened.

"If you still want me to learn what I can about your father, I need you to tell me everything you know, or were told, about his disappearance," I said.

The sisters looked at each other.

"But we don't know anything else," said Corrine at last. "It was the second day. The day the flood was at its worst. I remember Mama saying that."

"And after the fires started," Isobel said with excitement.

"That's right!"

"Neal had gone out to catch a glimpse of the fires. Mama didn't like it, but she was frantic."

I'd taken my steno pad out and was scribbling furiously. In my teens I'd refused to learn shorthand; I had no interest in being a secretary. Now, in light of how often I needed to make notes while people were talking, I regretted that stubbornness.

"She told him not to go past Bonner, but I doubt he obeyed. Neal knew she had too much on her mind to keep track of him."

"Jem — our little brother — was sick," her sister explained. "He had a raging fever. That's why Papa went out. To try to get to the drugstore and bring back something to help break the fever. We knew things were bad. We'd already heard talk of whole buildings swept away, turned over with people flung out to drown. We prayed we were high enough up to be safe here, and that he could get through."

"Where was the drugstore?"

With Alf dead, it was the best place I could think of to start. At least I'd know the direction their father had gone. But both women shook their heads.

"We usually went to one over on Apple, but Papa didn't get far at all before he realized he'd never reach it," Corrine said. "He zig-zagged and ran into Neal and sent him straight home to tell Mama he was going to try the other way, on Percy. Only...."

"He never came home," I said softly. I waited a minute. "Any idea why he picked Percy instead of some other street? Was there a store there you used sometimes?"

Corrine frowned. "No. We always went to the one on Apple." The silence of defeat engulfed her. Then she straightened. "Unless.... Where was that place with the horehound drops?"

Her question to her sister mystified me. Every drugstore I'd ever been in sold horehound drops for sore throats.

"Oh... I remember," said Isobel vaguely. "The man always gave us a couple. I didn't like them much, but they were better than no candy at all. But heavens, Corrie, we were children. I have no idea what street it was on, or even the direction."

Corrine scarcely seemed to hear, she was so intent on her thoughts.

"I think Papa knew the man who owned it. We were always with Papa when we stopped there. And - and Alf was there sometimes, I think. Papa *knew* the place. Oh, what was the name? Dolan's? Dobbins'? Something like that."

"That's good," I encouraged. "If you happen to think of the name, you can give me a call."

I needed to think through what I'd already learned before I determined what questions I should ask next. A wad of certainty that their father's disappearance merited at least a little more sniffing around was sticking to me.

"Just two more things right now," I said closing my notebook. "What did the police tell you about Alf's death? About how he died?"

In spite of everything they'd said about their stepfather, Isobel's eyes grew watery. She cleared her throat in order to speak.

"They said — they said he'd turned on the gas. They said he'd left a note."

My ears pricked up. "Did they tell you what it said?"

"Not... verbatim. Just that it indicated he was despondent. That he missed his wife."

I wondered if it had mentioned their legal dispute. Or hostility from his stepdaughters. If it had made any reference to me, I doubted Chief Wurstner would have let me off the hook.

"Your brother Neal, does he have any juice at City Hall?"

"Influence? Neal?"

Isobel started to laugh.

SEVEN

My clients might have stepped in something nastier than they expected. It made more sense than ascribing happenstance to the events that had taken place since they hired me.

Was a man's disappearance twenty-six years ago enough to worry somebody now? Or was my involvement stirring concerns over something more recent? Maybe Alf had been mixed up in something bad enough that word of his stepdaughters hiring a private eye had caused him to kill himself. Or for someone else involved to make murder look like suicide.

I chewed on all the possibilities along with a thick ham sandwich while I sat on a bench and watched the activity inside the downtown Arcade. The sandwich was fresh ham, which I liked because it had more flavor than the salty cured kind. Above me a glass dome spread like the hoopskirt of a Southern belle, covering a full city block. At ground level, housewives doing their marketing and downtown workers after a fast lunch swirled past small vendors selling everything from cheeses to pickles to cooked meats and dozens of bakery specialties.

I did some of my best thinking in the Arcade. As I watched two women debate the merits of one merchant's sauerkraut over that of a rival, I did my own debating: Murder or suicide? Linked to the long-ago flood or not? Crime or coincidence?

One thing made me increasingly sure it wasn't coincidence. Namely the complaint that had almost cost me my license.

Wurstner had intimated that the complaint — or at least the pressure to act on it — had come from somewhere above him. That could only mean City Hall. The complaint must have come from the mayor's office or one of the councilmen. That meant either they had a stake in this, or someone who was thick with them did.

"Nothing like stepping on big toes," I muttered under my breath.

A man passing with a cone of fresh French fries shot me a look.

My pal Jenkins had picked a lousy time to be off enjoying a three-week vacation. His work snapping photographs for the *Daily News* took him in and out of offices all over town, including City Hall. He might have been able to sniff something out, and we traded favors. Popping the last bit of ham in my mouth, I dusted my hands.

The threat of losing my license had frightened me plenty. If I had any sense at all, I'd back off. Instead, the anonymous complaint had produced the same effect as waving a red flag in front of a bull. I was going to pin my hopes on Chief Wurstner while I started digging.

***

Back in my office I kicked off my shoes and propped my feet on my desk to try a trick that probably wasn't prudent. If it paid off, though, it might provide something useful. Anyway, both curiosity and resentment were egging me on.

I found the number I wanted. I picked up the unsharpened pencil that protected my manicure. Fitting it in the various holes of the telephone dial, I made my call.

"George Maguire?" I asked when a male voice answered. Alf Maguire had two sons, but Corrine and Isobel had assured me it would have been George I met that morning, since he and Neal shared an apartment.

"Yeah?" he said curtly.

"This is the citizen complaints department at City Hall," I gushed. "Someone failed to log the time when you made your complaint. Could you please tell me what time you called? Approximately? We try to be very strict—"

"Complaint? I don't know what you're talking about."

"Oh, maybe it wasn't a formal complaint. Did you talk to someone in one of the councilmen's offices?"

"Look, lady, I didn't call about anything. I'm trying to set up a funeral." George banged down the phone.

He'd sounded genuinely vexed. As if he had no idea what I was talking about. Pleased with what I'd learned so far, I swivelled my chair. Why not see if my tactic could jar loose one more bit of information? I checked my notes from the Vanhorn sisters, looked in the telephone book and dialed the small factory where Neal Vanhorn worked.

"This is Dr. Pennington's office," I said. "We don't seem to have noted the time when we saw Neal Vanhorn after that little bump he got yesterday. Could you possibly tell me what time he got back to work? It will help us narrow it."

"Oh, yes. The one who'd injured his nose. Had blood on his shirt. Vanhorn, did you say? Let me check with the girl who does time cards and call you—"

"Oops. Doctor needs me. I'll call you back," I cut in.

As I hung up with one hand I grabbed the phone book with the other. In the event there really was a doctor named Pennington, I'd have to tie his line up with some creative dithering. That part would bother my conscience a little. But there wasn't. Chastened by the lesson that I sometimes ought to plan better before launching into a tall tale, I waited five minutes and tried the woman at the factory again.

"Three-fifteen," she said. "How lucky for him that he'd taken time off to go to the doctor anyway."

"Uh, yes," I said. "Thank you so much." We hung up.

So Neal had lied about his reason for taking off work. As I saw it, that more than canceled out my playing fast and loose with the truth. It confirmed my sense that Neal was untrustworthy. Unfortunately, the time he'd returned to work meant he couldn't have been the one eavesdropping in the kitchen, and made him a less likely candidate for killing the dog.

When he got off work, I'd be waiting to ask if he'd filed the complaint against me. Right now I was going to attempt to track down a drugstore which twenty-six years ago might have vanished into the Ohio River, then the Mississippi, on through the Gulf of Mexico to dispense its horehound drops to Davy Jones.

EIGHT

Dayton's main library had taken a beating during the flood. A librarian, a custodian and a couple of others had holed up there for three days and nights, enduring freezing temperatures without heat or food. They'd moved what books they could to ever higher floors as the water rose. Among items saved, or located since, were both the 1912 and 1913 editions of the City Directory. Ten minutes after sitting down with them, I hit pay dirt.

The Vanhorns had vaguely remembered a drugstore named Dolan's or Dobbins'. Going through those long-ago addresses on Percy, I found Dillon's Drugs. According to the listings it had stood between a menswear store and a sewing shop. I jotted down the names and addresses along with those of a few other nearby establishments.

When I switched to the latest directory, I discovered that not one of those places still existed. At least not in the original location. After more than a quarter-century some might have moved, but a trip through the phone book brought me to a dead end. I was fairly certain I knew where John Vanhorn had been headed the day he vanished, but the businesses that had been there then appeared to have vanished too.

Swept away in the flood?

The best way to find out was to go have a look. Most of the afternoon still remained. There'd be plenty of time to get to Neal Vanderhorn's place of employment and have a friendly chat with him when he came out.

***

As I left the reading room, a man who'd had his face buried in a newspaper got up too. He didn't bother to hang the wooden stick holding the newspaper back on the rack. Did I recall seeing him come in shortly after me? I thought so. He'd definitely been in the same spot reading his paper the whole time I'd been there. I picked out some novels to keep me entertained over the weekend. When I finished getting them stamped, the man was staring avidly at a display.

It reminded me about Otis Ripley, the ex-con threatening to even scores. With all that had happened since yesterday, he'd slipped my mind. There wasn't a suit in the world that could disguise Oats from ten feet away, though. Still, he might have friends. Or more accurately, people who owed him a favor. I found it hard to believe any of them would know the way to the library.

Outside on the steps, I pretended to reach down and flick some lint off my skirt. It gave me a quick peek back. The man was sauntering along, too far behind me for me to make out features and too nondescript of both build and attire to be much help. The light was red when I reached the corner, so I did a girlie spin, hugging my books and doing a quarter turn as if bubbling over with happiness I couldn't contain.

The man's steps hesitated. He decided to jaywalk, cutting across in mid-block. By the time I crossed with the light, he was going in a different direction than the one I was headed, leaving me to wonder if I'd only imagined something suspicious. I made a face at my vigilance and stretched my legs for a couple of blocks till I reached the gravel parking lot where I kept my car.

***

Percy was a pleasant little street southeast of downtown. It was only three blocks long, and consisted mostly of neighborhood shops, except for a couple of small office buildings. The area had a tidy look. Although it didn't trumpet prosperity, it didn't show the vacant storefronts and peeling paint that scarred too many neighborhoods since the Depression. Wayne Avenue, a much larger thoroughfare, split the street in two.

The address once occupied by Dillon's Drugs was on the western arm of the street. That lot and the one to its right which had housed the menswear store now held a single two-story brick building. Its lack of ornamentation suggested even to my untrained eye that it had been constructed sometime since the flood. The ground floor housed a bank branch. A separate doorway that opened into a small entry where stairs led up to what a directory indicated were medical offices, a dance studio and a lawyer.

Before my spirits could sag as much as they wanted, I turned toward the place on the left. It was smack on the corner where the sewing shop had been located. From the outside I couldn't begin to guess the age of the building. It was painted robin-egg blue with white trim around arched windows. It housed an upholstery place now. I opened the door, causing bells above the door to jingle softly.

"Gee, what a nice place," I said to a middle-aged woman seated behind an attractive desk that apparently took the place of a counter. "How long has it been here?"

"Oh, my, eighteen years now," she said with a laugh. "How time flies."

She stood up and came forward to greet me. Eighteen years wasn't long enough to help me. Through a door to a back room came sounds of rhythmic tapping.

"I'm trying to get in touch with the man who used to own the place next door back when it was a drugstore," I said. "Dillon's Drugs. Was it still here when you moved in?"

"Goodness no. Next door was already pretty much like it is now."

"What about this place? Was the sewing shop still here before you?"

"No.... Well, actually I'm not sure." She starting to frown. "Wally's parents were the ones who started the business. My in-laws. They'd had a shop before that, over on Richard. Wally worked with them, of course, and I helped out some, but I was mostly busy with babies." Her fingers trailed nervously over a bolt of brown plush with a pattern cut into it. "Is it important about the place that was next door?"

"It is to the two girls trying to find him. He knew their father." Maybe that would tug at her heartstrings. It seemed to.

"Oh. Maybe.... Wally?" she called over her shoulder.

The tapping in back stopped. A man emerged with tacks lined up between his lips.

"She's trying to find out about the place that used to be next door," his wife said. "A drugstore."

Wally plucked the tacks from his mouth one by one, thinking.

"Back when?"

"Twenty-five, twenty-six years ago."

He shook his head. "We haven't been here that long. But I do know this whole block burned down around then."

"Burned—" It wasn't what I'd been expecting.

He chuckled awkwardly.

"During the big flood. Hard to picture, isn't it? Fire you can't put out with all that water around. But I guess the gas line broke...."

"Yeah. I've heard about that. I thought it was downtown, though."

The night before, I'd talked to my landlady some about the flood. She'd told me a big patch of several blocks right where my office now stood had burned to the ground when the gas lines exploded. It made sense there might have been smaller fires elsewhere, yet I felt a tickle along my spine. The kind of tickle that told me something wasn't right.

My feeling had nothing to do with the couple in the upholstery shop. They were more than a little helpful. What bothered me was hearing there'd been a fire in the area where I was increasingly certain John Vanhorn had disappeared.

"Your wife said your parents were the ones who opened the shop here. Any chance they'd know?"

Wally's face told me the answer before he spoke.

"They're both gone now."

"I'm sorry."

"Old Mr. Brigham at the grocery store down on the corner might have been able to help. He was here then, and he rebuilt. I guess some of the shop owners didn't. But he died about a year ago. I can't think of anyone else who might know. You could try his son Sterling. He runs things now. Maybe he remembers his father talking about the old days."

I thanked them and asked them some questions about what sort of things they upholstered, to make them feel good. Then I made my way up their side of the street. For the time being I skipped the bank. Trying to ask questions there would eat up time since I'd have to speak to a teller and then a supervisor and on up the line. If I came up empty everywhere else, they'd be my last resort.

By the time I reached the grocery store on the corner, I hadn't found anyone who'd been in the neighborhood at the time of the flood. The owner of the grocery store shook his head in apology.

"If my dad were alive, he'd be able to help you. He'd talk your ear off. His store was right here where we're standing, and it got hit pretty hard. He lost just about everything. Had to struggle and scrimp to get going again. At least he didn't have fire damage like some of the places farther up did."

My attention sharpened.

"The fire didn't take out the whole block?"

His attention had drifted beyond me to something that was happening in the canned good section.

"Only about half," he said absently. "Three or four places down at the other end got the worst of it. More in the middle lost roofs and had damage. Don't know why it didn't spread all the way. Sorry."

He was starting to frown. I turned and saw the top cans on a pyramid had fallen. A kid who was scampering to catch up with his mama might have had something to do with it.

"Anybody still around who might be able to help me?" I asked.

"I don't think so. I was just a kid at the time, didn't notice the grown-ups much. I kind of remember a drugstore, but that's about it."

I crossed the street to try establishments on the opposite side. The waitress in a little café looked old enough to remember things, but she hadn't been in this area then. She brought me a piece of blackberry pie that was good except for too much lard in the crust. I couldn't bake a pie, but my taste buds had been to college when it came to eating them.

With energy replenished by pie and coffee, I worked my way through half a dozen more places of business.

"Sure I was here then," a leathery old fellow who ran a cobbler's shop acknowledged querulously. "Had a place across the street, but it burned. Don't remember nothing about the drugstore, though. Don't believe in pills and doctors. Now, have you got shoes to fix? I don't have time to yak."

My inquiries at an up-to-date looking drugstore two doors down got me information that they'd only been there ten years. And that the cobbler had never set foot inside.

"Puts all his faith in drinking buttermilk and sleeping with the windows open," said the owner.

The last building on that side of the block was a five-and-dime. It sat directly across from the cheerful blue upholstery shop. Bright and uncluttered, it featured a cosmetics section prominently at the front, with less enticing household items at the back. Compared with McCrory's the place was small, but from candy to sewing supplies it had most of the necessities of daily life. A man nearing fifty with a skinny, leading-man mustache balanced halfway up a stepladder, getting set to retrieve something for a customer who was pointing at the shelf above him. Toward the other side of the store a very young blonde was dusting a display of cheap leather wallets.

"May I help you?" she asked looking up with a smile.

Her dress had a Peter Pan collar. A bow held the waves of her yellow hair back at one temple. The shiny pink of her lips had come from a tube, but she didn't look cheap, just up-to-date and fresh and eager. I put her at about seventeen.

"I'm trying to find someone who might have known a man who owned a drugstore across from here before the big flood of 1913."

"Not me. I wasn't born then." She giggled, then covered her mouth with embarrassment. "If you wait just a minute Mr. Marsh should be finished. He can help. His family's owned a store around here since the time of the pilgrims, I think."

Her gaze had been devouring my hat, a pumpkin gold Robin Hood number with a long, wispy feather.

"Gee, that's a great hat. I have to scrimp and save to even get one of the little felt ones we sell here."

"It's tough when you're starting out," I sympathized. "I used to drool over hats like this. I'd have a million if I could afford them. I'd been eyeing this one for weeks — putting a quarter aside here and there — when it went on sale."

Her sigh was curtailed as she straightened, all business.

"Mr. Marsh? Could you help this lady?" She waited until he was close. "She's trying to find out about a man who used to have a drugstore across the street before the big flood."

Marsh, the man from the stepladder, gave me a sharp look.

"Sorry. Can't help. Don't know anything about it." Without so much as a phony smile, he started to turn away.

Perplexity crossed the blonde's smooth face. Before she could say anything to land her in hot water with her boss, I spoke up.

"Gee, that old cobbler a couple doors down told me you'd been around for the flood and the fire and could fill me in."

The lie didn't bother me in the least. The two disagreeable men deserved each other. Better still, it halted Marsh in his tracks.

"My folks had the store then," he said testily. "It was years ago. I don't even remember what was across the street — just the mess cleaning up. As to what that old coot claims to remember, I wouldn't trust it as far as I could spit." He noticed the young clerk, who was listening avidly. "Emily, when you finish that dusting, restock the candy. You've dawdled all day."

She moved on, but not before her eyes caught mine to signal I should talk to her. The five-and-dime owner had turned his attention to me again.

"Now, if that's all you came in for...."

"Gee, you've been a peach about helping." I gave him a smile so sunny it just about scorched him. "Since I'm here and you've got such a nice place, I think I'll just look for a new tube of lipstick to wear on my date tonight."

Marsh stared at me uncertainly, maybe wondering if I was unhinged.

"Uh, yes. It's right there."

I drifted toward the cosmetics, and when he'd put a few steps between us, I raised my voice.

"Hey, I saw this color I liked in a magazine, in a lipstick ad. I don't suppose you'd happen to know —"

"Oh, I bet I know the ad you're talking about!"

Emily didn't need a picture to recognize the opportunity I'd given her. Putting her feather duster down, she scurried to a rack of magazines and brought one over. Meanwhile I had moseyed into the cosmetics section, far enough away that the store owner couldn't hear us, though he had cast a watchful eye in our direction.

"This one right here," the girl bubbled, flipping some pages. I shifted to shield her as she dropped her voice. "Come back Monday between noon and two. Theda works then."

"Boy, you've got some memory," I said aloud, then under my breath, "Who's Theda?"

"Older woman. White hair."

"Do you really think I could wear that shade? The model's hair's darker." I changed volume again. "Why noon to two?"

Emily's gaze slid beyond me, making sure all was well.

"Want to look at it in the tube?"

She led the way toward a glass case and I had to strain to hear her reply.

"Some group he's in has lunch. Hears speakers."

Emily unlocked the case and we made the right lipstick chat while she got out a cotton swab.

"You get a commission if I buy one?" I asked quietly.

She nodded, flushed with embarrassment.

"Gee, I hope I look half as good in it as the girl in that magazine," I said for her boss' ears. "Go ahead, ring it up."

NINE

Getting information, or information leading to information, often costs money. Usually it's not a lot. Sometimes four bits, sometimes five bucks, on rare occasions more.

A tube of lipstick fell on the cheap end of things. For once I even got something fun out of the deal. Usually my outlay went to some sullen bartender or a down-at-heels character with a hard luck story. I hoped Emily made more than a couple of extra cents for selling it to me.

Back in my DeSoto I took my compact out and tried the new shade. It fell midway between the two colors I already owned, and having three to choose from now made me feel like a socialite. It made me look snazzy too, even though I'd lied about having somewhere to wear it. Maybe Neal Vanhorn would be so dazzled by my looks that he'd come clean about any shenanigans without the need to punch him again.

Asking questions on Percy Street had eaten up most of the afternoon. It was just about time to head across the river to Neal's place of work. I wanted to be there when the factory let out.

As I drove I thought about my visit to the five-and-dime. I'd learned more there than Marsh, the owner, probably realized. That wasn't even counting the tip from Emily about coming in Monday.

What I'd learned was that Marsh knew more about the time of the flood than he'd admitted. First of all, he must have said something about the event at least a few times for Emily to be so prompt in telling me he'd been around then. Next, there was his brusqueness, almost bordering on rudeness. Most business owners took pains to be cordial to anybody who might be a customer — even shoppers who weren't so cordial themselves. The cobbler I was willing to write off as a crank, but Marsh had been all pleasantries for the customer who needed something from a top shelf. Finally there was the fact that the grocery store owner, who'd been the same age or even younger than Marsh at the time of the flood, at least remembered Dillon's Drugs, if only vaguely.

Marsh had been too quick to answer. He was hiding something. Either that, or he'd been warned not to talk to me. The question was what? Or why?

***

With ten minutes to spare I pulled to the curb a block from the factory where Neal worked. It gave me a chance to study the street and spot a few beer joints where men coming off their shift were likely to head. Since I hadn't the least idea what

Neal's car looked like, or even if he drove it to work, my best move was to find a spot a few doors away from the factory entrance and try to look inconspicuous. The inconspicuous part didn't work so well.

A whistle blew, and men began to file out. They carried lunch buckets and some wore overalls, but they weren't covered with the soot and the grime spit by the machines at most factories. Whatever they made there possibly demanded a bit more skill or maybe just cleaner conditions. Most of the time they came out in groups of four, five, six. Most of the time someone in the group gave me the once over and nudged his companions.

A big guy with cowlicked black hair and a grin that had probably broken some hearts peeled off from his chums and strolled my way.

"That's some hat, sweetheart. Want to show it off over beer and a sandwich?"

"Hey, thanks for the nice offer, but I'm looking for someone."

"What's he got that I haven't?"

"V.D.," I said.

He took off fast.

A few minutes later Neal appeared with two other men. As they ambled up the street I stepped out of the doorway where I'd been waiting and fell in behind them. Neal was on the outside of the trio, which made it easier. Taking a couple of fast steps to catch up, I hooked my arm through his.

"Hi, Neal. We need to have us a little chat."

He tried to pull away as he recognized me.

"What the — You meddling piece of fluff. We've done all the chatting we're going to."

He jerked his head curtly at his companions. They moved away with frequent glances over their shoulders, torn between entertainment and fear of tripping over their feet.

"Now here's how it's going to work, Neal," I said pleasantly. "Either you answer a couple of questions without any guff, or I start screaming how if you don't marry me, my daddy's going to come after you with a shotgun."

His eyes took on an uneasy look. His Adam's apple bobbed.

"You're nuts," he said hoarsely.

I smiled.

"Who did you call at City Hall?"

"At... what?"

"To complain about me?"

His mouth opened and closed without sound.

"I never — Don't start screaming! I'm telling the truth! I never called City Hall. To complain about you or anything else. By the time those cops finished asking questions and said I could go, I was praying to God I'd still have a job. I didn't take time to pee, let alone make a phone call!"

He began to regain equilibrium. Cunning edged out his panic. His shoulders eased free of their protective curl and he waggled a finger closer to my face than I deemed polite.

"I'm warning you, though. If you bother me again, I *will* make a complaint!"

"Do you think Alf really killed himself?" I asked on impulse.

The whitening of his face was at odds with his returning swagger. His tongue licked out.

"How would I know? I was home in bed. I wasn't there!"

"But you know—"

"I don't know anything! I didn't even talk to him that day! Now let me alone!"

Wresting his arm free, he hurried away.

***

Back in my office I hung my hat carefully on the top of my coat rack. It had occurred to me that until I discovered the source of the complaint against me, it might be wise to stay in the good graces of the chief of police, so as soon as I'd switched my .38 to its holder under my chair, I put in a call to his office.

"Miss Sullivan?"

"This morning I neglected to ask whether you'd object to my looking into that disappearance from twenty-five years ago I told you about."

"With all the more recent things we have to deal with? I certainly have none." He paused. "Check with Lt. Freeze in case he feels differently."

"I will. Thanks."

I hung up and tapped my teeth with a knuckle. Freeze and I trusted each other about as much as two dogs circling the same bone. Come to think of it, that more or less described the situations in which we usually encountered each other.

Freeze worked hard and was smart enough to deserve his spot as homicide chief. It made sense to remain on his good side. I wanted to keep the chief happy too. And if for some reason Freeze did object, I could ignore him. By talking to him there was even a slim chance I'd learn whether they were looking at Alf Maguire's death as a homicide.

It already was a quarter to six, but Freeze and his unit worked late, especially when they had something fresh. I called and was told he was down the hall but would call me back when he returned.

Meanwhile I typed up my notes from that afternoon. When that was done I decided to treat myself to a drink. The pub in the bottom drawer of my desk was always open. I took out the fixings for gin and tonic. It was the only recipe I knew, but a tried and true one. I turned off my light and sat and enjoyed the sharp tang of gin and the gathering dusk.

As soon as Freeze called back I'd head for Mrs. Z's and see if Genevieve or one of the other girls wanted to go get supper somewhere. But Freeze didn't call. My stomach growled. I fixed myself another drink. When the hands of the clock nudged seven, I gave up and headed out.

The nature of my work had ingrained a low-level watchfulness in me that was second nature. If I was on the trail of something, or had a hunch I'd stirred up a hornet's nest, I stayed more alert. Tonight, once a glance in a shop window reassured me the crook who'd been sprung from the pen wasn't slinking along behind me in the shadows, I was free to enjoy the dance of the city where I'd been born.

The buildings I passed had long since emptied of
workers. Most people were home now, finished
with supper and putting their feet up. Reading the
paper or, if they had one, listening to radio. Half a
dozen blocks uptown, the well-off were dining and
dancing at the Hotel Miami or the Biltmore. Big-
wigs who invented things or owned the city's
manufacturing powerhouses were hobnobbing at
the Engineer's Club. Down where my office was, at
this time of day, streets were mostly deserted.

On days that I drove, I usually left my car in a
gravel lot between some railroad trestles and the
edge of the Fifth Street produce market. A casual
scan didn't show anyone else in the parking lot, or
any shadows moving between the cars. Under
FDR the Depression seemed to be loosening its
grip, but there were still plenty of desperate
people willing to wait and bash somebody over the
head for the coins in their pocket. I crunched my
way toward the DeSoto. It was parked with the
luggage trunk toward me. As I stepped around to
the driver's side, a hand closed around my ankle
and I felt myself yanked off my feet.

TEN

Even before my back slammed into the gravel I was reaching behind for my gun. My attacker had the advantage of surprise. He caught my wrist. It was too dark to make out his features, but I could see his free arm swing back to deliver a punch. I rolled toward him, catching him off guard with my direction. His knuckles got just the edge of my cheek and enough of my ear to make it ring.

I hurled myself in the other direction. It freed me long enough to scramble mostly to my feet. Then he was on me again, his grip on my wrist tighter this time, twisting my arm up hard. Rather than try to cover my mouth, he reached over my head. The fingers of his left hand pinched my nose shut, holding where I couldn't bite.

"Breathe or scream, girlie. Can't do both."

As I fought and tried to suck in air, I realized any yell I managed would be puny. Did I recognize his voice? Was he the hooligan I'd helped send to prison?

My left hand flailed ineffectually, unable to deliver a punch. Scratching him would be futile. Pain seared the arm he was twisting.

"Might as well give up, sweetheart." His chin pressed the top of my head as he gloated. "Dames aren't cut out for the big league."

I fumbled for the silk flower decorating my lapel, hoping it would serve the purpose I'd envisioned. On my second tug the extra-long stick pin topped with the flower pulled free of my suit. I rammed the pin back and up. The scream of the man imprisoning me raised the hair on my neck as I felt the steel shaft find its target — a cheek, an eye, I didn't care.

All at once I was free and gasping for air. I managed to fumble my gun out, but my newly freed arm was too weak to raise it. Turning in a circle, I saw no sign of my attacker. Movement on the street caught my eye as a car pulled away from the curb, paused to open its door, and roared off, switching its lights on. The off-kilter beam of one suggested it was out of alignment.

The nearly new hat I'd saved up for had fallen off in the struggle. Its feather was broken. I picked it up and unlocked the DeSoto.

The last thing my assailant had said, and his taunting tone, made it clear he knew me. Or at least my occupation. I was pretty sure it hadn't been Oats, so it was probably someone he'd sent.

The only alternative I could come up with was too far-fetched to contemplate: That the attack had something to do with Alf Maguire or the Vanhorn sisters.

***

Saturday morning seemed like a dandy time for a drive past Alf's place. Two brief paragraphs on an inside page of the morning paper said that a man in a Haynes Street duplex had died after being overcome by gas. He wasn't named, which was standard in cases of suicide, so if the police were still looking at the death at all, they didn't appear to be looking too closely.

It surprised me, therefore, to see a patrol car parked in front. I drove on, drumming my thumbs on the steering wheel in indecision. Freeze wouldn't be happy if he caught me poking around. Then again, since he hadn't returned my call yesterday, I'd never had a chance to ask if he minded. I did a U-turn and parked several doors away on the opposite side of the street.

The story in the paper had mentioned that occupants of the other half of the duplex had been roused in time to escape unharmed. Their side might be a good place to start. Several minutes of knocking and waiting brought no response.

"They're not home," called a voice from the sidewalk. A stout woman wearing carpet slippers held the leash of a mutt not much bigger than her footwear. "They've gone to stay with her sister a couple of days," she said as I walked toward her. "Until the gas smell clears out."

"Gas smell?" I played dumb.

Relishing the opportunity to share news of something so exciting, she told me about Alf's demise. The man in the other side of the duplex had 'some sort of job' at a dairy. He'd set out for work in the wee small hours, smelled the gas, and raised an alarm.

"If it was that girlfriend of his going back to Oregon or wherever it was last month that led him to do such a thing, then the poor man should have been counting his lucky stars instead," she concluded. "She was a cheeky thing. And between you and me, I think the police should be showing more interest in who came to see him that night."

That wrenched my attention away from her little dog, who was sniffing my ankle and some nearby bushes with equal enthusiasm.

"Mr. Maguire had guests?"

She nodded wisely.

"Not that I stick my nose into people's business, but Patches needs a tinkle or two in the night, so I bring him out. He won't use the back yard. A cat scared him once."

Right now I was hoping he didn't decide to use my leg.

"... so of course I know the cars that park along here. That night there were two that I didn't recognize. Just as I was thinking that was odd — it was after one — I realized there was someone sitting in one of them."

My heart began to beat faster.

"Well, I just walked on by, as fast as I could. I didn't want to attract attention. He tried to duck down, but I'd already seen him, and — oh, it was awful!" She pressed a hand to her throat, glancing over her shoulder as if fearful she'd be overheard. She leaned toward me. "He was an Eskimo!"

I wasn't sure I'd heard her correctly.

"An Eskimo?"

"I tell you, it scared me to death." She shuddered dramatically.

"Uh, what does an Eskimo look like?"

The woman frowned as though I were feeble minded.

"You know. Scary. Not like other people. Oh — Patches did his duty. Good doggie. We have to go."

Too stumped to ask anything else, I watched them traipse back to a nearby house. Maybe she used the word Eskimo to indicate a foreigner. Maybe she'd seen a Chinaman. I'd read a book once where a woman used the word to mean anything forbidden, like cussing.

Then again, maybe she was loony. It was interesting, though, that she'd seen two strange cars.

***

"Why on earth are you interested in the flood? That was back before you were born." Kate Leary wore a puzzled expression as she handed me a bowl of mashed potatoes. An unspoiled lake of butter cratered the white peaks.

I had a standing invitation to Sunday dinner at Kate and Billy's. Once every couple of months I took them up on it. Sometimes it was because I'd spent too much time wading through muck and needed to reassure myself the world had a good side. Other times it was to keep from hurting Kate, whom I liked and who was the only cop's wife who didn't grab her matchmaking bonnet each time we met.

Today there were five of us at the table: Kate and Billy; Seamus Hanlon, a gaunt, tall cop with wavy white hair; Mick Connelly and me. Despite Connelly's presence, I didn't suspect Kate of an ulterior motive. He probably sat at their table more often than I did. He was here because he was Billy's partner, just as Seamus was here because he'd filled that same role for so many years that he and Billy were almost inseparable. I explained about being hired to look into the long-ago disappearance. It drew the now familiar exclamations of disbelief.

"Well, I'll tell you about the flood — it was awful," Kate said, startling all of us by taking the lead. "Every policeman in the city called out, and not knowing what happened to any of them for days and days."

"What happened was all of us got trapped downtown — right in the flood plain!" Billy bristled.

He and the usually taciturn Seamus tripped over each other explaining.

Previous floods had always hit the downtown and surrounding neighborhoods hardest, sometimes bringing waters two feet deep. When the man who was chief in 1913 was warned of impending flooding, he'd summoned all his men from outlying precincts to help with the central area. Even as they fanned out door to door, warning residents to evacuate to higher ground, levees on the three rivers hugging Dayton's downtown ruptured. Waters surged to ten feet, then, as more rain poured unrelentingly down for the next two days, to twenty feet, then twenty-eight. The entire police force was trapped at the heart of the chaos. Help from and for outlying areas was cut off.

"Your mother and I called each other if one of us had a snippet of news," Kate told me, memories straining her face. "There we were, each of us alone with a toddler...."

Her gaze crept to a photograph of a twelve-year-old boy. He'd survived the flood only to die of measles not long after the picture was taken.

"All we could do was watch the water come up, and up, and try and reassure each other," she said softly. "Then the phones went out."

Our forks had been clicking away, consuming Kate's fine roast pork without the compliments it deserved. Connelly seemed as spellbound as I was. I tried to imagine my mother talking with someone — a friend. I'd never heard her use the phone except to make a doctor's appointment or ask if something was in at the grocery store.

"And when the cleanup started, Rudy Wurstner — he was just a constable walking a beat back then — he got stuck with disposing of all the dead horses," chuckled Seamus. "Now I'd have made him chief just for being man enough to do that."

It banished the somberness and we laughed and talked about how Cincinnati had lost again yesterday and was going to be out for good unless they did better today. I helped Kate with the dishes and said my good-byes.

"I'd better be off too." Connelly rose hastily, pecking Kate's cheek and catching up with me at the door. When it closed behind us, he cleared his throat.

"Guess I should apologize for putting your fur up the last time I saw you. If I said I made that all up about the Fourth of July, any chance I could ask you a favor?"

"Did you make it up?"

He grinned.

"Let's say I did."

I didn't like his answer, but I sensed an opportunity.

"I'd need one in return."

"Deal."

"What's the favor?"

"Remember a while back when Seamus and I had been listening to tunes and came in with me picking at one on a whistle?"

"Sure." Connelly hadn't been picking, though. He'd been whizzing along.

"And Rose said Finn should get his fiddle out?"

I nodded, mystified at where this was headed. Connelly shoved his hands in his pockets. He looked as close to shy as I'd ever seen him.

"Well, we've been getting together, playing some jigs and that. Thought it might be fun if we could find a few others who'd like to try some tunes together. Now and again. There in the back room."

At first I couldn't find my tongue. Of all the things I could have imagined he'd ask, this wasn't one.

"You mean... like a band?"

"Nah, just get together. Have fun."

Like my dad had adored, I thought swallowing. I probably couldn't count half a dozen times those evenings had happened, but I knew he'd lived for them.

Connelly examined his toes and ducked a look up at me.

"Seamus said if anyone knew who played, or used to, it would be you."

For several seconds the years peeled away from him. With shock I realized I might be glimpsing the real Mick Connelly, one buried deep inside the man whose easy-going ways camouflaged a hardened watchfulness that never let down.

In spite of that, I shook my head.

"I'd help if I could, but I don't know of anyone. There was a guy with a fiddle who used to come play with Dad now and then, but he's pushing up daisies. Don't know what became of the old guy who used to take his teeth out and play a harmonica. Never even knew his name. Wee Willie had an uncle or such who played something... a flute, maybe. But I've heard he doesn't know his own name most days."

I wasn't about to mention my dad's fancy lady.

Belatedly a face I hadn't thought about in years came to mind.

"There was an old woman who wasted six months or so giving me concertina lessons," I said slowly. "I can ask about her. But she was old then, so don't get your hopes up. Your best bet is to ask

Wee Willie. Could be he knows of some friends of his uncle's."

I shifted, feeling like a skunk to let him down when he'd been so eager. "Want a lift?"

Connelly smiled, his youthful look gone, but still in good spirits.

"Thanks, but it's too fine a day for stretching my legs. They'll forget what they're for. If you do come across anyone, tell them Thursday at seven, back room at Finn's."

He strode away on legs formed walking miles, not blocks. I knew he missed country lanes. Missed Ireland, though he never said as much. I watched until he turned a corner, and I heard him burst into his trilling whistle. Connelly had the gift of joy.

ELEVEN

I was wondering whether I'd learn anything by attending Alf's funeral that afternoon when I unlocked the door to my office on Monday.

A gun in my ribs couldn't have stopped me any faster.

"Couldn't call and make an appointment since you weren't here," said a razor thin man lounging to one side of my window. He always stood where he could watch the street as well as the room. I had a hunch it stemmed from his line of work. Not that anyone ever had put a name to that work. "You need a better lock," he said.

"The super and I aren't exactly pals. He said if I changed it, he'd have me evicted."

"Thought it might disturb your neighbors less if I waited inside." Pearlie bared the snowy teeth responsible for his name. It passed for a smile. It was also the look a dog wore when it might either lick your hand or bite it. He was edging toward attractive, and his suits cost enough that they fit to perfection, but he had the same air as a closed switchblade.

"Rachel okay?" I asked.

"Rachel's fine. She don't know I'm here."

I nodded. Rachel employed him. His last comment made me curious why he'd come, and more than a little uneasy. He opened the window beside him a couple of inches, then lighted a cigarette.

"Oats Ripley's looking for you," he said.

I gritted my teeth. If one more person told me that, I was going to scream.

"So I've heard."

"I could make sure he didn't bother you."

Some people might think Pearlie was hitting me up for a bribe. I was pretty sure he wasn't. I was also pretty sure his solution would be the permanent kind.

"Thanks, Pearlie. I appreciate it. I'd just as soon take care of Oats by myself, though. So people don't get the idea I can't."

Pearlie frowned. It wasn't an expression I'd ever seen him wear.

"Guy's a sneak. Doesn't have backbone enough to face somebody fair and square. He's the sort shoots somebody in the back."

"Yeah, but his aim's lousy. And anyone who wasn't deaf would hear him breathing through his mouth before he got close enough to try."

Pearlie regarded me somberly. He took a drag on his cigarette, tossed the rest out the window and lowered the sash.

"I figured you might not be receptive," he said, and walked out.

I sat down, amused by the final word, which suggested Pearlie continued his efforts to improve his vocabulary. I took off my hat and tossed it onto my desk. Before I had time to speculate on the meaning of Pearlie's visit, or his offer, my telephone rang.

It was Freeze.

"Sorry I didn't return your call on Friday," he said. "I was... called away."

His almost indiscernible hesitation snagged my interest. Indecision wasn't Freeze's style. I hadn't seen anything in that morning's paper to suggest Alf Maguire's death or anyone else's was under investigation. If a new case had popped up Friday afternoon, Freeze wouldn't be sitting in his office now talking to me. I waited a minute in hopes he'd volunteer more, but he didn't.

"Chief Wurstner suggested I call you," I said when I'd waited as long as I could without annoying him. "Remember at the Maguire place I told you I was there because his stepdaughters had hired me?"

"The stepdaughters who only recently had gone round with him in court over an inheritance," he said coldly.

"Just one small part of that inheritance, and the suit was settled in their favor. That had nothing to do with why they hired me."

Did I need to cross my fingers? Probably not, since I wasn't sure their dad's disappearance was even remotely related to Alf's death or the slop poured over me since. Before Freeze could turn too ill-disposed, I ran through the case I was working, omitting the women's suspicion Alf

Maguire had played some role in the disappearance.

"The chief said he didn't care if I poked around in something from that far back, but he said I should clear it with you first," I finished.

"If you want to follow a trail that cold, go right ahead. Just don't put your foot in anything we're looking at now."

"Does that include Alf Maguire's death?" I asked innocently. "Hard to put my foot in the right place if I don't know where the messes are."

"Don't play dumb. If you turn up anything you think might remotely be of interest to me, let me know, or you'll have more black marks against you than you can count."

***

My failure to learn if they were classifying Alf Maguire's death as a suicide miffed me. I took it out on routine chores: Paying bills that came in and sending some out to regular clients whose small retainers kept me going in lean times; cleaning out some old files. It didn't use up nearly enough of the time that stood between me and noon when I could return to Percy Street and talk to the clerk named Theda.

I eyed the desiccated plant decorating one corner of my office. Going upstairs to the ladies restroom for a glass of water to pour on it would take at least five minutes if I stretched it. Then again, the plant had been brown and lifeless for a couple of years. It would be cruel to get its hopes up.

Having nothing else to occupy me, I rose and paced the margins of my office. I opened the same window Pearlie had a couple of inches. I could hear the sounds of carts bumping over bricks at the produce market. Today the wind was right so I even caught the fragrance of apples.

I wasn't as cavalier about Oats Ripley as I'd let on to Pearlie. Oats wasn't a good enough shot or fast enough on his feet to be a first-rate thug, but he was mean as a snake. The kind who'd shoot you in the back, as Pearlie said. The kind who'd have no qualms about using a baseball bat or tying you up somewhere to starve or setting your house on fire. Needing to deal with him on my own was a matter of honor.

Even the slipperiest lawyer wouldn't have gotten him sprung if it had been a man who'd caught Oats standing over a woman he'd beaten to death with the bloody crowbar still in his hands. But it had been me. A judge had been persuaded that my failure to mention a missing button made my entire testimony unreliable. No doubt there'd been an innuendo or two — how a woman coming into a half-lighted warehouse on her own might have been understandably a little rattled. It didn't help that the other witness, elderly and nearsighted, was no longer quite so certain what he'd seen.

I drew a breath and let it out slowly, thrusting the thoughts away. It irked me that the need to keep an eye out for Oats Ripley blurred my focus on the Vanhorn case.

***

Since I'd been parked on Percy for the better part of Friday afternoon, I wanted to avoid notice this time around. I'd borrowed a neighbor's car which I sometimes used when my own might be too recognizable. By a quarter of twelve I was parked where I could keep an eye on the alley behind the dime store where I'd purchased my snazzy new lipstick.

I'd swung through the alley when I left the area on Friday, and again before settling in today. Both times a brown Desoto the same year as mine with white sidewall tires and a decal of some sort in the back window had been parked behind the dime store. Shortly before noon Marsh, the dime store owner, came out the back entrance, got into the car and drove away.

I waited ten minutes more in case he forgot something. When it appeared he was safely gone, I locked my borrowed car and headed across the street.

A couple of customers were browsing their way between counters. Emily's blonde head bobbed up and down behind the candy counter, maybe restocking it or maybe cleaning the cases; I couldn't tell which. A woman with silky white hair stood at the cash register. She had on a pretty mauve colored dress and her shape underneath it made me think of pillows. She greeted me with a cheery smile.

"Good afternoon."

I smiled back. "You must be Theda."

"Why, yes," she brightened even more. "And I'll bet you're the girl Emily told me about who wanted to know about the flood. How odd Mr. Marsh wouldn't talk to you. People are funny, aren't they? Then he *was* just a boy."

Glancing down to make sure her foot found the rung, she settled herself on a high wooden stool, preparing to chat. Her eyes made a businesslike sweep of the store first, making sure everything was under control.

"Oh, honey, I remember that awful flood like it was yesterday. My husband had a little butcher shop just around the corner from Brigham's grocery. Loveliest chops and roasts you ever saw! You just don't get meat like that these days. I helped out waiting on customers most afternoons, so I was in the thick of things, before and after. You ask away."

"It's the drugstore that was across the street I'd like to find out about."

"Dillon's Drugs."

"Yes. Do you know the name of the man who owned it and whether he's still around?"

Her eyes widened.

"His name was Tom Dillon — lovely old gentleman. Partial to lamb shanks. But honey, there was a terrible fire. Right during the flood. The whole place burned down, and him inside it, poor man. They said it looked like one of the big iron display units had fallen on him — pinned him under it."

She paused in her story to ring up a customer. It was just as well, since my brain was floundering under the implications of what she'd just told me. A vanished man who'd likely gone to the drugstore. A fire. A body. But surely Dillon himself would have turned up if the body in the store had been anyone else.

Emily had left the candy counter to help a customer with cosmetics. I hoped she made a sale. The drawer of the cash register slid closed and Theda climbed back on her stool.

"I guess they were sure the remains they found were Tom Dillon's," I said, keeping the question as casual as a question like that could be.

"Oh, yes. By a leg bone. One of his legs had been broken, you see, and healed a bit crooked. He limped." A frown at odds with her pleasant face marred her forehead. "Why are you wanting to know about Mr. Dillon? I'm sure he told me once that he didn't have any relatives."

"Two little girls who knew him then wanted to find out about him. He knew their father."

"Oh? What was the father's name?"

Here was an avenue I hadn't considered.

"Vanhorn," I said. "John Vanhorn."

She thought a minute, then shook her head.

"I can't recall hearing the name. You might.... Oh. Oh, my. Isn't that bad luck?"

"What?" I turned to see if she was looking at something behind me. She wasn't. "Isn't what bad luck?"

Theda's white head was shaking again.

"If only you'd come in this time a week ago! I was just about to say you could talk to Mr. Dillon's partner, only you can't now. He died just a few days ago. Friday, was it?"

An unsettling feeling started to crawl up my spine.

"What was his partner's name?"

"Maguire," she said. "Alf Maguire."

TWELVE

It wasn't something I'd expected, but it didn't surprise me. Maguire's sudden death before I could uncover this connection had just become all the more interesting. In my head I was dancing around like Shirley Temple, except without the ruffles and dimples. John Vanhorn's disappearance was, without a doubt, in some way related to Dillon's Drugs and to something that happened there the day the store fell victim to both flood and fire.

"How did they become partners?" I asked. "You told me Dillon didn't have any relatives."

"I think that's why he took Alf on," Theda said, thinking. "Not for mixing prescriptions; Alf didn't have any training in that. But Tom was getting older and I suppose he wanted some help. Someone who could learn the whole business — ordering, insurance, all the pieces. The two clerks he had — one was just part-time, filled in now and then — they were lovely with customers and had very good heads for ringing up sales, but there's a great deal more to running a business than that."

She spoke the last with the firmness of one who knew from experience.

"I don't suppose either of those clerks is still around?"

"Oh, goodness no. Married." Her fingers flicked to indicated that was the way of things. "I don't believe I ever knew their last names as it was."

She halted the conversation to help a customer. I looked at my watch. Nearly one o'clock. I needed to finish up soon in case the store owner came back sooner than expected. I didn't mind tangling with him, but I didn't want Theda to get into trouble for talking with me. Why her boss would object was a puzzle, but given how quickly he'd brushed me off when I brought up the flood, I felt sure he would.

"Why didn't he rebuild?" I asked when we were alone again.

Theda sniffed. "Too eager to make a quick dollar, if you ask me." She looked immediately abashed. "Oh, that's not fair, I guess. Plenty of others didn't rebuild either."

I glanced at my watch again to make sure time remained for a few more questions, and also to hide my interest in Theda's comment about a fast dollar. The store was momentarily free of customers. I beckoned Emily over and gave her some money and told her to pick out some nail polish for me and ring it up. I'd use it, and another sale would show their boss that they'd kept busy.

"How did he make a fast buck?" I asked.

Embarrassed, Theda tried to wave her comment away.

"Oh, I don't know that he did. It's just that I didn't like him. He and a friend of his always strutted around like they were such young blades. Looked down their noses at the rest of us, is how I saw it." She drew herself up like an enraged bantam. "They made fun of my younger son because he stuttered."

The nice old lady wasn't exactly impartial. I'd need to keep it in mind concerning the information I was gleaning about Maguire.

"Not that it's held my boy back. Not a bit. He's in charge of a laboratory over at Purdue University...."

Aware of time running out, I cut in.

"This friend of Alf's — did he work around here?"

"Cyrus? Oh, yes. His father had a menswear store next to Dillon's. Nothing fancy, but not overalls either. Just the clothing ordinary people need. It nearly killed his father, seeing the store destroyed after all the years he'd put into it. He didn't have the heart to start over." She sighed. "Life just doesn't make sense sometimes, does it? How fickle it is? Take those two boys. One dead now, and the other a big-time politician."

***

It was twenty till two when I got back to my borrowed car. I wanted to sit while I absorbed the import of what I'd learned from Theda. Instead, to eliminate risk of passing Marsh as I left the area, and having him recognize me, I put the car in gear and headed up Wayne with information bursting in my brain and my stomach growling. I could settle both of them down at a new place on East Third called Wympee.

The diner let you park up close, and the food came fast. Outside, its walls were curving, sleek-looking white ceramic tiles. Inside there was one long counter with stainless steel stools upholstered in green. The menu on the wall was short, but it stretched to a hamburger deluxe with extra pickles and a vanilla malted. Since the lunch crowd was gone, I had the place just about to myself as I worked my way through the food and what I'd learned at the five-and-dime.

The name of the friend young Alf Maguire had palled around with at the time of the flood was Cyrus Warren, though strictly speaking, the two of them hadn't been that young. Maguire had been in his late twenties and Warren half a dozen years younger, according to Theda.

Cy Warren's name had been vaguely familiar, though I couldn't recall what I'd read or heard about him. From what Theda said, he was clearly in politics, though maybe not quite as 'big-time' as she'd let on. I hadn't wanted to press her about him, because I knew I could find out plenty on my own.

I had no idea how, or if, he might be connected to John Vanhorn's disappearance.

I had no idea how, or if, he might be connected to Alf Maguire's death.

The idea I did have was that somebody mucking around in politics could be connected enough at City Hall to raise a stink about me and threaten my license.

"Everything okay with the food?" the man behind the counter asked nervously.

Likely as not I'd been scowling.

"Yes. Thank you." I smiled. "Just wondering if I should have a cup of coffee, and I think I will."

He brought the coffee. Two salesmen came in and sat at the opposite end of the counter, drawing his attention and leaving me to my thoughts.

Someone in politics would certainly be leery of anything coming to light about them that could queer things with voters, I reflected. Could it be as innocuous as a long-ago friendship with someone like Alf Maguire, who had rough edges and made bad investments and kept a floozie while his wife was dying? I couldn't buy that. Men were too willing to chuckle at transgressions by their own gender.

Could it be that Cy Warren had been mixed up in something shady with his pal Maguire? Maybe in the past, or even currently?

The only way to find out was to wear out some shoe leather.

THIRTEEN

I spent most of the next morning at the library, reading up on Cyrus Warren. There was plenty to read. He'd served one term on City Council eight years back but hadn't run for re-election. Since then he'd served on a couple of civic committees and the state real estate board. His face showed up in photographs alongside big-wigs including the mayor, two county commissioners, the state superintendent of education and a state senator. It appeared he was gearing up to run for a seat in the Ohio House.

Warren's business was real estate. He had an office downtown, which was going to be handy for me. His wife, who'd been photographed with him at a shindig or two, was a dreamy-eyed little thing at least a dozen years his junior. In all the photographs I came across, she gazed up at him so adoringly I needed Pepto Bismol.

This time nobody followed me when I left the library. Maybe the dust-up I'd had in the parking lot had discouraged whoever it was. I trotted on over to the county recorder's office to find out when Alf Maguire had become a co-owner of Dillon's Drugs and who'd bought the property after the flood. I left in under an hour, feeling frustrated.

Not surprisingly, property records from the time of the flood were jumbled and missing.

Lunch improved my spirits over the spotty records. There were other places I could poke, and one occurred to me that I hadn't thought of before. It would take some nerve, and I might get turned down, but the chance of success was enough to send me back to the office. My feet were tired, so I kicked off my shoes as I dialed.

"This is Maggie Sullivan," I said. "Could I please speak to Chief Wurstner?"

Somewhat to my surprise, he came on.

"Yes?" he said cautiously.

Since he hadn't used my name, I wondered if he had someone in the office with him.

"I have some questions about the Great Flood that other cops working then haven't been able to answer. I was wondering if you—"

"It is not the business of the police to do the job for private detectives," he said brusquely.

I didn't get a chance for a polite good-by.

He was right, of course. And I hadn't exactly been truthful when I told him no one else could answer the questions, since I hadn't even asked Seamus and Billy. I knew the beats they'd walked then, though, and they hadn't come close to the neighborhood where Dillon's Drugs had stood. Still, they might surprise me by knowing who'd worked there. I'd try them tonight; maybe stop by Finn's.

Meanwhile, I was going to pay a visit to Cyrus Warren. How could a politician pass up a chance to win a constituent's vote?

***

My first stop was the corner a block and a half away where I could usually find a tow-headed newsboy called Heebs.

"Hey, sis, I already sold you a paper. You stop back to see if I'd be your sweetheart?" he asked with a grin.

He wasn't old enough to shave yet. The sides of his shoes were coming apart, and his ragged jacket wasn't warm enough for the nights we had now, let alone when the snow started flying.

"I stopped by to see if you wanted to sell all those papers and make another four bits besides."

His eyes sparked with eagerness. "Want me to be your assistant again? Dress up in a vest and such?"

"I need your help, so yeah, I guess that makes you my assistant."

He was cocky enough as it was, but I figured most of that was bravado and he probably didn't get many chances to feel important. I was pretty sure he had no family and slept on the street.

"No vest this time," I said. "You'll just be yourself. But there's a pair of shoes in it for you, too, once we're finished. And there's two-bits for another newsie if he'll trade corners with you for the rest of the afternoon."

"Have to pick up the evening edition at four-thirty. Settle up on these." He indicated the copies of the early edition still in his bag."

"Okay. You'll be done at four then."

I explained to him what I had in mind.

***

Cy Warren's political office was on Perry Street not far from the bus station. At the front desk a girl in a tight sweater was pecking dubiously at a typewriter.

"Hi," she said looking up. "Are you here to volunteer?"

Across from her three tables were lined up. One held tall stacks of paper. A map on the wall wore red crayon lines carving it into chunks. On the wall by the secretary a swag of bunting adorned an oversized photograph of the current governor. Surrounding it was a virtual gallery showing Cy Warren glad handing him and other luminaries.

I tried my best to look bashful.

"Actually, I'm here to see Cy."

"Oh."

The girl frowned. Her gaze slid to an open door in the wall behind her. On the other side of it I could hear men jawing at each other, and the snick-thump of a card game.

"Um, if you'll tell me your name I'll see whether he can come out. He's in a meeting."

"That's okay. I'll just go on back," I said, sailing past her.

The room at the back reeked of bay rum and male privilege. Four men in shirt sleeves looked up from a poker game as I stepped through the door.

"Mr. Warren, I wonder if I could speak with you for a couple of minutes." I flashed my brightest smile at the man I recognized from the photographs. He was middle-aged, medium build and strikingly handsome. His dark hair swept straight back. White streaked the center and temples.

"Oh, Mr. Warren, I'm so sorry!" the girl from the front desk apologized, crowding in behind me. "She just brushed right past—"

"Don't worry. No harm done."

He waved a finger and she scurried off as he produced a chuckle which didn't quite mask irritation. Leaning back in his chair, he clasped his hands behind his head and eyed me with practiced pleasantness.

"I'm afraid you caught us boys being naughty. What can I do for you, sweetheart?"

I let the 'sweetheart' go for the time being.

"My name's Maggie Sullivan, and I'd like to ask you some questions about Alf Maguire."

His reaction was nothing except faint puzzlement.

"Alf Maguire...." he repeated slowly. "I'm afraid I don't recognize that name."

Since he hadn't done the gentlemanly thing and invited me to sit down, I helped myself to the chair in front of his desk and crossed my legs. All four men looked startled. Maybe they weren't used to a woman making herself at home back here. Or most likely anywhere else. I made slow circles with my toe.

"Kind of odd it doesn't ring a bell," I said. "From what I've heard, the two of you cut quite a swath together over on Percy Street."

Cy Warren stroked his chin with his fingers.

"Percy Street.... Do you mean Alfred from the drugstore?"

"That's the man."

One of his cronies started to clear cards and poker chips from the side of the desk where they'd been playing. The other two seemed mesmerized by my legs.

"Lord almighty. I haven't thought about him in years." Cy's indulgent smile hinted at memories of youthful hijinks. "What's this about?"

I leaned forward and slid him one of my business cards. He read it and frowned.

"Sam — track down Wilkins and talk to him about the northeast. You two, go through those records again," he instructed the two who remained seated. "Use a fine tooth comb. I want something I can use at that meeting." When all three were gone, he picked up my card and read it again. "What's Alf done?"

I noted his switch from Alfred to Alf.

"What makes you think he's done anything?"

The indulgent smile appeared again.

"That's generally why people come to politicians. They're in some sort of jam or need some sort of favor."

"Alf's not much in need of favors right now. Then again, maybe he is, since from what I've heard he may need to do some bargaining with St. Peter."

Cy's forehead wrinkled.

"Are you saying he's dead?"

"Bingo."

"When?"

"Thursday night."

He sank back with a sigh.

"Poor old Alf.   But I'm afraid I still don't understand why you're here—"

"I was hired to find out about a man named John Vanhorn. He went to Dillon's Drugs on the day it burned down and he never came home.   Alf Maguire knew him. I'm hoping you did too."

He reached for a humidor on his desk, brows drawn in concentration.

"I'm sorry."   He removed a cigar from the humidor and clipped the end. "It's not a name I recall—"

"Were you there on the day of the fire?"

"Was I...? No. Yes." He paused to get the cigar going, buying time. The pupils of his eyes had contracted when I mentioned Vanhorn. "Those three days — that whole damn week — is a jumble, if you want to know. But yes, I was there then.   Not during the fire, though.   Earlier. Everyone was. Everyone with a shop. Moving whatever they could to the attics.

"My old man was exhausted. I made him go home while his horse could still get through the water. Told him I'd carry the rest of the boxes of shirts and some cartons of underwear up and stick them under the eaves before I locked up. It was the best we could do. Someone came along in a boat as I was leaving, shouted for me to get in. I don't even remember where I got out or walking home."

He let out a long stream of smoke and regarded me through it. Some cigars smell marginally better than cigarettes. This one brought to mind a hot iron scorching a shirt.

"I don't suppose you can tell me why you're asking about something that happened that long ago?"

"No."

Cy glanced at the doorway into the front of the office. He stood and went over to look out for a moment. When he resumed his seat at the desk, he leaned forward, lowering his voice a notch.

"You knew I was lying when I pretended not to recognize Alf's name the first time you asked."

"I've had plenty of experience spotting liars."

His sharp look told me he didn't like being included in that group.

"I wouldn't expect you to understand the intricacies of politics," he said smoothly. "Voters are moody. Especially now that we have to win the votes of you ladies." He shot me a smile that was probably meant to suggest we gals were all bright as buttons. "Sure, Alf and I had some laughs when we were young. But he isn't — wasn't — the sort I'd want people to associate with me now. In and out of debt. Setting up house for a woman half his age while his wife was dying."

I thought Cy might be overstating his concerns about voters just a little.

"Tell me about the in and out of debt part," I said.

Resting his cigar on the rim of a brass ashtray, he shrugged with what I recognized as impatience.

"We'd run into one another a couple of times through the years. Had a drink together once, I think. Twice he came to ask if I'd bail him out with a loan."

"Did he say why he needed the money?"

The politician shook his head.

"Gambling?"

"I don't know. Actually...." He pulled at his chin again. "Now that I think, the last time he came, he mentioned legal expenses."

"When was this?"

"Couple months back."

When he was contesting his dead wife's bequest of the house to Corrine, I thought.

"And before that?" I asked.

"Eight, ten years ago?" Cy gestured vaguely, his dwindling interest apparent.

"Did you pay?"

"The first time I did. Not the last. I feel somewhat bad now, knowing he's dead." He began to shrug into his suit jacket. "I'm afraid I can't spare you any more time just now. Come back any time if you have more questions."

I stood up. So did he. Resting a hand on my shoulder, he began to steer me gently but expertly toward the door.

"If I ever have need of detective work, I'll keep you in mind. I can see you're very good at your work."

He gave me a smile which crinkled his eyes. I smiled back.

"Looks like you're good at yours, too — sweetheart."

FOURTEEN

I left Cy Warren's office and headed left toward the corner without looking back to see if anyone watched me. Across the street, at the opposite corner and two doors up where he wouldn't be visible to anyone in Cy's place, Heebs lounged against a building. At sight of me, he began to amble toward the intersection, yelling in his best newsboy style to "get the early news." I turned the opposite direction. Our paths never crossed.

Halfway up the cross street I turned into a hole in the wall that sold coffee and sandwiches. Chances of Cy and his cronies showing up here were just about nil. Their watering hole was much more likely to be a beer joint. Five minutes after I'd settled myself at a table with two mugs of joe, Heebs came in grinning.

"Easy as pie, sis. They even bought two papers just to get rid of me."

He ladled sugar and cream into the coffee in front of him. The cream was too rich to pour and mounded on his spoon like pudding.

"Two sharpies and a girl in the front," he reported, licking the spoon. "Didn't get her name. They just called her 'the girl' when they told her to pay me. She took money out of a drawer, though, so I guess they weren't making her pay. None of 'em looked too worried. Didn't look like they were having a pow-wow or anything."

He slurped some coffee, checking the temperature. His next drink was quieter.

"At first the gents said they didn't need any papers, they'd already read the early edition and the late one would be out directly. I told 'em they ought to have papers out where people could see them if they stopped in. Make it look like they kept right up to the minute. They chuckled, but they said 'no' again. So I moseyed over to the girl and called her 'miss' — that butters dames up — but she said 'no' too.

"Didn't matter, 'cause I'd been thinking the door behind her was closed, and I hadn't seen any guy with white in his hair like you described—"

"Heebs!" I'd told him not to take any chances.

"So I said to the girl, all innocent, 'Anybody back there? Maybe they'd like one.' Only by the time I finished saying it, I had my hand on the door. I just got a peek before one the men in front yelled for me to get away from there or he'd knock me into next Sunday. He'd stood up and was heading over. I backed off meek as could be, and said I hadn't meant any harm. That's when he told me to give the girl two papers and git. So I did."

He paused, and I suspected it was for drama. He did, however, take the opportunity to swallow more coffee.

"Saw somebody back there in the little bit I got the door open, though. White streak down his hair makes him look kinda like a skunk?"

"Yeah, that's him." An opponent or two might have called Cy a skunk, but I suspected this was the first time the term had been used to describe his looks.

"He was hunched over the blower, talking away to somebody," Heebs continued. "Near as I could tell, he wasn't too happy." He hitched forward on his chair and crossed his arms on the table, eyes sparkling. "Listen, sis, if there's something shady going on there, I got a plan to keep an eye on things for you."

"No."

"Aw, you ain't even heard it yet. Haven't," he corrected hastily, saving me from doing it for the umpteenth time. "See, first I trade Con, who sells down here and let him have my corner for a week. He'll do it 'cause he'll sell more papers on my corner, so you'll have to make up my difference there. Then I'll keep going in to sell those pols papers, but I won't do anything else to get them suspicious. I'll just get chummy. Tell 'em how I'm interested in learning politics, and I'll do chores for them for nothing if they let me hang around."

"Okay, I've heard it and the answer's still 'No.'"

As plans went, it wasn't half bad. His attempt to see into the back room showed he took risks, though, and I didn't want to be responsible for his taking more.

"Why not?" he insisted.

If he put his foot wrong around Cy Warren's crew, they'd have him shipped off to the orphans' home before he could blink. If they suspected him of snooping, they'd do worse. But if I told the kid it was too dangerous, he might take it into his head to do it anyway. I thought quickly.

"I need you to do something that'll help more. We'll use part of that plan of yours, though." I looked at my watch. "I'll explain tomorrow — once I've gotten everything you'll need."

"Equipment?" He'd been looking down in the mouth, but that perked him up.

"I guess you could call it that. Right now you can help me with something else. When I leave here, watch out the window and see if anyone follows me. Not necessarily anyone from the place you just visited."

His face grew sober.

"You in some kind of danger, sis?"

"Nah." I slid out of my chair and winked. "Just may have an admirer I don't want." I picked up my purse. "Don't forget to get over to The Good Neighbor and ask for Clarice. Tell her I said put a pair of shoes for you on my tab."

***

Heebs and I had met up so soon after my visit to Cy that I'd had no chance to think about what I'd learned. As I walked back to my office, I began to put that to rights .

I'd learned Cy knew about Alf's love nest, for one thing. Maybe he'd only heard about the set-up second hand, but I was willing to bet a dime or two he'd had more contact with Alf than he admitted.

Maybe a lot more.

I wondered whether he might be the friend Alf was talking to in the back yard that night when two little girls were listening up in the tree house.

I also wondered whether the conversation the Vanhorn sisters had overheard that night was as sinister as they'd imagined.

When I'd removed my hat and had a cone of water from the cooler at the end of the hall, I began to update my notes. Most still went on a typed page, but now I also had a single hand-written page I kept beneath my typewriter when I went out. I started one when a case began to turn risky or odd, just in case anyone decided to snoop in my office, which had happened at least a couple of times. It had names and tidbits I wanted to keep close to my chest while I decided whether they mattered or not. The notes on it switched back and forth between English and Latin, in part because not many people inclined toward burglary would understand Latin, and in part because keeping my skills up to snuff was fun. If anyone invested muscle enough to lift the heavy old Remington, they'd be more irritated than enlightened by what they found.

Looking over my two lists of what I knew so far, one ugly little gap stuck out its tongue at me. It galled me I couldn't find out more about Alf's so-called suicide. Had the homicide boys decided yet if it was one?

Maybe I'd have to bat my lashes at Connelly. Now that I thought about it, he'd promised me a favor. Except I owed him one first, and I'd forgotten it.

I reached for my telephone book and flipped though pages to find the one I wanted. As I started to lift the receiver, the phone rang under my fingers.

"Hello? Hello?" The voice in my ear was hysterical. "Maggie? Are you there?"

"Isobel?" I said uncertainly. "What—"

"Help me! Please, you've got to help me!"

"Isobel, what is it? What's the matter?"

"Corrine...." She hiccuped with fear. "They've taken — Someone's taken Corrine!"

FIFTEEN

I drew a breath, trying to make out what she was telling me.

"Isobel, what do you mean? Who's taken her? Where?"

"*I don't know!*" She sobbed once, but struggled and managed to keep on talking. "I got a call at work. Someone — a man — said they had my sister. He told me to go home and wait if I wanted to see her again. He said if I told the police, they'd — they'd—"

"Are you at home now?"

"Y-yes. And she's not here!"

"I'm on my way."

I shoved my page of notes beneath the Remington and retrieved my .38.

My brain raced faster than the DeSoto as I made for the Vanhorn house, so I'd gone at least three blocks before I noticed the gray Ford behind me. It was an older model with headlights still on stalks. The left one was slightly out of alignment. Spotting it, I uttered a string of words which if overheard would have caused Mrs. Z to kick me out permanently.

Maybe it was just someone heading home, doing business, something innocent. To test the theory, I went another block and turned right. At the first opportunity, I pulled to the curb and unfolded a map. Rarely did I use it to find streets, but it made handy window dressing.

The Ford rolled slowly past and continued until it found its own place to park. I ground my teeth. I didn't have time to play these games. Isobel was waiting. As soon as I had a chance, I eased back into traffic. All I could determine as I passed the Ford was that the driver appeared to be on the short side, and somewhat fleshy. He pulled out after me.

Circling, I got back on Brown with the gray Ford hanging back two cars behind me. I had a plan now. I dawdled until the car between us became impatient and passed me. Burns Avenue was just ahead. I slowed some. Sped up as I neared the intersection. Waited until the last minute. Then I cranked the wheel hard and shot left on Burns without sticking my arm out to signal a turn.

Behind me I heard brakes squeal. The rearview mirror provided a fleeting view of the intersection, just long enough to assure me my tag-along had come to a stop rather than risk being broadsided by the car I'd seen approaching.

With luck the driver of the Ford would think I was headed for Percy Street. If this had anything to do with that location, which seemed increasingly likely. I turned sharply into an alley, and watched in the mirror as the Ford went past at a clip that suggested he'd taken my bait.

I made my way to the Vanhorn place without picking up my shadow again and without any sign of him when I turned into their street. Before I got halfway up the walk, Isobel threw open the door. Her curly brown hair was disheveled, as if she'd been crumpling it with her hands. I could see she'd been crying.

"Why would anyone do this?" she burst out. "*Why?* To a woman who can't even see? It's... it's...."

Taking her elbow, I steered her gently back inside.

"They're trying to scare you," I said.

Or me, I thought grimly.

Someone didn't want any more digging into what had happened on Percy Street the day John Vanhorn had disappeared. Maybe they wanted to scare the Vanhorn sisters into dropping any further inquiry. Or maybe, having failed to scare me off with the threat on my license — and possibly the attack in the parking lot — they'd made an innocent woman a pawn to dissuade me. If that was their plan, it was much more effective than anything else they were likely to try.

Right now the only thing I could afford to think about was finding Corrine. Her sister refused to leave the hall, where she could reach their telephone in a flash. We stood there while I had her go through every detail, starting with the phone call.

"And you're certain it couldn't have been Neal?" I asked when she'd finished.

"Heavens no!" She looked at me in horror. "He has a short fuse, but he'd never do anything like this. Besides, I'd recognize his voice even if he disguised it."

Having played some roles on the phone in my time, I wasn't so sure. Still, I didn't see what Neal had to gain. Especially since I'd already established he couldn't have been the eavesdropper that first day I came to this house.

"I'm afraid they've already hurt her," said Isobel lapsing into sobs. She gestured toward the parlor, unable to speak.

I went into the room where I'd sat on my first visit. A lamp was broken. A chair near the door was turned over. The gleaming poker from the stand beside the fireplace now lay on the floor at least six feet away.

"They didn't even let her take her cane," said Isobel looking in from the hallway. Her voice broke. "She hardly ever used it once she got Giles. But without either one of them, in a strange place, she'll be utterly helpless!"

I eyed the white stick lying on the floor. Had Corrine hurled or brandished it in a futile effort at self-defense? Or had the intruders kicked it aside before she got the opportunity?

"They were probably afraid she'd wallop them with it the first chance she got," I said in hopes of bolstering Isobel's spirits. "Looks like she put up a pretty good struggle." There was no sign of blood, which was good, but I didn't mention that.

The phone rang. We both jumped.

"Yes?" said Isobel. "Hello?" She tipped the receiver so I could listen.

"Isobel? Oh, Isobel! Are you all right?" sobbed a voice.

"Corrie! Thank God! Are—"

"Come get me! Please come get me! Some awful men took me and drove me around and let me out and — I don't know where I am! *I don't know where I am!*"

***

I drove north against traffic carrying people home after work. Isobel sat white-knuckled beside me, so close to the edge of her seat that she'd go through the windshield if I had to stop fast. A man with a kind voice had taken the phone and told Isobel her sister had found her way into his shop. At first she'd been almost unintelligible, she was so scared. Then she'd calmed down enough to ask him to call. He gave Isobel an address.

It could all be a setup.

The address took us north of the river to a rough neighborhood of hard work and hard drinking and more than a few shady businesses mixed in with honest ones. In the angle formed by Valley and Keowee, I parked in the first slot I found. Just a few blocks away there were factories and machine shops, scrap yards and auto repair places. This was a commercial district of sorts. Small businesses and eating places were interspersed with boarding houses, private homes and a few beer joints.

The shop we'd been directed to sold sewing supplies. One corner showed off a brand new Singer, along with used ones. The rest of the place held bolts of cloth and bobbins and whatnot. Corrine sat next to a small table that held pattern books, her hands knotted tightly together. Almost as soon as we'd stepped in, she seemed to sense her sister's presence. She sprang to her feet.

"Isobel?"

Isobel ran to her and they embraced, clinging to one another. Corrine's fingers dug into her sister's back so deeply I winced, imagining the welts they would leave.

I thanked the balding, bespectacled man who came hastening toward us, and who doubtless was the one who had called.

"It's shameful. Shameful someone would be so cruel to a blind woman," he said. An accent I associated with Czechs and Poles edged his words.

There'd been a few customers in the shop when we entered. Two of them turned from a bolt of cloth to look at the embracing sisters, who were oblivious to them.

"Did you see anyone, a car that might have been involved?" I asked. I gave him one of my cards.

His eyebrows raised. "No, no one. But my window is small, you see. I don't see much back where I stand."

He spread his hands, indicating the counter where he cut cloth and rang up sales. A woman I took to be his wife stood there now.

"I think they must have pushed her out in the alley," ventured the man. "We tried to ask her some questions, my wife and I, but she was so..." He hunted for the word. "...agitated. She kept talking about an awful smell and stumbling over things." His head shook sympathetically.

I thanked him again and went over and stopped a few feet away from Corrine.

"Corrine, it's Maggie," I said softly. "I brought my car. Whenever you're ready, Isobel and I will take you home."

She pressed her handkerchief tightly against her mouth. Her usually smooth black bob was tangled and her dress and arms were smudged. After several seconds she nodded.

"Yes. Now. I...." Her head turned aimlessly.

"I've already thanked the man who helped you," I said. "You can call or stop in when you're feeling more like yourself again."

The thread of a sigh escaped her.

"Yes. Thank you. I've — been such a bother."

"You're not a bother. The men who did this to you are s.o.b.'s. And I'm going to find them and see that they pay for it."

SIXTEEN

"Corrine, are you able to talk about this?" I asked when she was settled on one of the needlepoint sofas in her own parlor with an afghan tucked around her. In spite of the wrap and most of a glass of sherry, she was shaking.

"No.... Yes.... I can. I must."

I wondered if those last four words had been a motto which she'd whispered to herself a thousand times over the years as she struggled to prove herself competent in a world she couldn't see.

"How many were there?" I asked.

She almost smiled.

"Thank you. For thinking I might be able to answer that. Most people wouldn't."

"I think you've got more on the ball than most people. How many, then?"

"Two, I think. Possibly a third who didn't speak. But maybe I only think there were three because every way I turned—" Her mouth crumpled. "I was so scared—"

"Can't this wait?" pleaded Isobel.

Corrine put out her hand.

"It's all right, dearest."

"From the looks of this room, you made them work pretty hard to take you," I said.

"I heard them come in, you see. The front door opening. I thought it might be Corrie coming home early, or Mrs. Blair from next door. So I called, but nobody answered. Then I knew — I knew someone was coming to hurt me."

"So you managed to get to the poker."

She nodded. "Only just when I did, one of them grabbed my wrist. My other wrist, but it hardly mattered. I hit him as hard as I could, but I only had one arm to swing with, and I couldn't tell how tall he was or what part of him I was hitting. I think I only hit his shoulder. Then one of them slapped me, and they put a sack over my head—"

"A sack?" I said, looking up from the notes I was making.

Her laugh was short and brittle.

"Ironic, isn't it?"

Not only that, but vicious, I thought. Sadistic. The men who'd taken her knew who she was. They'd phoned her sister at home and at work. I'd bet my bottom dollar they also knew Corrine was blind. They hadn't demanded money for her release. Their only purpose had been to terrify her, and they'd used the sack to add to that terror.

"What did they say?"

"Hardly anything. It - it meant I couldn't tell where they were."

While adding to her fear, I thought.

"When they first... when they first got control of me, one shoved his face into mine and asked 'What did he see?'"

"Who?"

"I don't know. That's what I asked. They jerked me up out of the chair they'd put me in and one of them shook me and asked it again. I said I didn't understand. That's when they dragged me out to the car. That was all until just before they shoved me out. One — the same one, I think — said 'Next time will be worse.'"

I struggled against the anger that would make me useless.

"Someone's warning you not to stir up the past," I said to both of them. "You might be wise to take their advice. This could have nothing to do with your father. It could be connected to Alf. Something he was mixed up in back then, or even recently. I've heard he's tried to borrow money a few times."

"But it could have to do with our father?" Corrine persisted.

With anyone else I wouldn't think twice about lying. It didn't seem fair to lie to Corrine. I chose my words carefully.

"It's possible," I admitted. "But even if there is a connection, it won't bring him back. Even if I could somehow find out Alf killed him, which is what you seem to think, there's no way of bringing Alf to justice now. "

The two women turned toward each other in that intimate gesture where they shared thoughts wordlessly.

"We want to know," Corrine all but whispered.

"Oh, Corrie, I'm not sure—" began Isobel.

Corrine extended the palm of her hand. She looked pale. Exhausted. Shrunken in on herself in a way she hadn't been the first time we met.

"Tell us what you've learned so far," she said wearily. "Then we can decide."

I nodded, remembering too late that she couldn't see.

"Before I do, can you remember the name of Alf's friend? The one you heard him talking to when you were in the tree house?"

These were not impulsive women. They thought several moments before shaking their heads.

"What about his other friends? First names? Last?"

Neither spoke.

"I'm sorry," Isobel said at last. "We - we didn't really like Alf, so we spent as little time around him as possible. Not because he'd replaced Papa. Because he was loud, and always too, well, hearty and chummy. When he and Mama were first married, he'd fling his arm around our shoulders and squeeze and - and he'd pinch our bottoms."

She looked down at her hands, her face flaming. I gave her some time to recover.

"One more thing before I tell you what I've learned," I said. "Have you ever heard the name Cy Warren? Cyrus?"

Isobel looked puzzled by this new direction.

"Didn't he run for City Council? Something like that?"

"Ran and was elected."

"Does he have some connection to this?" asked Corrine. The weariness in her voice was unmistakable.

"I don't know," I said. "Here's what I've learned so far. At the time of the flood, there was a place called Dillon's Drugs on Percy Street. Alf worked there. In fact he was part owner."

Corrine gasped and gave her hands a clap.

"I knew it!" she said, her excitement reviving her if only briefly. "Go on. Is there anything else?"

"The drugstore burned down the day your dad disappeared. The other owner died in the fire. Alf got what was left, which from what other shop owners in the area told about their places, can't have been much. Most moved out. Only one old lady remembered Alf and she didn't like him."

At any rate she was the only one who admitted knowing him, I amended silently.

"Oh, this is wonderful!" Corrine smiled. "That must be where he was headed. Can you find out more, do you think?"

"I'm not sure."

Half of me wanted to keep digging, mostly because I was sure I'd gotten the run-around from Cy Warren, and maybe one or two others. And because someone had been more than willing to ruin me to achieve their own purposes.

The other half was reluctant to expose these two women to further attacks.

Isobel rose and started to pace with jerky steps. "For heaven's sake, Corrie, what's the point? As Maggie pointed out, Alf's dead now. We can't do anything."

"If someone is trying to scare us, then there must be something to learn," her sister said stubbornly.

"It could have nothing to do with your father," I repeated. "Someone may think you know something you don't."

Isobel came to a stop behind her sister. Frustration overflowed. She drove the sides of her fists down onto the top of the sofa.

"Listen to what she's saying, Corrine! We may learn nothing — and what if those awful men come back?"

Corrine didn't answer at first. Her mouth hardened.

"Neal forgot Alf's shotgun when he collected his things Sunday. I know where the shells are. I know how to load it. I'll sit here, facing the door, and if I hear anyone coming in, I'll shoot. It won't matter that I can't see them. I can't miss."

Isobel was too horrified to speak. It took some time before I could.

"What if it's your nice neighbor lady, stopping in to check on you?" I asked.

"She'd call out to let me know who it was. She always does."

"And what if she called out just as you were pulling the trigger?"

Corrine was silent. Her sister was still shaken.

"Please, Corrie! I've already told you that you could come to work with me—"

"And sit all day being useless? Have everyone pity me when you have to take my arm and guide me whenever I need to use the restroom?"

"No—"

"What about your church—" I began.

"No! I'm not going to be an object of pity. I can — I can—"

All at once she wilted. Tears squeezed noiselessly from her eyes.

"I'll go to the institution. The home for people like me," she said brokenly.

I heard her sister stifle a small cry. Corrine turned her face toward me. The tears slid out faster now. She extended a hand to me, pleading.

"Please. If I do that so I'm not a - a liability, will you keep investigating?"

SEVENTEEN

My hands seemed welded to the wheel as I drove north on Brown from the Vanhorn house. I was furious that someone had humiliated a woman who'd fought so hard to be independent. Killing her dog. Then coming back to abduct her and mock her with a bag over her head.

I was going to find that someone.

I'd promised.

Maybe giving in to Corrine wasn't the smartest thing I'd ever done, but I was fairly certain it had been right. Nature had robbed her of her sight. I wasn't going to let someone rob her of her dignity.

The problem was, Isobel had argued vehemently against her sister taking refuge in a home for the blind even temporarily. Though she didn't say as much, I suspected she thought it might prove the final blow to Corrine's self-confidence. She was no doubt right, but letting Corrine remain where she was meant Corrine might again be used as a pawn to stop the very investigation she wanted.

The trauma of the abduction, and her need to escape into the oblivion of sleep, had begun to make the unfortunate woman intractable. No, she wouldn't have a bodyguard, even though I knew a couple of good ones. She cut off any mention of the police, whom I privately thought unlikely to help since she'd been neither assaulted or robbed. She wouldn't let Isobel ask for another day off work, which was probably good if Isobel wanted to keep her job.

Finally Corrine was persuaded to let the neighbor woman stay with her the following day. The problem with that solution was that the neighbor might also be subjected to any violence which occurred.

Surely, I reasoned, the hoodlums who'd abducted Corrine would wait for a few days before they tried anything else. They'd wait to see whether their scare tactics had put an end to my questions.

I wasn't as convinced as I wanted to be by that rationale, but it led me to one conclusion: The sooner I found out who wanted to put the kibosh on my questions and why, the sooner Corrine Vanhorn would be safe.

It was after six now. The only place I might accomplish anything useful this late in the day was at Finn's. First, though, I wanted to leave the photographs I'd borrowed from Isobel at my office. It was late enough in the day I spotted a parking space in the next block and walked back. As I reached the intersection, a big, black Buick swept up in front of me, cutting me off. The rear door swung open.

"Get in," said a voice.

EIGHTEEN

I put my hand on the roof of the car and leaned in through the open door.

"Gee," I said to the woman sitting behind the driver. "Last time you put me in here, you had this door welded shut."

"I'm working on being polite. Now get in."

Her name was Rachel Minsky. She had a cloud of black hair, a china doll face, and shimmering dark eyes that revealed her thoughts about as reliably as a cobra did before striking. The sable fur-piece circling her plum colored suit was fastened with a gold clasp. Somewhere in her expensive garb, where she could produce it in an instant, she carried a small gun.

She used it extremely well.

I got in.

Pearlie, the guy who'd come to my office offering to dispose of Oats Ripley, sat in the driver's seat. Rachel fitted a cigarette into a gold holder as the car glided off again.

"Pearlie's heard something about you that he finds alarming."

"Not that awful rumor that I'm not a virgin, I hope."

Pearlie snorted.

Rachel's eyes narrowed. "Don't be a smartass."

She cranked her window down with jerky movements and snapped a lighter, starting her cigarette. When she had it going, she cupped her elbow in the opposite hand and regarded me with displeasure. Shifting her jaw to the side, she blew a stream of smoke out the window.

"He says you won't let him solve the problem of Oats Whatever- his-name-is."

"It's not that I don't appreciate Pearlie's offer. It's that if I took him up on it, some people might get the idea I'm not tough enough for my kind of work."

She contemplated me some more. If anyone could understand my explanation, it would be Rachel. She owned a good-sized commercial construction company which she ran herself. The uncle who'd owned it before her had been crooked. I was pretty sure Rachel wasn't. Nevertheless, she could play as rough as she had to, whether on a muddy work site or competing for deals against big-wig businessmen. Her rivals didn't like her for several reasons: She was a woman. She was a Jew. She often beat them at their own game.

It was why she had Pearlie. She referred to him as her boyfriend. I took it for granted that was a joke.

I liked Rachel.

I liked Pearlie.

Their strange display of concern gave me an idea.

"If you want to improve my odds against Oats, there's another problem Pearlie could help me with," I said. "It would keep me from being distracted."

Rachel blew more smoke out the window.

"What kind of problem? What would he need to do?"

"Make sure nobody bothered a blind woman for a couple of days."

Pearlie tended to make people nervous as soon as they saw him. The way he dressed. The way he moved. The way his eyes watched.

Corrine wouldn't see him. If I could spin a story for her, it just might work, and I excelled at spinning stories.

The big black Buick meandered slowly down Monument, just inside the embrace of the river which a quarter century ago had spewed forth the chaos at the heart of my case. Its waters ran serene tonight. Across the way the Art Institute and the nearby Masonic Temple rose on their hills. Staring over the city, they were aloof from floods, aloof from the passing concerns of mortals. I told Rachel and Pearlie about the Vanhorn sisters. I outlined what I had in mind.

"What do you think, Pearlie?" Rachel asked when I finished.

He shrugged. "I like piano music."

We turned back through side streets where lines snaked into soup kitchens and families settled in to sleep in doorways. Rachel suggested a drink. I said it would have to wait; I had something to do.

They dropped me off in front of Finn's, which was fortunate. The man I wanted to see was just leaving.

***

"Something happen to your car?" asked Connelly as the Buick pulled away and I came to join him and Seamus.

"Car's fine. Some friends picked me up and we went for a drive. Glad I wasn't five minutes later getting here. I was coming to see if you two might want to go find some supper."

Seamus shook his silvery waves.

"Not me. Got me a sandwich and can of beans waiting." He pursed his lips thoughtfully. "Not something you wanted a word on, is there?"

I slipped my arm through his and gave it a squeeze.

"Everything's fine, Seamus."

"Well, then. I'd best not miss my bus."

Before I could speak again he was striding off at a good clip for a man with a bad knee. I didn't know what to make of it.

"Was that his way of playing matchmaker?" I asked.

Connelly chuckled.

"I saw him get the sandwich, and I know he bought a new record yesterday. My guess is matchmaking was the farthest thing from his mind."

I felt considerable relief. Seamus was the only person I knew who never tried to meddle. Not in my life, not in anyone's life. He was there for you, like a rock, never offering advice or opinion unless you sought it. Then it was worth hearing.

Connelly gave me a sideways look as we drifted along. I fought its effects. Memories of my mother's toxic discontent swirled up around me like the flood waters at the heart of this case.

"So. You want a favor, I'm guessing," said Connelly.

"Yeah. I do. And I haven't even talked to that concertina player like I promised I would. I had the phone directory out to see if she was listed when I got a call that one of the women I'm working for had been snatched."

Connelly stopped in his tracks.

"Snatched! You mean kidnapped?"

"No — and she's home safe now. Men came into the house and dragged her off and called her sister to say that they had her."

I filled him in on that part of my day, skipping over the details of being stopped by Rachel. By the time I finished my story, we were sitting in a place a few blocks away, waiting for our blue plate specials.

"Corrine was just about two breaths shy of falling apart completely," I said. "She didn't want the police, and I didn't think much would get done even if I insisted."

Connelly rubbed his chin with the back of a finger the way he was wont to do when thinking.

"No, probably not," he agreed at last. "No proof of damage done, no money demands. And if the two women got tagged as hysterics over that dog business...."

"Yeah."

Our blue plates came.

"So what's the favor, then?" Connelly asked when the waitress had gone.

"I want to know whether Alf Maguire's death has been written off as a suicide or whether it's getting a closer look."

He cut a piece of pork chop and ate it without switching his fork to the other hand. A more efficient way of eating, I thought. My dad and Kate and Billy had all abandoned it in favor of the American style. I wondered if Connelly would too, eventually. I doubted it.

"Can't see the harm," he said. "It may take awhile for me to find out since I'm just about the bottom of the pile and don't hear much of goings on at Market House."

Like all the other beat cops, Connelly worked out of Central Police Station which was a good half dozen blocks away from headquarters.

"You're thinking someone wanted Maguire out of the way?" he asked.

"Yes. But unless there was something odd when they found him, or Alf was shadier than his stepdaughters let on — and they didn't like him — there'd be no reason for the police to be suspicious."

Connelly drew a napkin across his mouth and pushed his empty plate aside.

"The men playing poker with the politician. You said he sent them out to do something when you gave him your card."

"I think he realized he'd be smart to have the rest of his conversation with me in private."

"Could he have been sending them over to scare the blind woman?"

It took me awhile to consider.

"I don't think so. Judging by when the men who abducted Corrine arrived — she remembered the clock striking shortly before they came — they'd have been there before Cy's pals even left."

"Okay, then who else even admitted to knowing Maguire?"

Connelly said something else, but I lost track of his words. Something was oozing up out my memory. The Vanhorn sisters had mentioned that Alf had two sons. Why did the pictures I'd gotten from Isobel just a few hours ago show only Neal and his stepbrother George?

NINETEEN

"Do you like cowboy stories?" Pearlie inquired.

"Cowboy stories?" Corrine said weakly. "I - I don't believe I've ever, ah, heard any."

"One brave lawman protecting a town against outlaws," Pearlie recited as if he'd read it somewhere. "I brought some to read so I didn't get in the way." He brandished a pulp magazine. "Thought I could read one out loud if you liked."

"Oh.... Why, that's very thoughtful."

She hadn't seemed frightened of Pearlie when I introduced them a few moments earlier. She just didn't know what to make of him. Neither did I.

"Please. Make yourself at home," she said, gesturing toward the parlor.

"I really appreciate your letting him come here so he didn't have to sit around his hotel room all day," I said when the two of us were alone in the hall.

I'd called Isobel last night and passed Pearlie off as a friend who'd come into town on business only to have his meeting delayed. Corrine had been more receptive to the idea of keeping someone else company than she had been to having the shoe on the other foot.

"Isobel said you wanted a picture of Franklin," she said as she moved unerringly toward the hall table holding the telephone. She removed an envelope and handed it to me.

"According to Isobel, he and his dad had a blowup and didn't speak to each other?" I said.

"Not for fifteen years or better."

"Any idea what caused the blowup?"

"No." She tried to smile. "Goodness. I'd better see to your friend."

We walked to the front door together so she could lock up. She'd recovered from yesterday's ordeal better than I expected. Her shoulders still drooped, though.

"Franklin was nicer than his brother and Alf," she said at the door. "He came back to see Mama a few times when he knew Alf wouldn't be here. When her illness got worse and we knew she didn't have long, we called him. He came that very evening."

***

It was only half-past nine, too early to call on the woman who'd given me concertina lessons all those years ago. I had other tasks to fill out the time. Too many to fit in the morning, in fact. At the top of the list was talking to Heebs.

He was at his usual corner hawking papers. By the lightness of his bag he'd had a good morning. His worn out shoes had been replaced by a sturdy second hand pair.

"Saving a paper for the girl with the best-looking legs in town," he called when he saw me.

When I got close enough I took one and slipped him money enough to cover the job he was going to be doing for me. I spoke quickly, my voice low.

"If I'm not in my office when you get finished here, stop in the sock wholesaler down the hall from me. The young clerk there's named Evelyn. She'll have an envelope for you. Sit out in the hall where her sourpuss mother-in-law can't see you and look at the pictures. I want you to keep an eye out to see if any of the men in the pictures go into Cy Warren's place. When you've had enough of a look at the pictures, slide them under my door."

"You behave yourself, now, Sis," Heebs said loudly enough for passers-by. He gave me a fresh-guy wink.

I walked off grinning at the kid's moxie. When I reached my building and started across the small lobby, the elevator door folded open and Boike's blunt shape stepped out.

"I was just up looking for you," the detective said in greeting. "Chief Wurstner told me to bring you this."

He handed me a slim business envelope.

Curious, but with no intention of opening it until I went upstairs, I took it.

"Thanks."

Boike cleared his throat.

"Chief says I'm to wait while you read it. Make sure you understand." He looked down at his shoes. "It's, uh, your official letter of warning."

My mouth opened but I managed not to say anything.   I'd thought everything was okay between me and the chief.

"Yeah, fine."

I ripped the envelope open. The single folded sheet inside contained only one line. It was handwritten. I read it and blinked. It wasn't what I'd expected. I read it again:

My wife would like you to stop by at eight this evening.

What the devil did this mean?

Boike, whose stolid manner seldom hinted at what he was thinking — or even noticing — wore an expression suggesting he'd rather be anywhere else.

"Tell the Chief I understand perfectly, and I'll do as instructed," I said. "And Boike — if you could find it in you not to mention this to anyone else, I'd be grateful."

What Chief Wurstner was setting in motion by sending him here was unusual, to say the least. I had a pretty good idea the message he'd sent had nothing to do with meeting his wife. Whether it did or not, the fewer who knew about this communication, the better, lest he appear to grant favors, or worse still lest it prompt tawdry speculation. If Boike believed his discretion might spare me embarrassment, he'd be less likely to mention this errand.

Boike mumbled he would and headed for the street as fast as decency allowed.

I felt bad for Boike. He was a good guy. I thought about how he'd tried to make amends for Fuller's obnoxious behavior over the dead dog, and the sadness on his face as he'd looked down at the unlucky animal. The memory suddenly hooked in to something I'd been contemplating, and I ran out after him.

"Boike!"

He turned at the sound of my voice. I caught up.

"Did one of the cops tell me once that you like dogs?"

"Crazy about them. Guess I'd have three or four if I could. Why?"

I didn't blame him for the note of caution in his voice. He'd just brought me a missive that he believed would upset me.

"I'll walk with you so you're not late getting back," I said. We fell into step. "That dog that got its throat slit the other day?"

"Yeah?"

"The woman who owned him's lost without him. It's not just that he was her eyes and helped her cross streets and that, it's that he... I don't know. Gave her confidence too. Maybe just being there with her. I thought maybe you knew somebody had a nice one they needed a place for temporarily. Even permanently. Their yard's plenty big to have two dogs. I just thought it would be company for her, make her feel better until she gets the kind you can train."

He stopped in the middle of the sidewalk, staring at me.

"Are you telling me that pretty woman was *blind*?"

Pretty?

Either Boike had been married a very long time or he didn't date much.

"Well, yes," I said. "That's just what I'm saying."

Boike removed the olive green fedora that was the only one I'd ever seen him wear. He pushed one hand through his pale hair as though to regain equilibrium and set the hat carefully back on his head.

"I never noticed that," he said glumly.

"Hey, I'm a detective too, and I didn't know till she told me."

That seemed to make him feel better.

"There's this old lady who takes in strays," he said as we began to walk toward Market House again. "Lives just outside of town. I go out on weekends and help her since I can't keep a mutt where I am, and working my hours. I'll see what I can do."

I said thanks and turned back toward my office to update my notes and get the photographs ready for Heebs. My mind, however, wasn't on Heebs or photographs or even getting a dog for Corrine. It was on the message from the chief of police. I didn't for a minute believe it had anything to do with his wife. I thought it meant he'd decided to share some sort of information.

TWENTY

Every minute until eight o'clock that night was going to be torture. Returning to the neighborhood where I'd grown up helped pass the time. I couldn't bring myself to drive past the house we'd lived in. The loss of it was still too acute. From a few blocks over it was no trick at all to trace the route I'd once walked to a wee little white frame cottage where Mrs. Brennan had made valiant attempts to teach me the basics of playing the concertina. Not the English kind where you got the same note regardless of whether you pushed the two sides together or pulled them apart. Her students, as might be expected, played the Irish concertina, where every button pressed could give two different notes, depending on whether the bellows were pushed or pulled.

I hadn't wanted the lessons.

I had no innate talent.

Truth be told, I wasn't that crazy about Irish music.

The lessons were my dad's idea. I liked to think it was the only time I'd disappointed him.

Going up the walk, my steps seemed to slow, just as they had when I was nine. The middle two sections of sidewalk still heaved up in a little hillock. I stepped onto the narrow stoop and turned the wings of a doorbell mounted in the center of the door. It jangled inside, and a minute later I heard footsteps.

The door opened. A stout, short woman with gray hair pulled up in a bun peered at me for several seconds. Her eyes brightened.

"Maggie Sullivan. It is you, isn't it?"

"Hello, Mrs. Brennan."

"Land's sake. Well, you'd better come in, hadn't you?" She swung the door wide, smiling.

Her front room wasn't much changed, only now I was old enough to recognize it reflected a woman who lived life to the fullest. It was chock-full of potted plants, an overflowing knitting basket between two comfortable chairs, and two straight-backed chairs suggesting she still gave lessons. In a row on top of her scarred upright piano perched four of the dainty hexagonal squeezeboxes which she played.

"You're looking well," I said.

She brushed the words aside as nonsense, but she did look nice in her house dress and bibbed apron. Like she had some fizz to her, although she was bandy-legged and tended to list as she walked. Maybe she hadn't been quite as old as I thought when I was a kid.

"Will you have some tea?" she asked, waving me to one of the easy chairs.

"Thank you, no. I can't stay."

"Are you here because you're wanting to have a go at lessons again?" she asked with a twinkle.

I laughed.

"It's a wonder you didn't pinch my head off the first time around. I don't think I'd better press my luck. I looked you up because a fellow I know is hunting up people who like to play some of the old tunes. Wants to get them together in the back room at Finn's pub — you know where that is? — on Thursday nights. Just for fun."

"You mean a *seisiún*?"

"Well, I suppose."

"Land, I haven't played with other people in I don't know when."

"It's just Mick — that's the fellow organizing it, Mick Connelly — and a couple of others. Finn hadn't played his fiddle in years. I don't know who else. When I mentioned you, Mick went wild." I wasn't sure why I was trying to sell his venture, but I was.

"Oh, child. My fingers are so crooked now, not half as nimble as they used to be."

"That would still be nimble enough for any two people," I said.

She made her dismissive gesture again, and I saw that her hands had, indeed, fallen prey to the swollen knuckles that went with aging. Her gaze slid toward the row of concertinas on her piano. Despite her protestations, her cheeks were as pink as a girl's.

"I'd muck it all up," she said. "But I have a girl coming to me for lessons. Twelve now, she is, and been coming since she was six. Plays like a demon.

Maybe I could bring her. See how she got on. I think she might fancy it, and I know her Ma and Da wouldn't object. You'll have to write the address, though. Thursdays, yeh? So they'll be there tomorrow."

***

Checking property records, which was where I wanted to dig around next, would take more time than was left of the morning. Instead I went back to the office to learn what I could about Alf's son Franklin. Heebs had picked up the photos as scheduled and slipped them back under my door. I studied the one I'd gotten that morning.

Franklin Maguire was lots better looking than his brother, starting with a nice square chin. Most of the time you couldn't tell hair color in pictures, but I'd guess his was light brown. His gaze was level and on the serious side, or it had been when the shutter clicked. I put the picture back with the others and looked at the phone number Isobel had provided.

She hadn't listed an address, and when I asked Corrine that morning, she hadn't even known what street. From the things the sisters had said, they might not have been there. Franklin appeared to be on better terms with them than the rest of his family was, though. Maybe better than their own brother.

I stuck my unsharpened pencil into one of the holes on the front of the phone and dialed the number from Isobel.

"My name's Maggie Sullivan," I said when a woman answered. "I'm trying to reach Franklin Maguire?"

"Yes?"

"Is he there, please?"

"Why no, dear. He's at work."

"Oh, of course. I didn't think. I'm helping his stepsisters tidy up after his father's death—"

"Gracious! We didn't know his father had died."

Interesting.

I wanted the address, but I also wanted to talk to this woman, who must be his landlady, as well as to whoever else 'we' included.

"I need to drop off some papers for him," I improvised. "I'm afraid I've misplaced the address...."

She told me and I arranged to stop by. Before heading there, I bought a couple of roast beef sandwiches to drop off for Pearlie. I had some concern that he'd get restless sitting around a house all day. If it looked necessary, I'd tell him the men headed for his fictitious business meeting had arrived. In that case I wasn't sure what my next step would be. Maybe spend the afternoon with Corrine myself, and get nothing done.

Remembering the car that had followed me the day before, I left my building through a door in the janitor's closet in back. The door had been there before the neighboring building was built. It no longer opened completely. Once through it, I had to crab sideways between the two buildings to get to the alley. The maneuver was a nuisance, but it meant that anyone watching my office wouldn't even be aware I'd left.

When I got out at the tidy gray house where Franklin lived, a man with tufts of hair in his ears and cheeks red from exertion looked up from painting the lattice work around the foundation.

"Tell her I'll be in directly to get washed up," he said in greeting.

"Sure. Nice day for that kind of job."

"Long as the leaves don't blow in it while it's wet," he grunted, absorbed in his task.

Franklin's landlady turned out to be a wiry little woman with frizzy hair. The house was immaculate, with starched curtains at the windows.

"Gee, what a nice place," I said when she'd let me in and offered a chair. "Has Franklin lived here long?"

"Six years last spring. Poor man. We didn't even know he had family, except for his sisters, and I don't believe he saw them that often. We've talked about it, the mister and I, how he's such a nice young man but doesn't seem to have any fun at all. Spends all his time working, except for his night classes."

"Isobel says he's quite keen on his work," I nodded. "Clerking, I think she said, but I can't recall where."

If I forgot as much as I claimed to, I'd be out of business.

"Watkins Plumbing Supply." His landlady frowned. "Don't you know Franklin?"

"No, just his sisters. As I said on the telephone, I'm helping them out. There's so much to do after a death. Oh, here are the papers I came to drop off. If he has any questions he can give me a call."

I stood. If I asked more questions, the woman might get suspicious, which I didn't want in case I needed to stop back. She glanced at the envelope I handed her. It was sealed, with Franklin's name typed neatly on the front.

Fishing could sometimes get just as much as questions could, and seemed innocent. I decided to risk a little.

"You seem fond of Franklin."

"Oh, we are. He lends a hand to the mister sometimes, when Franklin sees him moving a heavy ladder or something like that. Some renters wouldn't, you know."

"Then I think maybe it's okay to tell you. Franklin didn't have much to do with his father. The man was ... well, I hate to speak ill of the dead, but he was crude. Quite rowdy, really, from what I've heard. Spent a lot of time carousing and drinking."

Somewhere at the back of the house a door banged and someone clumped in. The mister coming in to wash up, no doubt. His wife was nodding wisely. Her voice became confidential.

"I'll bet that's who it was the one and only time we've ever had any trouble with Franklin. Two men, and the way they were shouting and late as it was, I just know they'd been drinking." One finger tapped my shoulder in excited emphasis. "The mister went out in his nightshirt and told them if they didn't leave he was going to call the police. Poor Franklin. He came in the next day and apologized. He was so embarrassed."

We'd been moving toward the front door. I stopped.

"When was this?"

TWENTY-ONE

"We just may, possibly, be getting somewhere," I told the DeSoto. I gave the steering wheel a perky little fingertip tap like Franklin's landlady had given me.

According to her, the incident with the men had happened about five months ago. No, she and the mister hadn't been able to hear what was said, except when Franklin raised his voice and told them he wasn't going to get involved. One of the men had replied with something quite crude.

I suspected the men had been Alf and George Maguire, or maybe George and Neal. The players mattered less than the subject. From the time frame, it could have to do with Alf's challenge to Corrine's inheritance, or it could have to do with his attempt to borrow money from Cy Warren — assuming that story wasn't utter malarkey.

Still chortling with my feeling of progress, I rang the bell at the Vanhorn house. Pearlie opened the door.

"Everything's O.K.," he said. "Miss Vanhorn's in the kitchen."

The fragrance of roasting chicken enveloped me as I stepped into the hall. Corrine came through the kitchen door wiping her hands on a tea towel.

"I brought some sandwiches by," I said, feeling foolish as I held up the sack.

"Oh, how thoughtful," said Corrine. "I'm afraid I've just taken a chicken out. Isobel and I were going to have it last night, but then it was too late and we didn't have much appetite. I didn't want it to spoil. Won't you join us?"

"Um, no. Thank you."

"I do believe Mr. Thomas has a knack for piano," Corrine was saying. Pearlie had instructed me to introduce him as Paul Thomas. "We had a lesson and he can already play 'Happy Birthday.'"

I looked at Pearlie. He gave his dog like smile.

"She's got some students coming this afternoon," he said. "Forgot to cancel them last night. I'll make myself invisible. Sit and read."

I felt as though I'd fallen into one of those Walt Disney cartoons where animals danced and sang.

"That's good," I said weakly. "Well, unless I hear from those people you're going to meet with, I'll stop by to pick you up around five."

His car was parked around the corner, but he nodded agreeably. I said good-by and got back in my DeSoto still holding the sack of sandwiches. At least I had lunch.

***

Talking to Franklin Maguire was now high on my list of things to do. Digging into his father's finances was higher still. Maybe I'd have a look at Cy Warren's too, while I was at it. The more you know, the more directions you can veer off in when you question someone, and the more you can pick up from something they say.

I spent the afternoon soft soaping clerks and looking at documents in public records offices. By the time I finished, my hand was cramped from taking notes and my face hurt from squinting at faded ink. I walked back to my office having learned a couple of interesting things.

One was that Alf Maguire didn't appear to be in any sort of financial bind. He owned a good-sized house up on Harvard, presumably the 'monstrosity' one he'd built after marrying Mrs. Vanhorn. Nobody held a mortgage against it, the taxes were paid and he'd been collecting rent on it for several years. Three years ago he'd bought the duplex where he'd installed his girlfriend. Everything was paid up there, too. The business he'd acquired when he landed a wife and stepchildren looked to be doing okay. I had no way of knowing his bank balance, or if he had gambling debts, or if he had other business ventures that weren't doing well, but from what I'd learned so far, I couldn't see him needing a loan.

The second thing I'd learned was how Alf and Cy had gone from being under the thumb of others on Percy Street to where they were now. That might include Alf being six feet under.

For both men, it had started with the sale of the properties destroyed in the fire. The fact that they'd sold wasn't in itself remarkable. A number of the owners whose businesses burned had done the same. After all, what were they going to live on while waiting for a new building to be constructed? Available funds might be better spent on restocking goods and equipment and renting space elsewhere. Alf Maguire and Cy Warren's father had been the first to sell though, and with each sale after that, property values had dropped.

It was what came next that intrigued me. Not six months after selling the lot once occupied by Dillon's Drugs, Alf had bought another lot three doors down. Shortly afterward, Cy's father bought two adjoining lots a block away. A few months later, Alf and Cy bought a lot together. Cy eventually became owner of record on the two his father had purchased, and still held those deeds. But the one Alf bought, and the one he and Cy owned together, as well as several others on the street, had been sold to an outfit called Swallowtail Properties.

Maybe Alf and the Warrens had simply seen an opportunity and seized it. Still, it made me curious.

Satisfying my curiosity would have to wait. Right now I needed to check in with Pearlie. Then I wanted to talk to Mick Connelly. After that, I was scheduled for a tête-à-tête with the chief of police.

Not many girls have such a varied dance card.

***

"I told her my business associates still hadn't shown up. She said I was welcome to come back tomorrow," Pearlie reported. While I thanked Corrine, he'd waited for me in my car even though his own was around the corner. He told me later she'd sense it if we didn't leave together.

"Fine," I said. "Her sister gets off at noon on Thursdays. I'll call around a quarter till and tell whoever answers that the people you're supposed to meet have just gotten in. Then I'll pick you up."

We'd reached his car. I stopped with motor idling for him to get out.

"Hope she has some lessons scheduled," he said. "They're interesting. Had a boy this afternoon she said was an absolute terror, but he musta been on his best behavior. Corrine couldn't believe it. Said maybe I had a calming influence."

Pearlie gave his smile. I grinned. The kid was probably on his knees right now vowing to mend his ways if he didn't cross paths with Pearlie again. He might even be entertaining thoughts of entering a seminary. Pearlie stepped back and I drove away.

I was running later than I liked, so instead of heading directly to Finn's, I decided to drive toward Ford Street Station. The day shift was ending and cops would be heading home, or downing a pint at the end of the day. If I could catch Connelly between the two places, I might save the time required to park and wait while Finn filled my glass before finding out whether Connelly had learned anything.

The Central Police Station, known as CPS or Ford Street, was a block-long warren of spaces and offices. Cells, booking, and interrogation rooms were headquartered there, along with most of Dayton's sworn officers. The only exceptions were headquarters brass, detectives and some special units over at Market House. Not far from the CPS entrance, a railroad siding ran parallel.

A block and a half before I got there I spotted Connelly moving along with his loose-limbed stride. Billy's short figure bobbled beside him.

Billy had a black eye.

I cut across traffic and pulled to the curb so abruptly that horns blared.

"Billy! What on earth happened to you?" I asked jumping out.

"Ah, it's nothing," he scowled as I took his arm and tried to get a better view. "Saw a couple of punks breaking into the back of a house. While Mick was scrappin' with his, the one I grabbed got his arm free and clobbered me. Couldn't get to my club without losing him, so I unsnapped my holster and gave the pipsqueak a tap with the butt of my gun."

"Pipsqueak was going on six feet," Connelly said dryly. "Hasn't been an hour since it happened, and Billy's making a stink over me wanting to see that he gets to the trolley okay." He raised an eyebrow.

"You're not taking the trolley," I said firmly. "You're riding with me."

"I don't need fussing over, or like it either!" Billy complained as I steered him.

"Gee, you get plenty of practice handing it out when other people don't want it."

Connelly quickened his pace for a few steps and opened the passenger door of the DeSoto for Billy.

"You coming to Finn's? I've learned something," Connelly said in my ear as Billy got in, his litany of objections flowing without interruption.

TWENTY-TWO

Connelly caught my faint shake of the head in response to his question. I needed to freshen up and get something to eat before I saw Chief Wurstner. Running Billy home was going to make my schedule tighter. I wanted to hear whatever Connelly had to tell me, though, and he picked up my cue when I offered to drop him somewhere after we'd delivered Billy. He climbed into the back.

"Guess it turned out kind of handy having your gun in that holster," he said solemnly to the white head seated in front of him.

"One time. Never going to happen again," Billy blustered.

I caught Connelly's eye in the rearview mirror and saw his mouth twitch.

Like most of the older cops, Billy had grumbled when new department regulations called for service revolvers to be worn in a holster on a Sam Browne belt. The sidearms previously had been carried in a policeman's jacket pocket. Loudly, freely and frequently Billy had shared his opinion that 'flaunting' a gun would only make people fear the police.

We turned Billy over to Kate, who sighed like she'd dealt with Billy's injuries and tantrums more than a few times.

"You take care of that shiner, Billy," I urged, giving him a soft little peck on the cheek as I said good-by. It always flustered him when I kissed him, but this was this first time I'd seen him injured. Minor as it was, it worried me some.

"He get hurt anywhere else?" I asked Connelly as we went down Billy's front walk to my car.

"Just his pride. Did I guess right that you wanted to hear what I knew while we drove?"

"Yeah. I've got an appointment with somebody who may have useful background for me, but I've got things that need doing first. I talked to the concertina player, by the way. She claims her fingers have gotten too old to keep up, but she talks like she'll bring a student of hers who's a whiz."

"Thanks." Connelly shifted, resting his back on the door and facing me as he spoke. "In addition to a note, the cops found a nearly empty bottle of whiskey on Maguire's kitchen table. He was on the floor next to the table. Looks like he passed out — from the booze or the gas — and fell out of his chair. It had scooted some.

"There was a broken glass with whiskey residue not far from his head. Could have been knocked off when he fell, or dropped when he hit the linoleum."

"Tidy."

"It is that."

"Innocent?"

"Homicide has concluded it is. They're calling it suicide."

"Ten bucks says they're wrong."

Connelly was silent.

"Anything in what you've heard that would make you question the suicide verdict?" I asked.

He rubbed his thumb across his chin and I could hear the rasp of stubble along his jaw. It made the confines of my car feel uncomfortably intimate.

"Nasty bump on the side of his head," Connelly ventured.

"Enough to knock him out while somebody turned on the gas?"

"Hard to say without seeing the scene. And he could equally have gotten it when he fell."

"Not much reason to question it when all the other trappings fit so nicely," I said.

"'Tidy' I believe is the word."

We were at Finn's. I pulled to the curb and he got out.

"If I pick up anything else I'll let you know," he said through the door. "What's the concertina player's name?"

"Brennan."

"First name?"

I thought for a minute.

"Mrs."

***

I set out for Chief Wurstner's house driving the same car I'd borrowed when I went to talk to Theda. The neighbors kept the car in a shed at the back and I went out the back door at Mrs. Z's to collect it. This time around the precaution was more for the chief than it was for me. No sense letting anyone know he'd done a private snoop a favor.

The house was handsome without being fussy. It was three stories tall, dressed in awnings, with a small balcony over the front door. A peppy middle-aged woman with spectacles on her nose answered the doorbell.

"Miss Sullivan?"

"Yes."

"How nice to meet you. I've read about you. My husband's in his study. Let me show you the way."

A sense of unreality made me unaware of details for a moment. I was in the home of the chief of police. The trance ended as I stepped into his wood-paneled study. There was a large desk in one corner, but he rose from a wing-back chair in the opposite one, putting aside what looked like a thick report of some kind.

"Miss Sullivan. Won't you sit down?"

"Thank you. And thank you for seeing me."

He had traded his uniform jacket for a cardigan over his white shirt and tie, the closest he got to informal, perhaps. I perched on the edge of a chair that faced his.

"I generally have a whiskey this time of evening," he said. "Will you join me?"

I hesitated. This was chummier than I'd expected. I wondered if he had some unseen agenda; if he was assessing me in some way.

"If you'll put a good deal of water with it," I said.

A small chest against one wall held an ice bucket and the various accouterments one could take with whiskey. He didn't speak again until he'd brought me mine.

"I reconsidered your request," he said, resuming the seat he'd occupied. He brought his glass of whiskey, which he drank neat, level with his eyes. He studied it without drinking. "I see no harm in speaking about things that happened in 1913. You appear to have ruffled feathers by your attempts to learn something about that time. I believe in your position I would be curious. I believe if someone appeared to be pulling strings to silence me, it would make me dig all the harder."

He took a sip of whiskey, watching for my reaction.

"Funny," I said. "That's just the effect it had on me."

His stern mouth smiled ever so slightly.

"May I ask what you've learned?"

"I've learned the man who disappeared was headed for a place called Dillon's Drugs on Percy Street. I've learned the man found dead last Friday — Alf Maguire — was part owner of that business. There was a gas explosion, nothing like the one downtown, but several businesses along there burned down, including the drugstore. The other owner of the drugstore died in the fire, his remains pinned down by an overturned cabinet. Maguire and a man who's now a politician were pals at the time, though they may have gone their separate ways since."

I wasn't sure it was wise to mention their property dealings. For one thing I hadn't seen evidence of anything crooked. For another, I had no idea how cozy Chief Wurstner was with various politicians. I drank some whiskey and water.

"That's about it."

Wurstner nodded. His eyes focused on distant thoughts.

"I don't suppose you'd care to name the politician," he said after a minute.

"I'd rather not."

He took a pipe from the stand beside him, filled it, and when it was ready, puffed.

"And what were the questions you wanted to ask?"

"I was hoping you might be able to tell me who was patrolling Percy Street at the time of the flood. If they're still around, I thought I might...."

He was shaking his head.

"I knew the man who walked Percy Street very well. We were friends. He died, oh, six years ago."

"What about records?"

"Record keeping, even of a rudimentary nature, wasn't high on the list of priorities for some time after, I'm afraid. The cleanup alone was.... My God, I can still smell the stench of dead horses. Fourteen hundred carcasses. That was my job. Heading a detail to cart them out of the city to a disposal site. I'd just made corporal."

He chuckled, but he was rubbing his forehead. His eyes were dark.

A tap at the study door interrupted.

"Rudy, I'm sorry to intrude, but you apparently promised to look at some homework."

Wurstner knocked back the rest of his whiskey and got to his feet. I stood too.

"I knew your father," he said. "He was a very fine man. Tenacious. You remind me of him." He opened the study door for me. "If I recall anything that might be useful, I'll give you a call. Charlie and I — the man who patrolled Percy — talked about the flood sometimes. When we were alone."

"Thank you." We shook hands.

"I'll see Miss Sullivan out," said his wife.

He nodded and started upstairs. Mrs. Wurstner walked beside me to the front door.

"I do needlepoint," she said. "If anyone asks. I'm working on a chair."

She was making sure I had a leg to stand on in case anyone learned that I'd been here.

"It's been a pleasure to meet you," I said.

They were a gracious couple, the Wurstners. Probably kind. Yet as I pulled away in my borrowed car, I couldn't help thinking the chief of police had gotten plenty of information from me, while I'd gotten nothing useful from him.

TWENTY-THREE

I'd had high hopes when I received Chief Wurstner's invitation. The next morning I rattled around my office feeling sorry for myself. As far as I could tell, I wasn't any closer to discovering what the Vanhorn case had stirred up than I had been before Corrine's abduction. I walked back and forth to the window. I kicked the metal wastebasket next to my desk. The wastebasket was acquiring a swell brocade pattern as a result of similar assaults.

Maybe talking to Franklin Maguire would shed some light on things. According to his landlady, he got home from work around half-past five.

Meanwhile, I wanted to see what I could learn about Swallowtail Properties, the outfit that had bought up lots on Percy Street, including the ones owned by Alf Maguire and Cy Warren.

There was something faintly familiar about the name. Did it only seem that way because of the property records I'd pored over yesterday? Or had I come across it somewhere before that?

The newspapers at the library. Maybe.

I grabbed for my telephone directory.

There it was. Swallowtail Properties. I tapped my teeth with a fingernail. When I went through the papers at the library I'd been hunting things on Cy Warren. His occupation was real estate when he wasn't politicking. That had to mean I'd come across the name Swallowtail in connection with him.

Did he own Swallowtail Properties? Had he and Alf been partners?

Grabbing my pencil, I dialed the number in the book.

"Good morning. Swallowtail Properties."

"Hi," I said in a breathless rush. "This is Sally. Is Cy in? I just need a minute."

"No, I'm sorry, he's already out and about. Who did you say—?"

"What about Alf?"

"Who?"

"Alf Maguire."

"I'm afraid there's no one here by that name."

"Oh, gee, did I get it wrong? I can't read what I've written." I tittered. "I'll try Cy at his campaign place. Thanks."

I hung up.

Gloating would be unseemly. Then again, there was no one else to gloat for me. I'd just linked Cy to Swallowtail. It sounded like he might be the owner. But Alf appeared to be unknown there. Had he sold out to Cy all those years ago when, on paper, they'd both appeared to sell to Swallowtail? Or had what looked like sales actually been the formation of some sort of corporation or similar legal entity?

And what did any of it have to do with John Vanhorn's disappearance?

The question put a crimp in my gloating. I thought for a minute and called Corrine.

"Do you remember your mother or Alf mentioning something called Swallowtail Properties?"

"Swallowtail Properties," she repeated thoughtfully. "I don't believe so. It's rather whimsical. Is it important?"

"It might be."

"I'll ask Isobel."

"That's okay. If it starts to look as if it is important, I'll give her a call. How are you and P— Paul getting along?"

"Oh, splendidly. One of my voice students came for a lesson this morning. I don't believe he enjoyed that as much as piano. He's so quiet most of the time that I almost forget he's here."

I thanked her and hung up. Since this was Isobel's half day at work, I'd be able to talk to her when she got home in a few hours. Right now I felt an urge to trot over to Cy Warren's headquarters.

Before I'd gotten my hat on, the phone rang.

"Yeah, this is Mr. Thomas," said Pearlie's voice. "Just checking to see if those gentlemen— They have? Sure, I can make it then. Could you call Miss Sullivan and tell her to pick me up at twelve sharp? Thanks. Tell her if she can't make it to give me a buzz and I'll take a cab."

"You want me to be there at noon," I confirmed. That was half an hour earlier than we'd arranged. Something was up. "Any problem?"

"No, no. That's all I need, thanks."

For several minutes I stood puzzling through the conversation. I couldn't imagine anyone getting the drop on Pearlie and forcing him to make a phone call. Even if they managed to do it, they wouldn't know about our subterfuge of his being in town for a business meeting. His gibberish had been for Corrine's sake. Reassured there was no crisis, I headed for Cy's campaign office.

***

A meeting was in progress when I got there. Several dozen men, mostly white-haired or bald, sat or slouched around the tables by the map that was marked with red crayon. A man with a stogie jammed in his mouth was talking to them. Another man was passing out mimeoed sheets.

The redhead who'd been in the back room with Cy the first time I showed up noticed me first. He went over and whispered to Cy, who was listening to the cigar smoker. Cy looked around. I waggled my fingers. I thought he looked a shade irked, but it was gone by the time he reached me.

"Miss Sullivan. What a surprise to see you again. Did you come to help put ribbons together? That meeting's this evening. Or do you just find me fascinating?"

It was either a joke or a warning. I smiled.

"Not enough to worry your wife."

Pinpoints of something appeared in his eyes, gone before I could even be sure I'd seen it. Did Cy have wife troubles? I recalled his seeming indignation over Alf's love nest. Maybe it had been real and the politician didn't consider playing around a subject for levity.

"Actually," I said. "I came to find out about Swallowtail Properties."

He looked at me without understanding.

"My business? It's commercial real estate. As I'm sure you must know. I can't see how this relates to what we discussed yesterday."

"I'm interested in its beginnings. When you and your pal bought up places on Percy."

"'Bought up.'" He rocked his head back and chuckled. "You make us sound like a couple of moguls."

Over by the map, the guy with the stogie was still going on. Cy made deliberate show of consulting his watch.

"I can't spare more than ten minutes. Let's go to my office." He glanced at the redhead who'd tagged along and was hiding a grin as he eyed me curiously. "Eddie, take over here. I'll be in back if you need me."

Cy and I didn't chat any more until he'd closed the door to what he called his office.

"First, let me assure you there's not an iota dishonest about my business dealings," he said, sitting behind his desk with force enough to suggest anger. "If there was any dirt to be dug up, believe me my political rivals would have done so long ago."

Once again he failed to invite me to sit. Once again I did anyway.

"I wasn't suggesting that," I said mildly. "As I told you, my only questions relate to Alf Maguire. When did he sell his interest in Swallowtail?"

I was going out on a limb with that, but my call to the Swallowtail office and the fact Corrine didn't remember the name gave me at least some confidence.

Cy removed a cigar from the humidor and clipped off the end. He lighted the end and drew a couple of times, letting me wait.

"Alf was never a partner in Swallowtail," he said. "I started it. I bought several lots along there, including the lot Alf owned. It's how I got my start."

"It wasn't the lot where the drugstore had been though."

"No. Like most of the others whose places burned down, Alf saw he faced a long wait to rebuild and start over. So did my pop. He had the idea of selling, and taking the money from that and what insurance paid and finding someplace he could rent instead. Alf thought that was smart, so he did the same thing."

"But then you both turned right around and bought again."

Cy removed the cigar he'd started and studied the end.

"The fire just about destroyed my father. Broke his spirit. He talked about starting over, but I could see his heart wasn't in it. Or maybe it was, and he just...." His hand waved vaguely. "He'd lost his energy. Worried constantly. Didn't sleep. My mother and I were worried about him. On top of that, places to rent were scarce, so much of the city had been destroyed.

"I persuaded Pop to keep enough money to live on and use the rest to buy vacant property and put up a building or two to rent. No cost for merchandise, no waiting on customers six days a week. Property along there was dirt cheap by then. The bank knew him. He was able to get a loan for construction. I think he put in a good word for Alf as well." He paused and smiled. "It turned out to be a very good move."

"And a few years later you, or your father, became Swallowtail."

"By then we saw the possibility of increasing our holdings. Having a business name made us appear more important than we actually were at the time."

He chuckled, an affable fellow looking back at how he'd succeeded, modestly hinting it was equal parts hard work and dumb luck. I wondered how closely his true nature matched the role he was playing.

"But Alf wasn't interested in being a part of it?" I asked. "You'd owned one parcel together."

"Ah. I'd forgotten. We bought him out, as I recall. Alf was impatient. Real estate was too slow a game for his taste. In any case, he'd married his winsome widow by then."

I gave him my sunniest smile and stood up.

"Thanks. You've been a real help."

And he had been. Without even knowing.

TWENTY-FOUR

Amid all the rest that Cy had told me, the word 'winsome' blinked at me like a neon sign. At our first meeting he'd attempted to give the impression that he and Alf had scarcely any contact after the flood, and that certainly they'd done none of the swaggering around together attributed to them earlier. Yet he'd known that Mrs. Vanhorn was a looker. Moreover, Cy's use of the possessive '*his* winsome widow' suggested Alf had been interested in her for some time before he'd married her, and that Cy had been aware of that interest.

Neither point struck me as something a man would mention casually on the street. It seemed even less likely if the two men meeting had been close once but no longer were.

On the other hand, it sounded very much like something one pal would confide in another over a few beers. If the woman in question was happily married, the enamored man might lament his lot and exaggerate her charms. I'd overheard enough conversations in Finn's and other gin mills to know such misery was usually met with the joking that passed for sympathy among men, followed by an off-color comment or two and maybe some prurient speculation.

His winsome widow.

I thought about it as I watched the car that was following me. It wasn't the Ford with the crooked headlight that had tried to trail me once before when I was headed to the Vanhorn place. This one was a nondescript black Dodge. Such cars were plentiful, and I wouldn't have noticed it except for having to keep one eye peeled for Oats Ripley. As near as I could remember, it had been behind me since I left the parking lot. As soon as I'd become aware of it, I'd jotted down part of the license number. This was still the same car.

The problem was, I was on my way to get Pearlie, and he'd made it clear I shouldn't be late, but I didn't want to lead anybody straight to the Vanhorns.

The occupant of the black car could be Oats, or someone he'd hired. It could also be one of Cy Warren's lackeys. Cy would know about the Vanhorns since I'd asked not only about Alf, but about John Vanhorn. Oats wouldn't. It gave me an idea.

After hopscotching several blocks, I cut back through an alley, then nosed in between some other cars parked at the side of a building. For several minutes I watched the intersection where I'd begun my maneuver. No sign of the black car.

There were only three blocks to the Vanhorn's street, but each was several times the length of those downtown. I recognized Pearlie's car at the end of Corrine's block. It was headed in the right direction for what I had in mind. And there at the opposite end sat a black car that looked a lot like the one that had followed me.

Corrine's perkiness when she opened the door assured me all was well. Pearlie was right at her heels.

"Come back any time you're in town," she said as he thanked her.

"You've been an exquisite hostess," Pearlie replied. His alertness as he ducked past me conveyed impatience to be under way.

"Isobel should be home in thirty minutes or so," I said. "Don't answer the door until then."

Corrine had two fingers over her mouth and was chuckling silently. Her attention appeared to be fixed on something beyond me.

"I'll be perfectly fine," she said waving aside my concern. "Mr. Thomas does use some odd words at times, doesn't he?"

"Uh, yes," I agreed.

At the curb Pearlie was leaning comfortably against my DeSoto.

"Some cop's coming over to see her," he said when I joined him. "Called her and asked if he brought some dogs by, would she give him advice. Said he had the afternoon off."

Boike.

"And you didn't want to chance being here," I said.

Pearlie shrugged. "Don't like cops."

"Mind helping me with something else for maybe fifteen minutes?"

"Sure." He opened the passenger door.

"There's a black Dodge parked up the street," I said as I went around to the driver's side. After I drop you off, I think it's going to follow me."

Pearlie was the only person I knew who not only didn't need warning not to look, but never appeared to do so no matter how casually. He flicked his cigarette into the street and got in.

"What do I do?"

"Fiddle around till he passes you. Check your tires or something. Then you follow him. I'm going to hunt for a stretch with a couple of parking spaces and pull into one. If he pulls over too, you block him in."

Pearlie wore a small smile of expectation. It showed only his canine teeth.

"What if he doesn't?"

I started my engine and executed a U-turn to deliver him to his car.

"Then you go on back to Rachel and tell her I said thanks."

***

This time the black car was cagier, but only because it kept a couple of cars between us. Either the driver was used to tailing Dumb Daryls, or he didn't have much experience at what he was doing.

I went up Brown instead of Main. Less traffic would get snarled if I had a chance to try my plan. Eventually I saw the perfect setup. Just ahead of me was a vacant parking spot. Four or five spaces beyond that, a car was pulling away from the curb.

Sticking my arm out the window, I signaled and slowed, creeping toward the newly vacated space. I couldn't see Pearlie behind the Dodge, but I had every confidence that he was. Motioning a car around me, I began to angle into the parking space. Another car went around me. Then all my attention, not to mention my muscle power, went into turning the steering wheel.

By the time I'd finished, I didn't see any black Dodge in my rearview mirror. What I did see was Pearlie's car stopped in traffic a few spaces back. His hand was out the window only as far as his wrist. One finger motioned languidly for people to pass. I heard a horn toot. I got out of my car and strolled back.

There wasn't room to kick up my heels between the car at the curb and Pearlie's car. There was, however, room for me to tap on the window.

The guy inside was medium build, with lank brown hair and nervous eyes. I didn't remember seeing him before, but lots of people had been at that meeting at Cy Warren's place. His eyes were bobbling this way and that, and the size of billiard balls with the realization he'd not only been spotted but trapped. His hands appeared to be stuck to the wheel.

I tapped again and gave him my most pleasant look.

His gaze slid toward the passenger door, trying to decide if he should run for it. Instead he swallowed and turned the handle to lower his window two inches. Somewhere behind Pearlie a car honked. I leaned in agreeably to talk through the window.

"Hey, it's flattering, having someone following me all morning, but I'm kind of shy. Tell Cy if he wants to know where I'm going, he can call my office. Give him this, so he doesn't need to look up the number."

I tossed one of my cards through the gap in the window. The man on the other side grabbed for it as if it were a glowing cigarette about to land on his privates.

I sauntered back to my car. Pearlie drove past me. I started the DeSoto and drove off.

Nobody followed.

TWENTY-FIVE

Picking up Pearlie had cost me a chance to talk to Neal when he came out for lunch. By the time he got off work for the day, I'd need to be elsewhere if I wanted to talk to his stepbrother Franklin Maguire, which I did. At half-past five I was parked near the house where Franklin rented a room with (his landlady bragged) its own tub and toilet.

Franklin was easy to recognize from the photograph Isobel had lent me. As I'd guessed, his hair was light brown. He walked briskly, a man who was either efficient by nature or on some schedule. He took no note of my car as he turned up the walk to the gray house with its freshly painted latticework.

My plan was to give him about twenty minutes before I went calling. He'd have time to wash up, maybe relax a little. It would make him more receptive to my questions.

Franklin had other ideas. He'd only been inside ten minutes before he came out again, wearing the same fawn-colored cap and tweed jacket he'd worn when he went in. This time, though, he carried a book and notebook. He set off with the same purposeful stride.

Recalling his landlady's mention that he took classes, I jumped out and hurried across the street to intercept him.

"Mr. Maguire?"

"Yes?" he said politely. The lack of hostility put him several notches above George and Neal in my estimation.

"I'm Maggie Sullivan. I left you an envelope."

"I'm afraid you forgot to put in whatever papers you intended. My landlady said it had something to do with my father's death."

"Yes."

His manner had grown more cautious.

"Could we do this tomorrow? I've a class to attend." He gestured with the book he was carrying.

"I have a car." I nodded toward my DeSoto. "If I give you a lift can we talk?"

A slight frown had appeared between his eyebrows.

"What's this about?"

"Some problems your sisters are having." I handed him one of my cards.

His head snapped up.

"Corrie and Isobel? What kind of problems? Don't tell me that idiot George is hounding them," he said sharply.

I liked it that he hadn't corrected me that they were his stepsisters.

"I don't think so." I indicated my car again.

This time he walked quickly around to the passenger's side and we got under way.

"Before I tell you about it, one question," I said. "Where were you last Thursday night?"

"A week ago?" His bark of laughter lacked humor. "That's easy. In a ditch somewhere between here and Waynesville. All night. With my boss." His eyes slid toward me and I thought I saw the ghost of a grin. "I expect the police have already checked with the farmer who found us. They asked the same thing.

"Herbert — Mr. Moore, my employer — was taking his truck down to pick up a secondhand display case that a place that had gone bust was selling cheap. He asked would I go along to help lift it. We had trouble finding the place, and getting it into the truck took longer than we expected. Then we got turned around on the roads and had to backtrack. Just when we thought we were finally on track, a deer came bounding out in front of us. Herbert hit the brakes, and I guess the display case shifted. Next thing we knew, we were in the ditch. Fortunately, we didn't roll or anything, but we were stuck there till morning when a farmer came along and saw us and pulled us out with his tractor."

I laughed. "I've heard some doozy alibis, but that takes the cake."

"Yes, doesn't it." Franklin was relaxing now. "That's why I headed out early tonight. I missed last week's class because of the trip. Another fellow in it said I could copy his notes, so we're meeting up for a sandwich." His expression turned serious. "Now, what's this about the girls having problems?"

I told him about being hired to look into what became of their father, omitting the fact that they thought his own father might have had something to do with it. When I mentioned an eavesdropper, he hitched in his breath. When I got to the part about the dog being killed, he swore under his breath and turned his face to the window.

"Poor Corrie," he said. "Poor, sweet— That dog was more than her helper, you know. He was her dearest friend, next to Isobel. Who in God's name would do such a thing?"

"Would Neal?"

He turned to me, startled.

"Neal? I don't think so. He's hotheaded, but — No, I'm sure he wouldn't. He wouldn't have the stomach for it. Besides, he's kind of soft on animals."

"What about your brother?"

"George?" He chuckled faintly. "He's even less likely. They both swagger and talk tough, but they're mostly hot air."

"And your father? Could he kill the dog, knowing how indispensable an animal like that is to a blind person?"

He was quiet a moment.

"Yes," he said at last. "I believe he could. And the dog didn't like him. But why—?"

I shook my head. I'd learned all I needed to know and I saw no need to shame him further.

"I wanted to talk to your father because he and John Vanhorn were cousins of some sort, and may have had friends in common. I'm trying to find out who those friends were."

Franklin glanced at his watch. We were only five minutes or so from his destination.

"You think someone my father knew killed Corrie's dog?"

"It's possible."

He looked at me thoughtfully.

"It's not just the dog, is it? What else has happened to them?"

"Let's save that for later. What I need to know, before you get out, is if you know the names of any of your father's friends. Ones who maybe came to the house when you kids were little."

He rubbed his thumb against his lower lip.

"There was a fat one who always slapped me on the back and called me 'laddie'. I hated him. I don't recall his name." He closed his eyes as if to see the past more clearly, then shook his head. "He had men over sometimes. To play poker mostly. Jokey sorts who laughed a lot. I don't remember hearing names, though. Can't even picture anyone except that one I didn't like."

I gave him a minute or two to dredge something more up, but he shook his head.

"What about someone named Cy?" I asked.

"Cy?"

"Or maybe Cyrus."

He rubbed his thumb on his lip again. "Possibly. Or maybe it's only because you mentioned it. I just don't know."

The business school where he took his class was just ahead.

"You never told me about the rest of the troubles the girls were having," he reminded.

"Can I tell you this weekend?"

Filling him in on Corrine's abduction wouldn't take long, but I had more questions, and time to think some before I asked them would be handy.

He didn't look pleased, but his head dipped in acceptance. "Sure. I guess. I'll be around."

I pulled to the curb and let him out. Another fellow about the same age who was waiting in front of the school started forward to meet him.

"Look, is there anything I can do to help them?" asked Franklin, leaning down and preparing to close the car door. "Besides talking to you, I mean."

"Yeah," I said. "Your sisters seem to enjoy it a lot when you visit."

***

My meeting with Franklin Maguire hadn't yielded much more than my visit to Chief Wurstner the previous evening. It now seemed likely that Alf was the one who had killed the dog, but that didn't tell me why someone wanted to halt further digging into John Vanhorn's disappearance.

Genevieve and I went for supper together. Then I washed out a blouse and some stockings. I had a fast bath and was entertaining sour thoughts as I wound my hair into pin curls when someone knocked rapidly on my door.

"Phone call," said Esther. "He wouldn't say who it was."

It was just shy of Mrs. Z's cutoff time for using the phone in the hall downstairs. I tugged my bathrobe tight around my waist and hurried down.

"This is Maggie Sullivan," I said warily. Only a handful of people knew my number at Mrs. Z's: Billy and Seamus, Connelly, Wheeler's Garage, Jenkins.

"I've been thinking about the man assigned to Percy Street at the time of the flood," said Chief Wurstner's voice without introduction. "I believe I mentioned to you that we were friends."

"Yes."

I was gripping the handset tightly, hoping this call meant he'd found something useful.

"I've remembered something he told me. At the time it seemed unimportant, just a child's chatter. Something to smile over when we needed it. After what you told me last night, I wonder if.... Anyway. There was a little girl. Six or seven, I think he said."

"And she saw something?" I couldn't restrain my impatience.

"Her family had come back afterwards to salvage whatever they could of their things. The officer — my friend — saw them and asked how they were. Made small talk. There was so little else you could do. He asked the little girl had she been scared when the water got high. She told him no, just sad when the men put the store dolly out by the barrel, because the dolly was going to be lonesome out there in the rain by himself."

A chill crept into me. A chill from the freezing waters of twenty-six years ago.

"A store dolly?" I repeated.

"He said her mother laughed and explained it was what she called clothing dummies."

"Mannequins."

"Yes."

I drew a long breath.

"Who would bother putting a mannequin out in the middle of pandemonium?" I asked.

"Exactly."

TWENTY-SIX

Friday morning I found myself pulled in three directions. Most tantalizing was the possibility of locating a little girl who might or might not have seen something on the day John Vanhorn disappeared. I also wanted to know the extent of the holdings of Swallowtail Properties.

The trail of the little girl would be stone cold by now. Without specific addresses, uncovering more on Swallowtail would require time, and most likely contacts I didn't have. That left number three, the easiest of the lot, talking to Neal again. The way he'd dissolved into panic when I asked whether he believed Alf had committed suicide had seemed excessive. At the time, I'd accepted it as grief and his inability to absorb the reality of his loss yet, let alone imagine it resulting from something sinister.

Now, after the attack on his sister and the car that had followed me yesterday, I wasn't so sure. Giving him a shake or two might jar loose information he'd kept to himself. If I started with Neal, I should still have most of the day left for heavier digging.

The sky was a brilliant autumn blue. Just beyond where my car was parked, the produce market gave off a cider-y scent of ripe apples and buzzed with voices. Grocers and restaurant cooks as well as housewives shopped at its stalls. Two women with overflowing shopping bags passed me, chattering about the jelly they were going to make and the wonderful grapes available today. It gave me an idea for upping the odds on an outing I planned later.

Temporarily ignoring the market's temptations, I drove to the factory where Neal worked. As I'd dressed that morning, I'd contemplated skipping breakfast in order to catch him on his way in. I'd decided against it. Making him worry he'd clock in late wasn't likely to improve his receptiveness to me and my questions.

As I'd guessed when I'd come here before, the inside of the factory was cleaner and less of a barn than most. Its small front office was well lighted. A brick wall at the back muffled thumps from machinery.

"Could I speak to Neal Vanhorn's supervisor?" I asked the woman who came to the counter to help me. I gave her a card. "Neal's family hired me to tidy up some loose ends on their late mother's estate. His sisters thought if I could speak to Neal for a a few minutes he might recall a couple of names that we need."

The woman pressed her lips together and looked toward a door in the back

"Um, just a moment, please. Let me check."

Hugging her sweater around her, she went to speak to a woman at another desk. They both looked in my direction, then conferred in low tones. The woman at the desk picked up a telephone. I waited. Several minutes passed before a man with heavy brows knotted together and a sour expression strode through the door. He made a beeline toward me.

"You looking to talk to Neal Vanhorn?"

"Just for five minutes. If they get some sort of break I can come back then."

I tried a smile on him. The effort was wasted.

"You can't talk to him then or any other time," the man glowered, folding his arms. "Didn't come back from lunch on Tuesday. Hasn't called to say he's sick. Not a peep. Plenty of others want work. I replaced him yesterday."

An alarm began to go off in my brain.

"Did anyone try to reach him? Call where he lives?"

The man regarded me with disdain.

"Like I said, there's plenty of men want a job if he don't."

He turned and left.

***

I sat in my car recovering my wits. What I'd just learned worried me. Maybe Neal had found a better job somewhere else. It was easy enough to imagine him walking out on his current employer without notice or explanation if he got a better offer. Except....

Except a neighbor out walking her dog had noticed two strange cars near Alf's place the night of his murder. Neal's insistence that he knew nothing about Alf's death had been almost hysterical. I didn't think he'd been involved, but what if he'd been there? What if he'd seen something?

Starting the DeSoto, I drove slowly away. With Neal unavailable, I might as well have a go at the two birds left in the cage: Swallowtail and the little girl from twenty-six years ago.

First I stopped at the office to call Corrine. She assured me she was doing fine on her own.

"Have you heard anything from Neal this week?" I asked.

I heard a dog wuff softly. Corrine murmured reassurance.

"Neal? No, why?"

"I just wondered if he'd gotten over being sore."

"He'll come around," she said cheerfully. "He just likes his sulks."

The dog wuffed again and she chuckled at something. I couldn't recall ever hearing her chuckle before.

"Okay, thanks," I said.

I swivelled back and forth in my chair for a while. The evening before, when Genevieve and I got back from supper, I'd called Neal's number. I was pretty sure it was George who had answered. He told me Neal was out and he didn't know when he'd be back. The last couple words had been fainter, like he'd been in a hurry and started to hang up while he was still speaking.

Talking to one of Neal's pals at the factory — maybe the one who'd offered to buy me a sandwich — began to feel vital. So did talking to George again, unless Neal was there the next time I called.

Still thinking about it, I adjusted the holster under my jacket so it rubbed a bit less and headed down to the produce market.

***

"A little girl?" The owner of the grocery store on Percy puffed out his cheeks as he thought. "There were a couple of girls, sisters I think, who used to come in with their mother. But I wasn't old enough that I paid much attention to girls back then." He gave a sheepish grin. "I guess the reason I remember them is that my dad always kidded me that the younger one was flirting with me. She'd stand and look at me and twist her skirt back and forth the way girls do."

"Was she around after the flood?"

He considered a minute.

"I don't think so."

"Do you happen to remember their name?"

"No. Sorry. There was another girl who lived around here who was in my class at school. But she would have been older than the girl you asked about, and in any case, her family was all in Columbus during the flood. Her grandpa was dying. What a nightmare. Losing a relative and then coming home to find everything ruined. They moved, but I don't know where."

I groaned silently.

"As to hearing anything about a clothing dummy...." The grocery store owner shook his head. Today he'd offered me a seat on an overturned orange crate and was in a chattier mood.

"Try Ray Marsh, at the dime store," he suggested. "He was a few years older than me and might have paid more attention to things. And there's a woman who helps over there — oh, even better, talk to Cy Warren. His dad owned a clothing store up where the bank is. They had dummies. Cy's still in town. Owns a real estate firm and was on City Council."

"And owns a lot of the buildings around here."

He nodded.

"But not yours."

"No."

I thanked him and crossed the street. From my first visit, I knew the woman who ran the corner café hadn't been here at the time of the flood. The grouchy old cobbler had, and Swallowtail owned his building, but I had something special planned for him. Before that, I was going to have some fun with Marsh at the dime store.

"Hi, remember me?" I sang as I marched up to him at the cash register.

He looked up from entering numbers on what appeared to be an order or inventory sheet. After a second his helpful expression gave way to a hard look. Before he could speak, I continued merrily.

"I was here last week asking about the flood in 1913, the one you weren't here for and don't know anything about."

"I never—"

"You must have been, what... eighteen? Twenty? Funny you can't remember. Cy Warren can't be much older, and he remembers plenty."

Marsh's mouth opened and closed so many times he looked like a fish.

"You've talked—"

"Now I'm hoping that the shoes you're wearing today don't pinch quite as much as the ones you had on last time, and you'll remember better." I propped my elbow on the counter so we were cozy as sweethearts. "What can you tell me about the day of the fire? Or about the little girl who talked about the clothing dummy?"

He'd jerked away as if I had a disease.

"I already told you. I don't remember. I was in back, on the attic stairs, hauling stuff up as fast as my father handed it to me. That's—" His blink told me his brain had just now registered something bewildering. "Little girl? What little girl?"

I waited.

"Did you say something about a dummy? What are you talking about?"

"Actually, she called it a 'store dolly'," I said carefully.

A customer came in. Emily, bless her, scurried to greet them. Marsh seemed unaware of it. He frowned in confusion.

"I have no idea what you're talking about."

If the little girl's family had been forced to relocate after the flood, it was possible no one on Percy had heard her story except for the cop on the beat, I realized slowly.

"There was a little girl who told people she saw men put a dummy out in the rain."

I was watching his eyes. They flared with curiosity.

"Don't worry, I won't tell Cy that you talked to me," I said before he could speak. "You won't get kicked out of this building, or that men's group you're both in."

The part about the men's group was a guess, but something in what I'd just said made Marsh redden.

"How dare you suggest Cy Warren is - is coercing me!" He gave his vest an affronted tug. "I don't have time to waste on greedy relatives trying to stir up a lawsuit over a building I barely remember. I can't even recall if we were still here moving things when it caught fire."

So that was how Cy had explained my questions on Percy Street; greedy relatives.

"I'll tell you something else." Marsh took a leather-bound ledger from under the counter and smacked it down, preparing to work. "Cy's a good man to know. He has influence."

***

My parking spot in the shade of a building had kept the big bag of grapes I'd left in my car reasonably cool. When I left the dime store, I retrieved them. Then I opened the trunk and took out a pair of shoes I kept for emergencies. The leather on the back of them was scarred and scraped from when I'd been dragged behind a car.

I kept them handy in case I needed to change a flat or walk through muck. With the bag of grapes in one hand and shoes in the other. I walked back to the cobbler's shop.

The wiry old guy who owned the place was tapping away on a bench in back when I came in. Still holding a hammer, he got up and came toward me. His eyes narrowed. He remembered me. And I remembered he'd told me if I wasn't a customer, he didn't have time for my questions.

I set my battered shoes firmly on the counter between us.

"I have shoes that need fixing."

TWENTY-SEVEN

"You're that woman was sticking her nose in asking questions," he said, ignoring my shoes. "Put people's backs up."

"Gee, the only ones who seemed to mind my questions were you and Marsh at the five-and-dime," I said with a grin. "You said you were busy and only had time for paying customers. I'm kind of hoping you might have a little more time today."

I set the bag of grapes on the counter. These weren't your thick-skinned blue-black Concords. These skins were more pink than purple, and the globes were big and sweet.

"Happened to be in the produce market on my way here," I said. These looked so nice, I thought you might enjoy a sack."

He grunted.

"Still don't have time for lollygagging." He eyed the grapes. "Closing for lunch so I can go in back and relax, open the door a crack for some air." He gave me a hard look. "Go on. Clear out."

He came around the counter with energy enough to make me think he intended to shove me out if he had to. I retreated. Had he been sending me a message or was he merely closing for lunch? With a shooing motion he herded me out the door.

It slammed behind me so quickly I wondered if the hem of my skirt would be trapped. I heard the sound of a key. By the time I turned, a placard that read CLOSED FOR LUNCH was swinging back and forth in the window next to the door. The surly old codger was hotfooting toward a partition in back.

For a good thirty seconds I stood staring, still unsure whether his talk about going in back had been a cue. It didn't require much pretending to act peeved. I crossed my arms. Finally I stalked up the street to my car.

I drove away, vaguely toward downtown. It gave me time to think. If I was right, the cobbler didn't want to be seen talking to me, which meant he was willing to talk, but was wary of some kind of consequences if he did. I doubled back to a residential street a block behind his shop.

The alley behind the shop was deserted when I got there, and the door of the shop was ajar. I walked quickly. The cobbler sat facing the door. His feet were propped comfortably on a footstool and he was eating a sandwich. The bag of grapes sat on an unused bench next to his elbow.

"Whose back was it that I put up?" I asked without preliminaries. I didn't figure he was one for small talk, just as I'd figured dangling money wouldn't loosen his tongue.

He sniffed, dismissing the question.

"Grow my own grapes," he said. "In the back yard."

He was letting me know he couldn't be softened up with a bag of grapes, but I also thought the contrary old coot might reward me with a tidbit or two if I passed some sort of test.

"Grow your own, huh? Concords?"

He nodded. I looked around and found a wooden stool that wobbled when I sat on it.

"Can't beat a Concord," I said. "But these aren't bad either. Anyway, I got a bag for myself, and since I was coming here, I thought you might enjoy some for the vitamins and that. You not being a believer in pills and doctors."

He took a single grape and chewed it. He grunted.

"Guess they're okay. What makes you so interested in Dillon's Drugs?"

"A man named John Vanhorn was headed there the day it burned. He never was seen again."

The cobbler shrugged. He shoved three grapes into his mouth and talked around them.

"Lots of people got swept away in the water. Name's not familiar."

"Anybody question whether the body they found in the store was really the owner?"

"It was him alright. We were clearing debris when we found him. Burned down to nearly a skeleton. I saw the crooked bone in his leg. Got broke when he was a kid and wasn't set right. Gave him an awful limp. Had to lift what was left of some steel shelves to get to what was left of him."

He popped more grapes in his mouth and followed them with a bite of sandwich.

"Any other bodies turn up?"

"Any others?" He looked startled. "Not around here. Why?"

"A little girl who lived around here told a policeman she'd seen two men carry a clothing dummy outside and leave it just before the fire started."

He chewed complacently.

"All kinds of gossip. Rumors. Me, I don't listen. Mind my own business."

His helpful streak was running out. I stood up.

"You never said whose back I'd put up asking questions."

"No point. Like I told you, I mind my own business."

"And since Cy Warren's your landlord, he could kick you out if you got on his bad side."

That won me a truculent look.

"I don't kowtow like some."

"Like Marsh at the dime store?" When he didn't respond, I switched tactics. "The other day you told me you'd owned your place across the street."

"I did. And when Warren and Maguire were crazy to buy up lots around here, I saw a chance to make a smart deal." The old codger cackled. "Saved what I would have spent on rebuilding. Money in the bank drawing interest for my old age, and a lifetime lease."

"If you crossed him, though, he could double your rent."

"Nope. Can't raise it more than two percent a year, written into the contract." He tapped the side of his nose. "Cy Warren wasn't as smart about real estate then as he is now."

A man's vanity regarding his cleverness yields information questions won't. So does giving him an opportunity to correct you.

"Huh," I said. "The way I heard it, Alf Maguire was the smart one."

He snorted.

"About as full of brains as he was ambition. Cy's the one who called the tunes." His mouth clamped shut, not because he'd told me anything unwise, but because he'd been more helpful — or maybe agreeable — than was his habit. "Now clear out," he said, my gift of grapes forgotten. "Come in the front in fifteen minutes and pick up your shoes."

***

When I came in the front, my shoes were no longer on the counter where I'd left them. The cobbler wore his leather apron again, and was standing at some sort of machine. He left it whining as he came to help me.

"Shoes weren't worth fixing," he said, slamming them on the counter.

I don't know if he intended for me to stalk out in a huff, but I did.

***

I found a pay phone and called to make sure Corrine was okay. I had lunch, then caught up at the office. Well before quitting time, I was parked where I could watch men leave the factory where Neal had worked. His pal with the coal black hair was half a head taller than most of the others, making him easy to spot. I got out of my car and started toward him with a wave.

One of his buddies saw me first and gave him a nudge. The big guy dodged a couple of cars as he crossed the street. His steps slowed as he drew near.

"You still hunting Neal?" he asked awkwardly. He was leery of being the bearer of bad news.

"Yeah, I am. And I already know he hasn't been in all week, and that he got fired."

He frowned.

"Why are you here then?"

I gave him a card. He read it slowly, his lips working silently over the word 'investigator'. Finally he looked up.

"You're a cop."

"Detective. Private. Not a cop."

His handsome head was starting to shake.

"I don't rat. Don't know any more than what I've already told you anyway."

"Listen. Neal's family's been having some trouble. I'm worried about him. A week ago he talked as if he was glad to have this job. Doesn't seem like he'd just up and vanish."

The big guy talking to me wiped a hand across his mouth, thinking.

"It's Friday," I coaxed. "End of the week. I've got a thirst for a beer. I'd buy you one too."

The high-voltage grin split his face

"Can't say other girls haven't been eager enough for my company they did the inviting, but I never expected an offer from a classy tomato like you."

I put out my hand. "You know my name from the card. What's yours?"

"Donnie. Donnie Williams." He started to shake the hand I'd offered, then hesitated. "I guess you made that up, what you said when I first met you? That you had a disease?"

TWENTY-EIGHT

Donnie vetoed the watering hole nearest the factory, saying it was sort of scruffy. He strutted a little as he led the way into another place farther up the street. From the greetings, it was clear he was both known and liked there. The place was crowded. Most of the men wore overalls or other rough work clothes. Besides me, there were three other women.

In spite of his boast about women asking him out, I knew Donnie would probably dig in his heels if I tried to order, so I slid him a buck and asked would he get our beers. He'd persuaded a couple of acquaintances to give up their table in favor of spots at the bar. He brought back the beers and we made small talk until he began to relax.

"About Neal," he said, watching me over the rim of his glass. "He in bad with the law?"

I shook my head. "Not as far as I know. As I told you, his family's been having trouble. A couple of days ago somebody roughed up one of his sisters."

He'd just taken a mouthful of beer. He went still as a statue before he swallowed.

"You think something happened to him?"

"Maybe. Or maybe he got scared and ran."

Donnie processed that for a minute. He wasn't slow, just thoughtful. There was an openness about him which I liked.

"Tuesday noon when we came out for lunch, a man was waiting for him."

"Someone he knew?"

"I don't think so. Anyway, it made Neal real jumpy."

"Tell me what you remember. What happened?"

"This guy was waiting, and he called Neal by name. Started ambling over."

"Was the man alone?"

"I guess. Didn't see anybody else. Anyway, Neal told the rest of us to go, he'd catch up with us. And he did. But he drank a lot and he seemed real nervous."

I drank some beer, but it didn't allay my growing uneasiness.

"Any chance you can describe this man?"

Donnie thought, then gave his head a rueful shake.

"I didn't pay attention, is the thing. I think he had dark hair, but his hat had a brim, so that could have been shadows."

"Build?"

"Kind of boxy." He brightened. "He was shorter than Neal. Does that help?"

"Sure." I felt like a fool, but I asked it anyway. "You know what an Eskimo is?"

"Those people that live in little round houses out of ice?"

"That's it. Anything about him make you think of one of those?"

He squinted at me.

"I know it's a screwy question," I said. "But a woman who saw something else told me there was a man who looked like an Eskimo."

"Oh. Well he wasn't wearing one of those coats with fur around the face. He was dressed like an American."

We'd run out of beer. Donnie got us replacements, and a couple of sandwiches to go along with them. Meanwhile I wondered whether what he described as a boxy build could be what the neighbor lady meant by Eskimo. It didn't seem likely.

The sandwiches turned out to be better than the beer, which was pale German stuff. I asked about the car Neal's visitor had been driving, but Donnie hadn't noticed whether he'd even had one.

"You think something's happened to Neal?" he asked again after an interval.

"I'm hoping he's just lying low. When I leave here, I'm going to check where he lives." I switched gears. "Anybody around here involved in politics?"

"You mean union talk?"

"No, city. State. That kind."

Donnie snickered. "Yeah, I kind of have my eye on running for governor." He drank some beer and started to nod.

"Okay, this isn't nobody here, and it may not amount to a hill of beans, except that you asked, but Neal claimed his dad was."

"Involved in politics?"

"Yeah. Well, not that his old man himself was, but that he had connections. Bragged about it a couple of times, but then Neal was always trying to sound important. It may not even be true."

My ears perked up.

"Any idea if he meant his own father or his step-dad?"

"Whichever one died last week."

I jumped up, not because what he'd told me was urgent, but because it had generated a thread of excitement. Thinner than that thread, but visible now, was one that maybe, just maybe, tied Neal's disappearance to Cy Warren, or at least to one of the politician's associates.

"Hey, I've got to run," I said. "Thanks for the help.

"Wait," said Donnie, overtaking me as I made for the door. "Do you like to dance? There's a nice place I could take you tomorrow. Respectable—"

"Thanks, Donnie. I wish I could, but I can't."

"What about next week?"

"The thing is, I've got a boyfriend."

"I've edged out a boyfriend or two."

We were already halfway back to my car. He kept just a fraction ahead of me, grinning down with a good-natured roguery almost guaranteed to make girls forget common sense. I laughed.

"I'll bet you have. But we're practically engaged. Anyway, he's not somebody you'd want to irritate. He's a cop."

I hoped my tongue didn't blister.

***

Neal and his stepbrother George lived together in a three-story brick apartment building on Brown Street. The top had a fake edge to make it look like a castle or maybe like someplace Spanish, but the front was flat and ordinary. Inside was just as plain, but clean. Mailboxes adorned one wall of the entry. In a burst of civic pride, the opposite wall held a lithograph print of the Wright brothers making the world's first powered airplane flight. I climbed the stairs.

The apartment I wanted was on the third floor. I knocked at the door and waited. I'd hoped against hope I'd catch Neal or George — or both — between getting home from work and heading out for the evening. No one answered my knock, so I tried again. I put my ear to the door and listened for sounds on the other side, but there were none. No water running, no radio playing. As I tried for a final time, a thirty-ish looking fellow came out of the apartment next door.

"They're not here," he said. "Saw one of them coming out when I was getting home."

"Which one?"

"The one with the sissy chin." He pinched his fingers together in pantomime.

"What about the other one? Have you seen him around lately?"

"Can't remember." He started off, eager to get somewhere. "They're always out Friday nights. Most nights. Come around earlier," he called over his shoulder.

As I was about to try the neighbor on the other side, a door across the hall opened. A woman with a mop of gray curls put one foot out, her mouth drawn up in disapproval.

"All of them along here come and go all the time, and all hours too. No respect at all for decent people. Just out for a good time."

"I'm looking for Neal," I said. "The taller one who lives here. Have you seen him?"

"Not lately, and just as glad of it, impertinent as he is." She looked me up and down. "I suppose you're some girlfriend here to make a scene because he jilted you. Or worse."

"No. Why?" She'd caught my interest. "Did another girl make a scene?"

"Oh yes. With that one you were just talking to. And number six, he's had two here crying around. I don't know how the Robinsons in number eight stand it. They claim they don't hear a thing, but you'd need to be deaf as a post...."

I thanked her and left while she was still lecturing.

She probably thought me impertinent.

***

My uneasiness over Neal was starting to increase. Skipping out on a decent job was bad enough. The fact no one where he lived had seen him recently upped the ante. I drummed my thumbs on the steering wheel. If I hurried, I might be able to start some serious checking into his movements.

This time I was able to park just a few doors away from the joint where I'd left Donnie. To my relief he was still there, though he'd moved to join a table of other men near the back. I waited just inside the door, knowing men would start to notice me and the ripple would reach him. When one of the men at his table said something that made Donnie turn, I inclined my head toward the door.

Polishing off what was left in his glass, he stood and shouldered his way through a room more crowded and more boisterous than when I'd left it.

"Hey, you decide that cop wasn't so interesting after all?" he asked with a grin.

"I swung by Neal's place. None of his neighbors have seen him these last couple days," I said in a low voice.

His face went serious. We stepped outside, squeezing our way past two men who greeted Donnie by name.

"So why'd you come to tell me?" he asked, baffled. "I honest to God don't remember anything —"

"I know. But I hoped you might help. You know the spots Neal usually went to have his beer? Have some fun?"

"Yeah. Three or four."

"Know some of the men he'd be with?"

"Sure. He didn't come down here on weekends, though. Went places with his brother or step-brother, I think."

"That's okay. It's someplace to start. If I give you five bucks, think you could find it in your heart to visit those places tonight or tomorrow? Buy a few beers, ask around, find out if anyone's seen him since Tuesday?"

I held my breath. He was a smart guy, and he had pride, and I felt pretty sure that underneath the kidding he'd nursed at least a small hope I'd fall for him.

"Doesn't seem right, taking money from a woman," he said finally. "But I guess it'd be like working for you. I guess I can. Neal's kind of an idiot, and I don't like him much, to be honest, but I hate to think of him ending up with his head knocked in."

"Thanks, Donnie. People wouldn't talk to a stranger like me the way they will you."

I opened my purse and gave him a fin. He took it and stood looking down at me for a minute.

"I know I'm not your sort, but you were nice enough not to say it. You're okay."

I put out my hand. His callused one engulfed it as we shook.

"You're okay too, Donnie."

TWENTY-NINE

Jolene's parents had come into Dayton for some kind of meeting. They'd dropped off a jar of her mother's fresh apple butter, which we demolished with our toast on Saturday morning. It fortified me for my short drive down to the brick apartment house I'd visited the previous night.

As I went up the stairs, I saw a woman letting herself in with groceries several doors down on the second floor. One floor up, I went down the hall and knocked where George and Neal lived. It was a few minutes past ten, late enough that they should be up, but before they got out and about, judging from what I'd heard of their fondness for nights on the town.

If I woke them, I didn't much care.

This time I was certain I heard sounds inside. I also heard one suspiciously like a door easing open a peep width from the direction where the nosey neighbor woman lived. Lest she think me unfriendly as well as impertinent, I waved without turning as I knocked again.

"Yeah, okay. Keep your pants on," mumbled a voice.

The door opened and I had the pleasure of seeing George's unshaven face. He squinted at me.

"Hi, George. Remember me?"

The fact he was still half asleep, and possibly somewhat hung over, didn't make him any faster on his feet. He stepped back automatically as I walked past him.

"Hey," he said as his brain woke up enough to allow the stirring of indignation. "I never said you could come in. I know who you are now. You're that - that woman Neal doesn't like. The one who came nosing around the morning my dad died."

"That's right, George. I'm a private investigator. With a license. That means I can be here."

Most people have no idea what gumshoes are allowed to do. If George had been dressed and fully awake he might have challenged me, but he was in his undershirt and trousers, barefoot, with hair uncombed. Even morning stubble couldn't make his nub of a chin look tough. Nevertheless, he clenched his fists.

"I'm not here to make trouble," I said. "I just need to see Neal. I've tried calling and never could raise anybody."

I sat down on the sofa, noticing that the small living room was surprisingly orderly. A newspaper lay unfolded as if waiting to be read. A jacket draped the back of the room's only easy chair.

"Neal's not here." His step-brother glared at me. "Haven't seen him for a couple of days."

"Since when, exactly?"

"I don't know." He pushed a hand through his hair. "Look, can I get some coffee? I wasn't even dressed when you came pounding on the door—"

"Sure. Get your coffee. I know how that is."

I could see through the doorway separating a small kitchen tucked in one corner. George had his back to me, rattling dishes and opening the Frigidare. On weekends I liked comfortable clothes. My pleated wool skirt with a blouse and cardigan didn't exactly lend themselves to wearing a holster, so my gun was in my purse. I unclasped the purse and tilted it slightly. Just in case.

George leaned around the door with a mug in his hand.

"You want some?" he asked grudgingly.

"If there's plenty, an inch or two would be swell. Black." Regardless of what someone's drinking, they feel more relaxed if you join in.

George brought two mugs out and handed me one. He lowered himself to the easy chair, took a swallow of coffee and made a sound of relief. He had another drink, then ran a hand through his hair again, this time with better results if smoothing it down was his intent.

"What was it you asked about Neal?" he said.

"When's the last time you saw him?"

"Oh. Yeah." He squinted, hunched over his coffee. He lowered its level some. "Monday, I guess. Monday night late." For the first time, he seemed to grasp the import of what I was asking. "What's this about?"

"That's what I want to know. He hasn't shown up at work since Tuesday morning."

"What? No."

George's mouth was hanging open.   He'd forgotten his coffee.

"He went out for his lunch break. A man came up and talked to him. The fellows Neal works with say he was acting jumpy when he finally caught up with them. Nobody's seen him since."

George was shaking his head. He swallowed a couple of times.

"Are you saying something's *happened* to him?"

"I was hoping you'd know. Did he tell you he was going someplace? Leave a note?"

"No! He just didn't come home when he usually does the next day. Tuesday, I mean. I got tired of waiting.   I fried up some bacon and made a sandwich. Then I went out and had a couple of beers. He still wasn't here when I got back, but I figured he'd come and gone."

"Has he done anything like this before? Gone off without telling you?"

"No. Made me kind of sore. We usually do stuff together."

"Was he scared of somebody? Worried? Acting different?"

His head swung in denial at each question.

"I mean, he was down in the dumps, same as me. Because of my dad, but.... Oh, no.... Jesus, no!"

"What?"

He'd remembered the coffee. He took a big gulp, but it sounded as if the gulp was masking a sob. When he met my eyes, his face was pale.

"Monday night we went out. We drank more than we should've. A lot more. Because of my dad, and the funeral and—"

"Sure."

"When we got back, there was a bottle sitting there on that table. We'd had a few belts before we left, and there was only an inch or so in it. Neal said we should finish it, drink a toast to my dad. So we did. Then all of a sudden he started bawling. It didn't make sense — and then I thought it was only because he was drunk—"

"What did he say?"

George hung his head. His shoulders heaved a couple of times. When he raised his face, his eyes were moist.

"He said, 'Alf didn't die. Somebody killed him.' But that's nuts, isn't it? That's not what the cops say."

I leaned back to ease the prickle along my spine.

"That's not what the cops say," I agreed.

I wasn't sure if it would make him feel better. I wasn't sure if what Neal had told him was true. If it was, though, and Neal was a witness, it could explain his abrupt disappearance. The question now was whether that disappearance had been voluntary.

"Are any of his things missing?" I asked.

George was holding his head in his hands.

"What?"

"Did he take any clothes, his razor, things like that?" I said patiently.

"Oh. I don't know."

"Could we look?"

He led the way to a bedroom with twin beds, one on each side of the room. One, presumably vacated by George not long before my arrival, was a tangle of sheets and blankets. The other was more or less made. George opened a closet.

"That's Neal's side," he said pointing.

He surveyed a shelf above the hangers.

"That space," he said. "It's where he kept his valise."

***

I found some encouragement in the fact Neal seemed to have disappeared voluntarily. Once George had begun looking, he'd discovered his stepbrother's shaving gear missing, along with two shirts, some underwear, socks and his hairbrush. The contents of drawers were scrambled, as though items had been snatched in a rush.

Two places where Neal might have gone to ground came to mind. He could have persuaded somebody from work or from one of the bars he frequented to take him in. If that was the case, I trusted Donnie's inquiries to bring it to light. Several rungs lower on the ladder of possibilities was that he could be with Franklin. Franklin seemed like a decent sort, and if Neal had turned up on his doorstep scared, especially after my visit alerting him to the problems the Vanhorns were having, he might have welcomed him.

It was easy enough to check, since Franklin and I had already agreed to talk more this weekend. When I got to the place he lived, though, after assuring me he'd be around all weekend, he wasn't.

Frustrated, I went and had lunch. It gave me time to wonder if I'd been too quick to trust Franklin. Alternating with that, I wondered uneasily if something might have happened to him as well.

Before leaving Mrs. Z's that morning, I'd called Isobel to see if I could stop in early that afternoon. I mostly wanted to let them know what I'd learned and see how they were doing. Now, in addition, I'd have to let them know about Neal, though I knew it would worry them.

I'd barely rung the bell when the door opened.

"Come in, Maggie. Lovely to see you," invited Corrine.

"How did you know it was me?" I asked curiously.

Had she already learned the particular sound of my DeSoto? Her mouth gave an impish quirk.

"Franklin happened to be at the window. He said you were here."

"Ah."

While I was trying to hide my surprise, and realizing foolishly that I didn't need to, she laid a hand on the head of a brownish mutt that was pressing against her.

"And this is Des. Well, I don't know what his real name was, of course, but I thought of Odysseus, wandering. That nice Detective Boike stopped by day before yesterday with Des and another dog, asking if I'd keep them for a week or so. A woman he knows finds homes for strays, but

M. Ruth Myers

she got called out of town and he was helping her farm them out until she gets back."

I suspected where this was headed before she rushed on.

"I told him I could only look after one, since we've had such upheaval. This one had something special about him. I'm going to keep him. He's quite intelligent. I think he may be capable of training for harness. If not, we actually do have plenty of room for two dogs."

The dog had positioned himself between us while she spoke. I couldn't tell whether it was possessiveness or desire to protect her. I followed them into the parlor. Franklin rose from one of the needlepoint sofas as I entered.

"I just went by your place," I said.

"I know, I told you I'd stick around and then I didn't. After I talked to you, I started to worry about Corrie and Isobel, here alone. When I called last night and Isobel told me the whole thing — how Corrie was kidnapped and stranded — I couldn't stand it. I came over this morning to see what, if anything, I could do. I got a wonderful lunch in the bargain." He smiled somberly.

"Actually, I'm glad you're all here together." I sat down in one of the chairs. I drew a breath and plunged in. "Neal's disappeared."

All three of them regarded me in stunned silence.

"What do you mean?" asked Isobel in an unsteady voice.

I told them. The man who'd made him nervous. His absence from work. What I'd learned from

George at their apartment that morning. Finally, I told them about Neal's drunken rambling, and the neighbor's report of two strange cars parked on the street late the night Alf died.

By the time I concluded, Corrine and Isobel had joined hands for support. Across from them, their stepbrother sat with elbows on knees. He looked at me and cleared his throat.

"It sounds as if Neal might know something — might have seen something — about my father's death. Something that indicates it was a - a—"

"Yes."

"And that's why the man came to see him? That's what's behind everything that's happened to Corrie and Isobel?"

"The trouble for Corrine and Isobel happened before Alf died," I reminded. "I think the whole mess, Alf's death included, is related to something that happened the day their father disappeared. Something that happened back at that drugstore where he was headed."

THIRTY

The Vanhorn sisters wanted me to find Neal. Somewhat to my surprise, they also wanted me to continue my inquiries into their father's fate — and to make that my priority.

"Neal's a grown man," said Isobel, her voice wavering. "If he's too big an idiot to go to the police or come to us, there's no sense dropping everything else to look for him."

So on Monday, early, I sat at my desk, reading the morning paper and fortifying myself with two cake donuts and a mug of joe from a hole in the wall across the street. The owner didn't usually let his mugs walk out the door, but he liked me and knew I'd bring it back.

I'd skipped my usual morning fare at McCrory's because Donnie was supposed to phone before he punched in at the factory. I didn't want to miss him. My fingertip was busy capturing cinnamon-sugar crumbs from the first donut when he called.

"No luck," he reported.

None of Neal's pals from work remembered seeing him since noon Tuesday. Neither had any of the bartenders Donnie had talked to at various places Saturday night. All he'd gotten for his efforts was the complaint from one bartender that Neal hadn't settled his tab at the end of the week the way he usually did.

"If I get wind of anything, I'll give you a call," Donnie concluded.

"Thanks, Donnie. You were swell to do it."

"Sure. And any time you change your mind about that cop, call me."

I laughed.

On to today's agenda, then.

Item 1: Look for Neal.

Item 2: Hunt a will-o'-the-wisp who'd told a cop about a mannequin.

Today was Theda's day to work at the dime store. If anyone recalled a little girl who claimed to have seen a clothes dummy carried out in the flood, she'd be the one. But I couldn't talk to Theda until her boss was safely out of the way at his weekly business luncheon.

Frustrated, I went and stood in front of a large city map I'd hung on one wall. I crossed my arms and stood staring at it, waiting for inspiration to strike about where to hunt for Neal. Inspiration was still putting its shoes on when the telephone rang again.

"I've got to talk fast, before Mr. Marsh gets back from the bank," said a voice I realized belonged to Emily at the dime store. "I heard you asking him something about a little girl when you were here Friday. I thought you might come back today to talk to Theda, and he's not going to his meeting —

he didn't say why. And Theda's not here. She quit."

"What?"

"She's gone to live with her son."

A chill seeped into my blood. Neal's disappearance concerned me only because he might have scraps of information to add to my patchwork, and because his sisters cared. But if anything had happened to cheerful little Theda, who'd been so willing to talk about the past, it would be my fault.

"Oh! Here he comes!" said Emily in a rush.

"Wait — do you take the trolley home? What number?"

I wasn't sure I caught what she said before she hung up.

For several minutes afterward, I stood with arms braced on my desk. Not a full week had passed since I'd talked to Theda. She'd mentioned her sons, yet she'd given no hint that she was thinking of leaving. Something in Emily's call reinforced my sense the older clerk's departure had been abrupt. It was one more thing that was too convenient. Too coincidental.

I sat down and swivelled my chair back and forth. Increasingly, I was starting to think this case had nothing to do with Swallowtail Properties or real estate shenanigans that made somebody rich. I'd made it a point to drive past Cy Warren's house, and I'd seen plenty fancier. His suits were well-made, but not upper crust. I got out my notes from the library and went through them again. Nothing I'd found in the newspapers connected him with the kind of large-scale developments that turned men into moguls.

Money hunger was the disease that most often led men to lie and commit acts of violence or murder. Greed, the great leveler. It made corporate chairmen who swindled their shareholders exactly the same as down-at-heels hustlers and muggers.

Yet my work had taught me other reasons could make men equally ruthless. Revenge. Ambition. Jealousy. Even pride.

What did Cy Warren want enough to commit murder? Or to arrange one? What was so precious that he'd use any means necessary to block a close look at his youth?

I picked up the phone and called Rachel.

"You pay any attention to politics?" I asked when she came on. "Not FDR. Local and state."

"Some. It can come in handy in business, just like rubbing shoulders with the competition can," she said cautiously.

"What would keep you from getting elected?"

Rachel's laugh was something to hear. Rich and throaty, it gave a rare glimpse into a woman who was a sphinx.

"Apart from being a woman and Jew?" she said.

"I was speaking in generalities."

"Getting caught with your hand in the cookie jar might make it awkward. Bribes that could be traced from or to you, maybe; not sure on that one. Skeleton in the closet." She thought for about five seconds, which at her speed counted as an eternity. "That should about do it."

"What about being a lush? Keeping a mistress?"

"Boys will be boys."

"How big would the skeleton need to be? Murder? Manslaughter?"

Another eternity.

"Something close to that scale, I imagine. An accident, maybe," she mused. "Membership in a group that blew something up or burned something down. Greek love. I'm only guessing with any of this. You'd need to talk to someone in politics up to their dingus to get a reliable answer. Or better still, someone with money to spend who finds picking candidates more fun than picking horses."

"You're at least as smart as someone in politics up to their dingus," I said.

***

Before I owned a car, I'd depended on trolleys or walking to get me wherever I needed to be. Once I hung out my shingle, a finely honed knowledge of how long it took for a bus to get from one stop to another sometimes became crucial. The fact four different companies ran trolleys in Dayton added to the challenge.

When the dime store on Percy closed for the day, I was on a trolley four stops before the one that was closest for Emily. If I'd understood her last words on the phone, and if Marsh hadn't let her off early or kept her late, she'd get on there. That added up to a lot of 'ifs', but it was the best I'd been able to think of before she hung up on me.

"Hey. Mind moving that?" asked a chubby guy, his forehead shiny with the effort of climbing aboard. His finger stabbed petulantly at the shopping bag on the seat beside me.

Aware seats would be at a premium this time of day, I'd brought the bag to discourage company until Emily boarded. Another bag sat on my lap.

"Oh, gee, sure, long as you don't mind holding it," I replied. "I been sick at my stomach all day, so I brought it along to keep handy in case... you know."

He moved past with amazing alacrity.

As we approached the stop where I expected Emily to get on, I turned my back to the window. Being seen with me might not be a good idea this close to Percy Street. A moment later I spotted her fair hair bobbing amid new passengers headed down the aisle. She looked around with a small frown, which could easily indicate a girl merely hunting a seat.

"Here, let me move this," I offered when she got almost abreast. As I leaned toward the shopping bag at my side, I also lifted the horn-rimmed glasses I'd donned.

Her eyes widened.

"Thank you." She sat down. When the trolley began to pull out, she whispered, "I wouldn't have recognized you."

Amazing what cheaters, along with a messy French twist and a dowdy hat, can do for a girl. I folded the all-but-empty bag I'd moved and shoved it into the one on my lap.

"Tell me about Theda."

"There's not lots to tell. She came in late Friday to pick up her pay for the week and didn't say a thing. Then this morning, Mr. Marsh called me over and said in that fussy way of his, 'Emily, if you know anyone dependable who's interested in working two afternoons a week, I need a replacement for Theda. She quit. I'll skip my meeting today so you're not alone.'" She'd crossed her arms while she mimicked his supercilious tone. Now pink tinged her cheeks. "If I'd thought faster I could have told him that I'd manage. Then if you'd come in—"

"It's okay. Where did you hear the part about her going to live with her son?"

"Oh, from him. Right then. It startled me so I said something like, 'What do you mean, she quit? Why?' and that's what he told me. He said she'd called him at home."

"What else did he say?"

"That's all." The girl considered a minute, then nodded her certainty. "That was everything."

"Theda didn't come in?"

"Not since Friday."

"Had Mr. Marsh seen her?"

"After she called him? I don't think so. He seemed kind of huffy." She chewed her lower lip a couple of times. "All the people you've been talking to along the street... the way Mr. Marsh clammed up when you mentioned that flood... is Theda in some kind of trouble?"

"She hasn't done anything herself, if that's what you mean. But yes, she could be," I said honestly.

Emily swallowed. She peeped out the window, possibly eager to see her own familiar stop after what I'd just told her.

"I liked Theda," she said. Her voice broke. "She was nice to me."

"Yeah," I said. "And I don't want anything to happen to you. No reason it should. You're not old enough to know anything about the mess I've been asking about. Still, stay on your toes for a while. Don't go walking around on your own if you don't have to. If anyone comes in the store when Mr. Marsh isn't around and you think they might mean you harm, get over to the cosmetics counter and squirt perfume in their eyes. It'll blind them long enough for you to run."

She nodded.

"Do you happen to know where Theda lived? Could you find out?"

"That street we just passed," she said turning and pointing.

Before I looked back, I made sure to identify the street just ahead, and a couple of nearby businesses.

"This side, about a block and a half. The right hand side of the street — a green house." The trolley began to pull over, but it wasn't Emily's stop yet. "I got off and helped her a few times last winter when she had groceries," she said as passengers shuffled off and on. "I was scared she'd slip."

Not long after, she pulled the cord for her own stop. The only others who got out with her were a mother and child. It reassured me as I watched her blonde head bob away in the gathering dusk.

I rode half a dozen blocks more before I got off. Then I walked some, ditching my horn-rims in my purse. I shrugged into the jacket that was folded in my shopping bag and made my way back to the green house. All of it had been somebody's home once. Now it was carved into four apartments. A businesslike FOR RENT sign occupied part of one downstairs window.

"Hi," I said to the woman who answered the front hall door beside the window. "Which one is Theda's place? My sister's kids were screaming so when she called, I did well even to get the address."

The woman was wiping her hands on a tea towel. The specs on her nose weren't for decoration.

"Oh, dear. I'm afraid Theda's moved. Gone off to Indiana."

"No kidding? I talked to her Thursday and she didn't even mention it."

She dropped her voice the way some do to convey sympathy for the person discussed.

"She'd had a terrible fright, poor thing. A pair of young hoodlums came out of an alley and grabbed for her purse. She yanked it away and started to yell. They ran, which is a mercy, or I hate to think what might have happened. She took an awful tumble, though. All scraped up. I was out here using the carpet sweeper when she came in. Shaking like a leaf, she was. Too upset to even tell me what happened until the next day."

My mouth felt dry.

"Sounds like punks who knew she got paid on Fridays," I said, fishing.

She nodded and sighed.

"I expect she'll be fine, once she settles in. Her son was awfully good to her. Came and got her for Christmas and a couple of weeks every summer. He'd been trying to coax her to come live with them."

"You'd met him, then? I never had a chance."

"Oh yes. Lovely man. Tiny stutter, but it didn't bother him." She paused to look at me with sharpening interest. "You wouldn't be interested in a nice apartment, would you?"

Unexpectedly, I felt the tug to have a place of my own. A real place, not just a room.

"I couldn't afford it," I said. "How much?"

THIRTY-ONE

As I'd expected, the rent for the small apartment Theda had occupied was beyond my means. Even though it was no surprise, it deepened the glumness infecting me as I sipped my stout at Finn's.

Theda had left an address for forwarding mail. I could take a train to Indiana, but even if I managed to talk to her, I doubted I'd come away with anything except more expenses for the Vanhorns. The abruptness of her departure showed how scared she was. Her story about someone wanting her purse might be a lie to hide getting roughed up while somebody warned her to keep her mouth shut. It was equally possible someone who knew old women were easy to frighten had sent a couple of punks to do just what she'd described.

In any event, it sounded as if she really was with her son, which meant she'd be safe. Unfortunately she hadn't left a phone number when she left the address.

I wasn't bursting with confidence I'd have any more luck locating Neal, but at least I'd concocted a plan. What I needed now was to run it by someone I trusted to see if my reasoning held up. If Billy and Seamus, or maybe Connelly came in, they might have some suggestions as well. My Guinness was half gone when Seamus and Connelly came through the door.

"Buy you gents a pint?" I offered, waving.

They ambled over. Connelly was grinning.

"When she's buying, she wants information," he said, giving Seamus a nudge.

"Yep, I need help from men with vast knowledge of this city's seedier drinking establishments."

"Can't turn down a lady in distress, can we, Seamus? I'll fetch the pints."

Seamus lowered himself to the chair on my left. I heard his knee pop.

"How's Billy's shiner?" I asked. "How come he's not with you?"

"The eye's faded so you wouldn't notice it, except Billy likes you to." Seamus had the sweetest smile. Not a mean bone in his body. "He went right home 'cause he'd promised Kate he'd take her to buy a second-hand rug she's had her eye on."

Connelly returned with their Guinness. He hooked a chair out with his foot and set the glasses on the table. For a while we traded the lazy, inconsequential chat that makes sitting with friends at the end of the day a renewal.

"Now then, what's this about seedy bars?" asked Connelly, leaning back in his chair.

"First, I need to ask Seamus, is anybody named Vanhorn in lockup?"

His mouth pursed a few times, leaving his gaunt face still more sharply chiseled as he thought.

"Nope," he said. Because of his knee, Seamus did mostly desk work now. He saw the jail booking register, and his mind stored it up like a camera.

"Vanhorn," said Connelly. "Those women who hired you?"

"Yeah. Their brother's gone missing."

"When?"

"Tuesday, near as I can tell. A stranger talked to him when he came out for his lunch break. The men he eats with say he was jumpy afterward. He didn't go back to work, and nobody's seen him since. He took his valise and some of his clothes, though."

"So you think he's hiding."

"Yes."

Seamus, less given to words than Connelly, grunted and dipped his silvery head in agreement.

"That's why you want to know about unsavory spots," continued Connelly.

"I might have razzed you a little with the unsavory part. There are plenty worse. These are just a mite on the rough side."

I took three lists from my purse and spread them on the table before them.

"These are places Neal went with his buddies from work." I touched one list with the point of my pencil. "No one's seen him there." I touched the second list. "These are where he went with his stepbrother George. George called this afternoon to say he'd checked and Neal hadn't shown up at any of them."

"And you trust George?"

"Yeah, I do. Ask that about Neal and I might sing a different tune.

"Now. From what I know about Neal, after work he didn't do much except sit and shoot the breeze while he had a few beers. I don't think he'll know what to do with himself except that. He's not especially smart, but he's not especially dumb either, so I'm guessing he'd have sense enough to avoid his usual places. But he'll hunt places like them — places he feels comfortable. Not too fancy or he'll feel awkward. Not up with the Poles and the Czechs where not speaking the language would make him stick out."

Connelly thumbed his chin.

"Makes sense," he said at last. He glanced at Seamus.

Seamus nodded. He already was eyeing my third list. I tapped it.

"So these are places I think he might go. I'm hoping you two might add a few more."

They conferred. They added a couple of pubs. They came up with a little area I hadn't considered.

"But why stick around?" Connelly argued. "Why not put more distance between himself and whoever he's in Dutch with?"

"Probably doesn't have money enough, and hopes the whole thing will blow over or get sorted out. Neal hasn't had to deal with much so far in life."

***

Late next morning, as I was standing in front of my map contemplating which of the areas the three of us had come up with was the likeliest place to start looking for Neal, the phone rang. When I answered, I heard a female voice, high and muffled.

"You the one who's been looking for a little girl who lived near the drugstore during the flood?"

"Yes. Who—"

"Know where Stainton is?"

"Yes."

"North end. Three down on the east side. There's apartments upstairs. Try the front one. Come between four-fifteen and four-thirty. Women are home fixing dinner; men aren't coming home yet. Nobody's on the street. Got it?"

"Yes—"

"Four-fifteen to four-thirty. Any later and nobody'll be home. Come by yourself."

The sound of a dead line buzzed in my ear. I sat with pulse accelerating. Had I just heard the voice of the little girl herself? At least I knew she was real now, and somebody knew who she was or knew something about her.

Unless the whole thing was a setup.

Tapping my teeth with my fingernail, I tried to think. Whoever she was, the woman I'd spoken to had sounded nervous. You could fake that, of course. I'd probably done it myself when I was wangling information.

I got up and tucked the Smith & Wesson under my jacket. There was too much to gain if the call had been genuine. It might well represent my only chance to find the kid who'd talked about a clothes dummy. What I could do, though, was look the place over, check the layout, see if anything triggered a warning of something amiss.

Stainton ran north and south just past where Third forked into Linden Avenue and Springfield Street. Streets were small here, and most of the houses could have used paint. The Depression had hit this area hard, since most of the men had worked in nearby factories, some of which had closed. Things were picking up under the New Deal. I even saw a HELP WANTED sign in a café.

The stretch where I'd been directed had a mom-and-pop grocery store on the corner. Across the way and a few doors down, a man in an apron was sweeping the sidewalk in front of a bar, probably spiffing up for noontime customers. The building I was hunting housed a second hand store, or it had. A sign on the door said CLOSED, and the place looked as if it had been that way for a while.

To the side, narrow stairs led up to apartments above it. Starched white curtains hung in the window of the front one. The glass sparkled. I drove past without changing speed. There was no sign of movement. The place looked occupied, though, and well tended. I figured I could chance one more pass around the block, and did.

Then I parked a few streets over and put on my glasses and dowdy hat. I walked back to the place next door to the closed second-hand store. It sold pipe and plumbing fittings. I had to wait for two customers before a round little man at the counter was free.

"Um, hi," I said. "Does that place next door have apartments over it?"

"Sure does. Why?"

"I just started a job down the street." I gestured vaguely toward Linden. "I'd sure save bus fare if I could find something closer than where I am now. Do you happen to know if they're rented? If maybe somebody might be looking to split the rent?"

He was shaking his head.

"Widow woman lives in one, I think. May have seen another woman come and go sometimes, or maybe a couple. You might go up and check."

"Okay. Maybe I will. Thanks."

He'd given me all the information he thought necessary. If I asked for more, I'd rouse too much attention. I went on my way and spent a few hours visiting spots on my list of places to ask about Neal. Forty-five minutes ahead of the rendezvous time, I returned to park on Stainton and sit watching its rhythms.

The woman who'd called me had a good feel for the beat of her street. At twenty till four a matron came huffing along with a grocery bag in one hand and a toddler holding the other. An older boy skipped ahead of them. They turned into a narrow house with fading blue paint. Over the next ten minutes, two more women came hurrying home with bags in hand.

Nobody went up or down the staircase leading to the apartments above the defunct second-hand-store.

At four-sixteen I took a final look along the street. The only pedestrians were two teenage girls walking slowly along with their heads touching as they shared a book that appeared to be mesmerizing. Something told me it wasn't a class assignment. As soon as they were past, I crossed the street and climbed the staircase. I knocked on the door of the front apartment.

Heels clicked toward me. A woman's heels, staccato and hesitant.

"Yeah? Who is it?"

"You called me this morning," I answered.

The door opened on a chain. An eye surveyed me. I couldn't tell much about the woman it belonged to, except that the eye was blue.

"You alone?" she asked.

"Yes."

She closed the door and there was the rattle of a chain being undone. The door opened and the woman stepped back. She was thin and brunette. It was all I noticed about her before the edge of my vision caught a blur of motion behind me.

I dodged, but not fast enough to avoid something hard crashing down on my head. Stars exploded and I felt myself sag toward the floor. Hands jerked me upright and a fist drove into my belly.

THIRTY-TWO

The pain of the punch revived my fading consciousness. My lungs worked independently of my brain, gasping air to replace the breath driven out of me. It cleared my head enough to take in disconnected images like those from a movie reel jumping off its sprockets.

There were several people in the room besides the woman. The one in front of me, a short mug with a bulldog jaw, drew back his arm to hit me again. I grabbed for the front of his shirt and my weight, added to momentum from his swing, pulled him off balance. It spared me the worst of the punch, but that didn't win me any favors.

"Hold her arms!" he snarled.

Someone — two someones — imprisoned my arms.

"Smart girl, huh?"

This time he slugged me in the face. I turned fast enough that the blow caught my cheek instead of my nose, and felt my lip split. I'd been worked over before, but never by fists this lethal. My cottony brain told me this one was wearing brass knuckles.

"Too bad you're not smart enough to keep your nose out of places it don't belong." Bulldog thrust his face forward, taunting. "You've been asked nice, but you must not hear good. Don't dig up the past."

I had to fight now, before the metal encasing his fist began to break bones. As his arm drew up and he leaned in for another punch, I toppled back onto the arms of the goons restraining me as if onto a bed. In the same movement, with my top half momentarily supported, I drew my knees up and drove my feet out toward Bulldog's belly.

They didn't connect hard enough to do much except surprise him. The men behind me crashed down on the floor in a tangle, bringing me with them. The pileup freed my arms, though. I rolled over one of the goons so I was no longer between them.

The guy with the knuckles, the one who was calling the shots, half tripped over one of the men on the floor as he swore and aimed a kick at me. I tried to scoot away but wasn't fast enough, and it got my ribs. Pain immobilized me. His foot drew back and he planted another one. I heard a whimper which I knew came from me.

He straddled me, reaching down to yank me upright for another taste of brass knuckles. Bursts of black distorting my vision, and flat on my back, only self-preservation gave me strength to push up with my elbows. I threw my left arm in front of me, maybe to ward him off, maybe in an attempt to distract — my brain didn't know.

My right hand went beneath me. Found the reassuring contours of my gun. Brought it around. Without aiming, I fired at the man above me.

I heard a high-pitched howl.

I felt a spurt of wetness on my hand.

I heard a woman's scream, and high-heels clattering off in retreat.

I fired again.

"She's nuts!" a man's voice cried. "The dame's gone crazy!"

"Shut up. I'm hit," another voice gasped. "Oh, Christ, I'm hit bad! Get me out of here!"

I wanted to fire again so nobody took another punch at me. Instead, I sagged back and lost track of everything.

***

I came to long enough to see a woman's shape hovering in the doorway to the landing. It wasn't the thin brunette who'd let me in. My unfocused vision managed to make out that the woman looking in at me was dumpy and her hair had the tight little knobs of a perm.

"What are you doing in Lucille's apartment?" she demanded shrilly.

"Some men beat me up," I managed through swollen lips.

"You don't belong here," she said as though she hadn't heard me. "Lucille moved out last week, and you don't belong here. I heard gunshots, too. I'm calling the police."

"Yeah, fine," I mumbled, and closed my eyes.

When I came to again, no cops were in evidence. I knew time had passed, but I didn't know how much. I hurt too much to check the pretty lapel watch pinned under my jacket. Blinking my eyes a few times cleared my vision enough to see it was twilight outside. The attack which had seemed to go on for hours had probably lasted only a matter of minutes. At least half an hour had passed since the men responsible fled. It must be around five.

An interval elapsed while I gathered all my willpower to make myself move. Gritting my teeth, I sat up. My head throbbed. So did the side of my face. My ribs felt several times worse. Trickling around them, nudging the pain back like a snake oil tonic that worked, was my anger.

I scooted on my haunches until I reached a chair. Gripping the seat for support, I pushed myself up. Then I sat for a minute. I'd gotten worse knocks on the head than this latest one, and was increasingly able to think. Just as well the woman who'd peered at me hadn't called the cops like she'd threatened. It saved time and questions. The woman must be the other renter up here, the widow who lived in the back apartment.

With several pauses to lean on the wall, I made my way to her door. I put all the pep I had into knocking. After a minute the door opened just wide enough for her to peer out. Right away she tried to close it, but I had my foot in. If she nudged my toes just a little, I'd fall flat, only she didn't know that.

"I'll give you four bits if you call a taxi and help me downstairs," I said as well as I could through lips the size of sausages.

I thought it would either appeal to her greed or shame her. All it did was make her hesitate in her attempts to force the door closed.

"If I don't, some cops are going be visiting to ask why you didn't call them when you heard shots."

She stopped torturing my foot.

"You better not come back making any more trouble," she said sticking her hand out. I dropped the change into her waiting palm. "And you can get downstairs yourself."

The door slammed.

I leaned against the wall to recoup my strength. Then I walked to the stairs and sat on the top one. Still on my backside, I made my way down, setting my jaw at every bump.

When I stepped out into what was left of daylight, I noticed a dark stain on the back of my hand. I remembered the spurt of blood from the man with the brass knuckles. My bullet had hit him somewhere in the groin, I guessed. Maybe the femoral artery. Since I wasn't inclined to use my skirt, I wiped the worst of the residue off on the wall of the stairwell. Taxi drivers take it badly if you get blood on their seats.

***

At the end of the previous year, when my bank account had been flush from a big case, I'd bought myself some Blue Cross insurance. The patching up I got at the hospital seemed likely to make it money well spent. A sawbones whose gray hair and world-weary face assured me he knew his business put some stitches in my lip and poked and prodded. He said two ribs were either cracked or broken.

"As long as they didn't puncture your lung, the treatment's the same," he said giving my thigh a cheerful pat. "Nurse Molloy will hold your arms up for me while I tape the ribs nice and tight."

Nurse Molloy had been in the same class with me at Julienne. She'd been shy and we hadn't said 'boo' to each other, but at least I hadn't antagonized her. She hovered, removing my blouse and my slip and standing by the whole time the doctor worked on me. When he finished taping my waist so tightly I could scarcely breathe, she gave me a packet of painkillers and helped me to a chair where she whispered something to the nurse working at a desk beside it.

"Who shall I call to come get you?" the new nurse asked

Exhaustion was catching up with me, and maybe the little paper cup of something liquid the doc had told me to swallow as well. I tried to think.

I wasn't about to upset Billy or Seamus by letting them see the shape I was in. I didn't know Rachel's number at home. None of the girls at Mrs. Z's had a car. That left one person. Swallowing pride couldn't feel half as bad as brass knuckles or stitches, so I gave her Finn's number.

"Hiya, Rose. Connelly around?" I asked as casually as I could.

"Maggie?"

"Yeah."

"You sound strange. Hang on. Let me fetch him."

Briefly I heard the comforting sound of glasses and voices.

"Maggie? What is it?" asked Connelly's baritone. He knew I wouldn't be calling without a good reason.

"I had a flat. Can you borrow a car?"

"Sure. Where are you?"

"Miami Valley."

I heard his sharp intake of breath as he guessed the truth.

"Be there directly," he said.

***

I was half asleep in a chair in the waiting area when he arrived. He was noiseless as fog, but I sensed his presence before my eyes opened. Muted profanities issued under his breath.

"Who did this to you, Maggie?"

I started to shake my head, but it hurt too much.

"Don't know," I said thickly. "But you might ask a nurse if anyone's been in who got shot in his thigh or groin."

He strode off buttoning his collar. Much as I tried to deny it, Connelly in uniform was an impressive sight. He wasn't especially tall or muscular, but there was a hardness about him which other cops lacked. It had been forged by what he'd witnessed, and done, growing up in Ireland. Within minutes he came striding back.

"Nope," he said, "and I hope the s.o.b. bleeds to death." His voice turned gentle. "Let's get you home then."

THIRTY-THREE

Genevieve helped me upstairs and into bed. She said I cussed a lot. All Wednesday I took pills from the doctor that made me woozy. In between them I slept. Thursday morning Mrs. Z. let Ginny make me a coddled egg with some bread crumbled in it, which was about all my sore lips, not to mention my jaw, could handle. After I finished it, I slept some more.

By Thursday noon I was bored. More than that, I was angry, impatient to nail the men who had caused my suffering. I'd settle for whoever sent them.

"Maggie, don't be a fool," chided Ginny as she helped me dress. "You're in no shape to go to your office."

"I'll take a cab. There's an elevator. I'll only stay there a couple of hours."

I'd taken only half a pain pill that morning. My head felt clearer. A mug or two of coffee would make it feel even better.

"You're weak as a kitten," she argued.

"I won't get any better if I baby myself."

"How would you know? You haven't tried it since I've known you."

In the end I won. It required agreeing that Genevieve could accompany me. By the time we got downtown, I was glad she had. She settled me at my desk and went across the street for my java.

"Promise you'll call if you start feeling wobbly," she said when she'd delivered it.

I nodded. "Thanks, Ginny. You're a pal."

When she'd gone, I sat sipping coffee. The solidness of my desk, the street sounds, the familiar knock of my radiator all seeped into me. Strange tonic, maybe, but one that worked for me. My ribs still screamed and the cut on my lip burned like it was fresh, but knots eased out of my muscles and I felt steadier. In control again.

Whoever had sicced those men on me in the vacant apartment had sent me a warning in very large letters. Too bad I wasn't in the mood to read. Not when logic was telling me I got the rough treatment only after I'd begun asking about the little girl. That, on top of Theda's frightened departure, made me think I was getting close to whatever someone didn't want me to find.

The little girl must be real. She must also be close enough I could find her, talk to her. That meant whoever was trying to stop me knew her identity. That meant she could now be in danger.

Having thrown a fit to get down here, I had to admit to myself I wasn't in shape to do much of anything. The only thing which came to mind was checking on Corrine and Isobel. I'd wanted to yesterday, but hadn't been able to face going downstairs and back to use the telephone.

"Oh, we're doing splendidly," assured Corrine. "Any news of Neal?"

"I was on the sick list yesterday. May be for a couple more days, if you want to get someone else —"

"No, no. I don't think we'd trust anyone else." One of her students was warbling a vocal exercise in the background.

Corrine said it was wonderful having Franklin around again and that the new pooch was settling in fast. We hung up.

Maybe I should get a dog, let him guard my office, I thought. And me, when I was in this kind of shape.

I preferred cats.

Cats weren't exactly in the same league when it came to protection. Maybe I could get a vicious one like Mrs. Z's. One that would sink its teeth into every set of legs that came through the door. Possibly not good for business. And possibly my thoughts weren't quite as coherent as I'd believed when Genevieve was trying to reason with me.

I forced myself to get up and take a lap around my desk. I tried to clear my head by breathing deeply, only to have the effort blocked by the bandages imprisoning my ribs. Finally, after thinking some, I called Rachel.

"Want to meet for a drink?" I invited. "I'll buy. Make it someplace dark."

***

Rachel's movements were uncommonly slow as she slid into the seat across from me in a nondescript bar on Third Street. Her midnight eyes began to glitter as they scanned my face. Forgetting her lighter she ripped a match from the book on the table and started a cigarette. Still studying me, she blew a stream of smoke over her shoulder.

"You look like dog puke."

"So nice to have a friend to cheer me up." I knew from the sting of my stitches I must have grinned.

She cupped her elbow in the opposite hand.

"Four-thirty did strike me as early for cocktails. Now I see why. Not that I'm complaining."

"Better for pain than little white pills," I said giving a small salute with the old fashioned I was sipping through a straw.

She inhaled some more and blew smoke out her nostrils.

"When did this happen?"

"Tuesday."

Rachel summoned the waiter and ordered a Gibson.

"Was it the man Pearlie expressed concerns about?" she asked when we were alone again.

"No. Somebody sent by a man who doesn't like some questions I'm asking, I think."

"Last time we talked, I got the impression you might be scratching around a politician."

"Yes."

"Care to share a name?"

"Only if you and Pearlie promise not to get involved."

"You're a big girl. You don't need us."

"That's the kind of wiggle I'd do to keep from making a promise."

Her smile spread in a slow line with no hint of a curve except at the ends. No matter what else it conveyed, it always held a hint of challenge.

"Very well. We won't poke in unless you invite us."

"It would complicate the little dance he and I are doing."

"What's the dance?"

"One where he needs to prove he's smarter than I am."

Rachel grinned.

"Does he know you're leading?"

Her drink arrived. The waiter asked if I wanted another. With some regret I decided against it.

"Cy Warren," I said as we settled in again.

"Swallowtail Properties. Commercial landlord. He doesn't build much, and when he does, the projects are smaller than we generally handle."

Rachel's company built small apartment buildings, private schools, offices for doctors and lawyers.

"Any whispers of his being crooked?" I asked.

"None that I've heard. Like me to make a few discreet inquiries of people I trust?"

"I'd appreciate that."

"Anything else that Pearlie or I could do to be useful?"

"I could use a driver tomorrow."

I was pinching bits from the cherry that decorated my old fashioned, easing them into my mouth, which was still too sore for much wear and tear. My empty stomach didn't have much sympathy for my mouth. Rachel eyed me shrewdly.

"What have you eaten today?"

"An egg. Coffee. Getting back on my feet."

"Sure you are." She knocked back her Gibson and stubbed out what remained of her cigarette. "Come on. I'll give you a ride home."

"That's okay. I'll take a taxi."

"A while ago you said we were friends. It's what friends do. Just let me make a phone call first."

On the way out, she noticed me favoring my side, but made no comment. She said we needed to make a stop on the way. It turned out to be at a good-sized building I'd never seen. One wall had a string of symbols I thought might be Hebrew, and two spotless delivery trucks were pulled up next to the door.

Rachel got out. When she returned, she shoved an open pasteboard box in my lap. Inside were a spoon and what looked like a squat, wide-mouthed vacuum bottle of stainless steel.

"Catering place," she said briefly. "The owner's a friend. He makes the best chicken soup you'll ever taste. Things in it are matzo balls. Good for what ails you."

THIRTY-FOUR

Rachel was right on all counts about the soup. The next morning I felt considerably better. By the time Pearlie picked me up, the other occupants at Mrs. Z's had left for their jobs, which was how I'd planned it. My mouth hadn't looked quite as swollen when I checked the mirror, and my lips weren't as sensitive. I figured I was up to oatmeal.

Pearlie let me off at the door nearest McCrory's lunch counter. He sauntered in ten minutes later to check on my progress. When he saw I was just about done, he brought the car around and helped me in. He argued some when he let me out in front of my building.

"Sure you don't want me coming up with you?" he asked for the third time.

"Nobody's going to jump me in the middle of the day. Except maybe you and Rachel."

"Okay. Twelve-thirty then."

"Thanks, Pearlie. Don't forget to give that Thermos back to Rachel, and tell her the soup was first-rate."

Heebs was supposed to check in with me. He might have stopped by to tell me something while

I was laid up, but in any case I wanted to pay the kid for his week's surveillance. And I wanted him away from Cy Warren.

In the meantime, while I still wasn't up to running foot races, I could make phone calls. I got out the list of beer joints Connelly and Seamus and I had brainstormed. Most wouldn't be open for business yet, but they'd be sweeping out, washing glasses, overseeing deliveries for another day's trade.

"Oh, hi. Could you take a message for Neal Vanhorn?" I bubbled when somebody answered. "This is the dry cleaners. He left a ten dollar bill in the pants he dropped off. We thought he might want it."

"Who?" said a voice on the other end. "Honey, this is a bar."

"Oh, I know. Neal said he had a swell time there." I gave what I thought was a giggle. Giggles had never been my strong suit. "I figured if he got the money back, he'd be spending some of it there."

"Sorry, don't know any Neals."

"He's kinda new, visiting or something. Maybe if I described him...."

I did. After repeating the same act half a dozen times, I still hadn't had any luck, although one guy had generously offered to come fetch the money and hold it for Neal in case he came in.

Someone knocked at my door. I leaned back and let my hand dangle conveniently close to the pocket under my chair as I called a greeting, but it was Heebs. He looked up from closing the door and stopped in his tracks.

"Holy smokes, Sis! Someone roughed you up bad."

"Yeah, but I shot him," I said to allay his dismay.

He came toward me, all traces of his usual sauciness vanished.

"Was it Cy Warren's mugs did it?"

"Nah," I lied. "Some girls have a fan club. The one they started for me is people lining up to break my nose. Learn anything on that black Dodge?" I'd asked him to keep an eye peeled for the car Pearlie and I had boxed in.

Still eyeing me solemnly, Heebs sat on the edge of a chair. He shook his head.

"Nobody ought to punch a woman like that, Sis. On the Dodge, what I learned is whoever drives it must not be pals with Cy. If you got the tail number right, then I didn't see it, not even once. I went past a couple of times in the evening, too, when I knew they were having meetings."

"Heebs—"

"Thought you might like this, though."

Reaching into his pocket, he brought out a torn scrap of paper and gave it to me with a flourish. Penciled on it were a dozen license plate numbers, each followed by the kind of car that wore it.

"Started keeping track of them the first day I was down there," he said proudly. "Ones parked in back of Cy's place and ones that parked along the street but people went in. A check mark means they were there more than once. Two marks means they were there most every day."

"Nice work, Heebs, but you took too much risk, snooping around in the alley. They might have spotted you, gotten suspicious."

He grinned, more aware than was good for him that he had an aptitude for my kind of work.

"Guy's got to walk back where he came from when he's done selling papers, and he's got to find somewheres in an alley to relieve himself now and then."

I started to chuckle, but gasped and pressed an arm to my side.

"You're good, Heebs. No question. Most of all, your malarkey. But you have to scram. You're making my ribs hurt. I'll give you a buck to run some errands for me, though, if you're willing."

"No need to give me lettuce to do you a favor, Sis."

I did, of course. Mixed in with my phone calls to bars earlier, I'd called a second-hand shop called The Good Neighbor. The woman who ran it appreciated some help I'd given her and she'd been more than willing to lend me a canvas cot for a couple of days. Having a place to stretch out would help me manage until I was back to full speed. By the time I'd made more unsuccessful calls about Neal, and Heebs had returned with the cot set it up with me explaining how it went together, I was more than ready to give it a test run.

Clarice had included a blanket when she sent the cot. Folded under my head, it made a good pillow. I closed my eyes, but my brain kept working.

Where was Neal?

Who was the little girl?

Why hadn't the black Dodge that had followed me several times shown up on the list from Cy Warren's headquarters?

Could the latter anomaly have anything to do with the fact Alf's neighbor claimed she'd seen two cars the night he was murdered? If there had been two cars....

That was as far as I got before falling asleep.

***

"There... and there." As Pearlie drove slowly down Percy, I indicated the spots where Dillon's Drugs and the menswear store owned by Cy's father once had stood. "It would have been put out somewhere behind those two buildings."

That wasn't necessarily the only place a kid might have seen what she thought was a clothing dummy carried out. Still, the stinging of my stitches told me it was the right place. Pearlie continued to the end of the block where he stopped to let a mailman cross with his bag. I thought of Wee Willie making his rounds somewhere, and wondered if he cut up any on his route. At the end of the next block, which was shorter and the last block on Percy, we turned into the alley and started back to get a view from the rear.

"Kids have good eyes. Need a feel for how far away the girl could have been," Pearlie observed.

I nodded. He'd brought Rachel's big Buick this afternoon. It was comfortable as an easy chair. I was sitting across from him instead of in back the way Rachel did when he drove.

"Alley angles some. Can't see the back of those places."

"Until you get about here," I said a moment later.

It was his turn to nod.

"And she would have been on the second or third floor, maybe the attic."

Even as I thought aloud, Pearlie was already squinting up at the houses that backed on the alley. I tried to dismiss the unsettling thought that his measure of how far you could see might be how far you could see to draw a bead on someone.

"What about the other side of Wayne?" I asked. "Could someone see from there, do you think?"

"Never smart to think when you can check."

We spent more than an hour surveying the area and debating lines of sight. After our first few passes, our attention focused on a single block of houses on the street north of Percy. They all backed on the alley, and though Pearlie expressed doubts about those farthest from the old drugstore, we agreed all the houses there were a possibility. I thought the house kitty-corner to the drugstore but on the other side of Wayne was a possibility too, and maybe a house or two on either side as well.

"Not unless there was a hotel there. Something high like that," Pearlie said.

The houses on the corner were well maintained, but they looked old enough to have predated the flood. So did the ones in the block that was my primary interest. Most of them were two story; a couple were three. We drove down the street in front of them again. The one behind where the drugstore had stood was painted white. The one next to it was pale green.

"What next?" asked Pearlie.

He meant driving directions.

"Next I find someone who knew the families who lived in these houses back then," I said.

Somewhere in the course of this ride-around I'd hatched an idea where to start.

THIRTY-FIVE

Pearlie dropped me off at Mrs. Z's around four. It was early enough the other girls wouldn't be home yet to pester me with questions when they saw my puss. The day had used up most of my energy. I hadn't realized how much breath stairs required until halfway up when I felt myself getting lightheaded. I gripped the bannister and lowered my head to get blood going.

"Maggie?"

I'd forgotten that Jolene left around this time to get to the club where she worked as a cigarette girl. She bounced down the stairs toward me.

"Oh jeez, Maggie, you got beat up. Here, sit down." She took my arm and sat down beside me.

"It didn't just happen," I said. "I'm okay — just get a little short of breath sometimes because I've got some ribs taped."

Her blonde curls bobbed wisely.

"It squishes your lungs so you can't breathe. Then you faint. Happened to me too. When I was a kid I got kicked by one of the cows. Good thing it wasn't my head, huh, although my brother used to claim that it was when he thought I was acting dumb. Anyway, my folks were scared it might have busted something inside me, so they bundled me into the truck and drove me in to the doctor..."

It always intrigued me wondering how long Jolene would be able to go on without pausing for breath. She should have been an opera singer, but they didn't pack as many words in.

"... and all the jouncing around coming home didn't seem to hurt quite as bad as I remembered, although since I'd blacked out going I didn't remember much. But then after a few days, when I started running around, I kept fainting. Head out to the henhouse and boom — I fainted. Run down to the barn to help feed the pigs and boom — I fainted. Well, Dad said no daughter of his was going to faint, not when any fool could see that everything else about me was working just fine. He told Mom to get out her sewing shears and cut those bandages off my ribs, and she did, and they didn't hurt any worse and healed just fine, and I never fainted again." She cocked her head as an idea struck her. "Want me to run get my scissors and cut yours?"

I managed not to laugh, mostly because I knew it would hurt like sin.

"I don't want to hold you up right now, Jolene, but thanks. I just might take you up on it in the morning."

She got up to leave.

"And hey, when people ask how you got that cut lip and bruises, tell them you got in a car wreck. They'll believe that quicker than saying you fell down some stairs."

It was a sad day when Jolene concocted a better fib than I did.

***

Jolene's coaching came in handy the next day when I called Billy.

"One of the girls told me you'd called about me a couple of times, but the cough syrup I was taking made me so woozy I was afraid to try and make it down the stairs." I coughed for effect. "Thought I'd better call and let you know I was on the mend so you didn't think I'd died or something."

"Well, I don't mind telling you, you had us worried. Mick said you had a bad cough, but it wasn't like you to be laid up for a week if it was no more than that."

"Trouble is, the friend who gave me a lift down to get the cough syrup got in a wreck, so I got banged up, too. Nothing serious. Didn't go through the windshield or anything."

He made concerned noises and I reassured him. I hung up in fine spirits. Genevieve had been home the previous evening, and she'd cut my bandages off. As Jolene had predicted, my ribs didn't feel any worse without bandages. It felt glorious breathing again. On top of that, no bandages meant I'd been able to take a bath. This morning I'd walked to the trolley and ridden it to the beauty shop I used sometimes, and got a shampoo while my stitched lip stayed nice and dry.

By afternoon I should be up to driving. I had an idea how to locate the little girl who'd lived somewhere around Percy Street. The sooner I did, the sooner I could warn her she might be in danger.

***

Wee Willie Ryan lived in the same white frame house his parents had lived in when we were kids. I swallowed the river of memories that wanted to come as I walked from my car to the door. It was late afternoon and the air had the sort of bite that makes kids tuck their cold fingers under their armpits and ignore its sting on their cheeks so they can keep playing.

"Maggie!" Willie's wife Maire burst into a smile the instant she saw me. Then she got a look at my face and her own face fell. "Jaysus, Maggie, are you still scrapping with people?"

We shared a chuckle. Maire had chestnut hair, with cheeks and lips as pink as rosebuds. She'd been a year behind Willie and me in school, and got into more trouble than she deserved for being an avid onlooker at most of our hijinks.

"How've you been keeping, Maire?"

"Better than you, by the looks of it."

"Car accident. Nothing serious. Look, I apologize for barging in when you're probably busy fixing dinner—"

"It's in the oven, and you'd better stay for some. Go on. Have a seat."

A cute little girl of four or thereabouts had been peeking round the kitchen door. Three boys, two older, one just a toddler, thundered in past her.

"Ma, where's our ball?" asked the tallest.

"Same place it always is. Say hello to Miss Sullivan."

The little girl had joined the bunch. They chorused as instructed, then ran to retrieve a softball from a pretty dish that looked like it had been meant for a more genteel purpose.

"I want to throw," the little girl begged as they started out.

"Girls don't play ball," said one of the older ones.

A tiny foot snaked out and sent him sprawling.

"Ma, Kathy tripped me!" he howled.

"And why'd you torment her with nonsense about what girls do and don't do? Let your sister play too or put the ball back. And if it comes near any windows, you won't see it again until spring."

They clattered out.

"That girl shows promise," I said.

Maire's eyes rolled heavenward. "Out of the four of them wouldn't you just know she's the one most like her father?"

"If I can just have a word with Willie, I'll be on my way."

"You won't escape that easy, but I'll tell him you're here." She stepped into a small hall and raised her voice slightly. "Will, Maggie-the-devil's here."

Irish girls named Maggie are a penny a dozen. There'd been three of us in my class, and at least that many in all the others. To keep us straight, the nuns added last names. Our peers preferred nicknames. I wasn't sure who'd given me mine.

Willie appeared, wiping his hands on a bandana which he stuffed in a back pocket. With his small stature and in ordinary garb instead of his postman's uniform, he looked like a kid again. He was opening his mouth to speak when he halted with a startled look. He came a step closer, pretending to squint.

"Are those stitches, or are you already sprouting hair on your face like my mam?"

Maire nudged him.

"Shush, now. She was in a wreck. Thank St. Christopher it wasn't worse."

After the fussing from everyone else, Wee Willie's cheerful assumption that I was resilient assured me I was.

"How about a taste of whiskey?" he offered. "It's not often Maire and I get to sit and visit without that crew of ours under foot."

"Just a dab," I said. "Plenty of water."

He left to get it while Maire and I talked. I wondered how she managed to keep her living room neat as a pin with kids running around. When all of us had glasses, we toasted the old times.

"Now," said Willie. "What brings you around?"

"Thought you might be able to run down some information for me."

"Something for one of your cases?" Maire's eyes sparkled. "I can step into the kitchen if you want it private."

I shook my head.

"It's for something I'm working on, yeah, but nothing hush-hush. I was wondering if maybe you could find out who was delivering mail in the Percy Street area back in 1913. Maybe a few years before that."

"Before the big flood." Willie wiped his lip with the back of his finger. "Looking to learn about someone who lived around there, is that it?"

He'd always been a quick little devil, but without much interest in actually studying.

"That's exactly it." I saluted him with my glass.

"Sure, I'll ask around. You'd be surprised how many old postmen there are. All that walking and fresh air keeps us healthy as horses."

The four kids pounded in again.

"Ma — it's cold," complained the girl.

"That's what happens this time of year, love." Maire whisked a hanky from her pocket and wiped the girl's nose.

"When's dinner, Ma?" asked one of the boys.

"As soon as you all wash your hands and I have a look at them."

They scampered off and I stood to go. Maire and Willie rose too.

"Come on, Maggie, stay and eat so we can have a proper visit. I made enough for an army. Meatloaf, mashed spuds, cooked carrots. That'll go easy on your poor mouth."

How could I resist?

THIRTY-SIX

Willie called me Sunday afternoon to say he'd found the man I needed to talk to. The gent was retired now, and Willie called him Old Ben, though he didn't appear a lot older than Billy and Seamus. We met in the little café on Percy Street the next morning. Old Ben was wiry like Willie, but taller. When he talked you could see he was missing a top tooth on one side of his mouth.

"How's the pie?" I asked once we'd introduced ourselves.

"Too much lard in the crust."

"That's what I thought too."

I ordered a slice of gooseberry, though, along with my coffee.

"Willie Ryan tells me you're a private detective." The retired postman pulled his eyebrows together in a way that warned me a lecture was coming.

"That's right."

"Doesn't seem like the right kind of work for a woman to do."

"Plenty of people tell me so."

He held his frown for several more seconds, then shrugged.

"Your funeral, I guess. Me and my wife raised three girls and none of 'em works. All found good husbands." He ate some pie. "So what is it you want to know about this neighborhood before the flood?"

"I'm trying to locate a family who lived on the street behind Percy. On the alley side of the street. Or possibly just across Wayne on the corner. They had a little girl."

"What was their name?"

"I don't know. I was hoping you would. That or which house they were in."

He gave the exhale of the long suffering.

"I switched from that route to one near downtown ten, fifteen years before Willie got hired. That's why he didn't know I'd ever had it, I reckon. Once you start learning names for a new route, it doesn't leave space for those old ones."

I felt my hopes teeter. He shoved his saucer away and scrubbed at his mouth with the paper napkin, rolling the napkin into a ball and tossing it down in a sign he was finished.

"Still," he said as he got to his feet, "walking that bit of the route might bring something back."

***

When I'd called to make arrangements with Old Ben, I'd offered to pick him up at his house. He'd said that after all those years spent walking, he now got a kick out of riding the trolleys. That's when we'd agreed to meet at the café.

Now, as we retraced his long-ago footsteps, I could see he enjoyed it. I found myself mesmerized by his rocking pace. Its gentle rhythm could carry a person through miles and more miles in the course of a day.

"Looks like they took a big old tree root out there. Used to be an awful hump in the sidewalk," he noted when we'd left the little business district for the residential street behind. Several minutes passed, and then he chuckled. "This house here had a silly little dog that would open an eye and look at me when I came, then go right back to sleep. Now that one over there — and I know you're not interested in that side — but those people had one of the meanest dogs I've ever seen."

He continued in that vein while we walked both sides of the block I was interested in and then crossed Wayne.

"Was there some sort of tall building here on the corner?" I ventured.

Old Ben tipped his cap back and peered into the past.

"Just a two-story house, like most along here. White. Not as big as this new one they put up, but it had a wrought-iron fence and the sweetest-smelling lilacs." He thought a minute. "It was kids you was interested in, wasn't it? Two little scallywags lived here. Boys, though. Used to hide in those nice bushes and jump out whooping like red Indians."

We went back to the block behind where the drugstore had been. This time Old Ben frowned at the houses we passed the same way he had at me.

"The trouble is, I remember children at some of the places," he said. "But I can't say if it was before the flood or ten years after, right before I changed routes."

"That's okay," I encouraged. "Just point out any that come to mind."

"Boys there..." He pointed and muttered. "Boy and girl there, but must have been older. He joined the Army during the war.... Nice family back there. I think they had a girl, and it was the saddest thing...."

He recounted the same tale the grocer had told me about a family that had gone to be with a dying relative when the flood hit.

"Now this house here had a couple of kids and a baby, but I don't remember when. And there..." He stopped in front of a gray house two down from where the menswear store would have been. With hands on his hips he nodded his head. "The ones who lived here had two girls. Perfect little ladies. Didn't play outside much."

I thought of Maire and Willie's daughter, running out on a raw autumn day and holding her own with her brothers.

"And I know they were here before the flood. Afterward, when it drained and was nothing but muck, when I started my rounds again, I remember passing here and seeing the doll carriage they used to play with caught in the bushes. The water had carried it out of the house with a doll baby in it."

Gooseberry pie lurched in my stomach. What if that was the doll the little girl had been talking about?

I jerked my thoughts away from that direction. Too much had happened since I started asking about the girl. This was no goose chase over a doll. Besides, her mother had told the policeman that the girl had been talking about a mannequin — not a toy.

"Did they come back after the flood?" I asked hoarsely.

The old postman shook his head. "Don't know where they went. Lots moved in with relatives, if they had any who'd been lucky enough not to get hit hard themselves."

"What about a name?"

He squinted at the door of the gray house as if expecting the two ladylike little girls to come through it pushing their doll buggy.

"Ames?" He said uncertainly. "Avis?"

By unspoken accord we began to walk back toward Percy Street, where I'd left my car and Old Ben would be only a short distance from a trolley stop. I wondered if either name he'd come up with was close enough to get me anywhere if I made more inquiries.

The soothing rhythm I'd come to enjoy stopped suddenly.

"Amos," he said. "Their name was Amos."

***

Back at the office I reacquainted myself with the cot. In a couple of days I'd return it before I got too attached.

After a late lunch I returned to the street with the gray house. I started there first. At least my face was looking considerably better. Remnants of bruises that hadn't quite faded, a couple of scabs on my cheek and ends of stitches sticking up like barbed wire. Other than that and the fact I couldn't wear lipstick, I was a regular glamour girl.

"Hi," I said when a woman in her mid-thirties opened the door. "I'm looking for the Amos family who used to live in this house. Are you a relative by any chance?"

She was about the right age to be one of the girls.

"Amos?" she repeated blankly. "No. I'm sorry, I don't even recognize the name. We bought the house from people named Tisdale, and that was—"

She broke off, speaking to someone inside with strained patience. "Dorothy, wash the polish off before you start buffing!

"I'm sorry, what was I telling you? Oh, yes. We bought the house from people named Tisdale, and that was before our oldest was born, so at least ten years ago."

Her eyebrows raised, inquiring silently if she might return to household duties. I thanked her and left.

I tried the houses in one direction from where the Amos family had lived. Then I tried the other direction. The results were much the same as those at the first house. Only one woman had grown up on the street, and she'd been a baby at the time of the flood. Her parents were both dead, and she didn't recall ever hearing the name Amos. Most of the people I talked to had moved there in the last twenty years.

The most unpleasant woman I encountered turned out to be the most helpful, but only after a fashion.

"I have no idea where those people went. Snooty as they came, that Mrs. Amos. Snubbed me every time we met."

She slammed the door in my face.

At least I was confident now that Old Ben had remembered the name correctly. Running low on optimism as well as energy, I decided to have one final stab before I gave up. I'd try the four houses across from where the Amoses had lived. If that didn't turn up anything, maybe I'd come back tomorrow to try the remaining houses on that side, and maybe I wouldn't.

When I reached the second house, as I was making my way up the sidewalk, a woman with nicely cut gray hair appeared from the side of the house. She wore a canvas butcher's apron over her dress and carried a trowel in one hand.

"May I help you?" Her tone was cool. "I've noticed you knocking on all the doors. Are you selling something?"

I attempted a smile.

"Actually, I'm hunting some information. I promised my aunt I'd try to find the woman who used to live in that gray house. Mrs. Amos."

"Lorraine?" She started to thaw. "Goodness. I haven't thought about her in years."

"They were chums," I said. "Their girls played together, I think. They lost touch after the flood, and my aunt's been down in the dumps since my uncle died...."

The woman filled in the blanks. Her tongue clicked in sympathy.

"Dear me. Just let me think. They moved, of course. All the houses along here had so much damage. First floors completely under water, and inches deep on the second."

And this street was just on the edge of the flood, where waters were lower, I thought. The woman with the trowel was telling me how she and her family and some of the others had simply lived in their attics during the long months of cleaning and making repairs.

"But I know Lorraine and the girls stopped by one day, after things had begun to settle down. She told me where they were living, too." She pursed her lips. "If only I...."

Her face cleared suddenly.

"You know, I do believe she wrote it down. Yes, I'm sure she did. I remember now. She asked would I send any mail along if it turned up, and tell anyone who might come looking for them. I think I might still have that slip of paper, too. Why don't you come in while I have a look?"

Depositing her trowel in a basket on the porch, she wiped her shoes like crazy on the doormat before going in. I did too. While she disappeared upstairs, I sat down in a front parlor furnished in heavy oak pieces. The loud tick-tock of a mantle clock filled the space around me.

Sooner than I expected, my hostess returned. Her smile was triumphant. In her hand was a leather-bound address book, its corners worn.

"I thought I might have tucked it in the back of this, and I was right."

She held out a scrap torn from nice stationery. The ink had faded with time but the information on it was clear:

Lorraine and Simon Amos.

Followed by the name of a street and a number.

THIRTY-SEVEN

Heebs had sold nearly all of his morning edition when I approached his corner for the second time in an hour on Tuesday.

"Thought I already sold you one of these," he grinned. "You back to flirt?"

"Back to see if you might be interested in making some money. Do you think you can go into maybe a dozen bars and ask a few questions without getting tossed out? They're pretty rough places."

He crossed his arms.

"Do I look wet behind the ears? My ma sent me into plenty of dives hunting my old man before he took off."

His mother had taken off too, when Heebs was, what, nine or ten? How he'd managed not to get picked up and tossed into an orphans home was anyone's guess. Maybe because hard times had left so many like him out on their own that the orphanages were full. I waited as a customer approached and handed him three cents for a paper.

"Okay, then," I said. "I'll pay you two bucks."

His eyes widened.

"Two bucks and a date with you, Sis? I must be dreaming."

***

Once I'd arranged a time and place to pick up Heebs, I returned to a trail that was growing more visible. The phone book didn't list anyone named Amos at the address left with their former neighbor, and it didn't list Simon Amos at all. I looked under Lorraine, although most women, even if widowed, kept the listing under their husband's name. No luck there, either.

The thought of repeating yesterday's round of knocking on doors didn't thrill me, but I'd known tedium went with this job when I hung out my shingle. I got gas for the DeSoto and drove to the address I was hunting. The street reminded me of the one I'd been on yesterday, except it was farther from downtown and some of the houses looked newer. I rang the bell on a door with an oval of frosted glass centered in polished wood. Through it I could see a woman and little girl come downstairs to answer.

"I'm sorry to bother you," I said, "but I'm trying to locate the Amos family who used to live in this house. It's about an inheritance."

For some reason people are more apt to help when they think money's at stake, even though they're not the ones who stand to profit.

"Amos," the woman mused. She had a hairbrush in her hand. One side of the little girl's hair was neatly braided; the other a mass of tangles. "I don't think I've ever heard of them. We've only been in the neighborhood a few years."

I tried a second house, where a woman was vacuuming to beat the band, then a third where a tired looking young woman greeted me two kids whining behind her, and another so close to arriving she needed a basket.

"You might try Mrs. Little, in that brick house over there." She pointed. "She's lived there a long time."

With a sigh of overdue hope I thanked her and crossed the street.

The woman who answered the door wore a hat and a suit like she was about to go out, and violet-pink lipstick which didn't make her look any younger.

"Oh, my yes. Of course I knew the Amoses. *Lovely* people. Lorraine and I used the same dressmaker, so we'd chat up a storm when we met there. Her older daughter, Jane, was in the same class as my girl. The younger one was an odd little thing — not feeble minded or anything, just sort of moony. She certainly married well, though, so there you go."

Foreknowledge was climbing my spine.

"Would you happen to know how to locate any of them?" I asked, although I had a feeling I already did.

"Lorraine passed away. I think someone told me her husband was poorly and living with Jane. Oh, if only I could remember what Jane's married name is." Her violet-pink lips pursed. "Well, no matter. You'll have no trouble finding Tessa. She married a man named Cyrus Warren. They say he's going to run for the Statehouse."

She started to close the door.

"I couldn't help noticing how perfectly that suit of yours fits," I said quickly. "I don't suppose you'd give me the name of that dressmaker you were mentioning. I've been looking for one."

Sometimes flattery buys as much information as money. It halted the closing door.

"Wanda Meecham, but she's not taking new trade." She preened at her privileged status and started to close the door again.

"Oh, gee. I'll bet she has an assistant, though. Maybe she'd take customers. Is that the Mrs. Meecham with a shop on Main?"

***

By the time I finished lunch I'd sorted through the pros and cons of the next step I wanted to take. Then I shrugged them all off and went with instinct.

I waited till mid-afternoon before driving up Salem to the half-timbered Tudor Cy Warren owned on Harvard Avenue. The area wasn't as swanky as Oakwood, but it was a neighborhood favored by doctors and other well-to-do types. The street curved around, showing off nice-sized yards and houses.

A couple of driveways had cars in them. Cy Warren's didn't. If he was the sort who occasionally came home for lunch, he wasn't here now, which was part of my plan. I parked on the street. Except for one other car, mine was the only one relegated to public space. Two concrete steps led up to a sidewalk set in a long front lawn. I followed it and went up another set of steps where I turned the polished brass doorbell.

After several minutes a sad-eyed colored woman who looked as if her knees hurt opened the door.

"I'd like to speak to Mrs. Warren, please. It has to do with her husband's campaign."

THIRTY-EIGHT

For one fleeting instant the maid's eyes noted my fading injuries.

"Yes, ma'am. Please step in and I'll tell her you're here."

She made her way laboriously down the hall to a room on the left. I'd been in entry halls larger than the one where I waited, but this one was beautifully furnished. The pale blue carpet looked as if it had been put down yesterday. An impressionist painting of couples strolling past a lake adorned one wall. Tessa Warren had a fine eye for decorating.

Several minutes passed before the woman I'd seen in newspaper photos appeared. She seemed to float instead of walk. The dreamy semi-smile she wore looked permanent. Her head cocked prettily.

"How lovely of you to want to help with my husband's campaign." The softness of her words was almost hypnotic. The handshake she offered had just enough energy to convey sincerity. "I'm afraid you need to go down to his headquarters if you want to sign up. Do you need the address?"

"Actually I've already been there. This is about Mr. Warren's early days. On Percy Street. He's told me a few things, but I'm hoping you can fill in some details."

"Percy Street?" Confusion drew her brows together. "I was only a child..." A note of petulance crept through her serenity. "Cy should have told ... Dear me. We'd better sit down, I suppose." Her hand flicked vaguely toward a parlor on the right. "I just need to... take care of something first."

As she turned to go, something caught her attention.

"Olivia, get that nasty doll out of here. I've told her a dozen times to keep it where it belongs. If I see it down here again, it goes in the rubbish."

"Yes, ma'am."

I hadn't noticed the battered rag doll at the foot of the stairs until the maid whisked it under her apron and began to climb ponderously. Tessa Warren glided away as if she'd forgotten my presence — which maybe she had. Her vicious-ness over a kid's toy startled me. The fact her serenity didn't so much as waver as she issued orders was downright unsettling. She behaved like a fairy tale princess inhabiting some world apart from the rest of us. Was it an act? Had she overdosed on something stronger than Miles Nervene? Or was there something else about her I was missing?

With the maid upstairs and my hostess vanished, I gathered an offer of tea wasn't on the agenda for me. I went into the parlor to wait. The carpet was the same soft blue as the hall, but the silk upholstery on the Queen Anne sofa and chairs featured a darker hue. In front of the sofa a low table held a vase half-filled with water. A handful of assorted flowers lay scattered as though forgotten on top of the florist's paper which had held them. Just as I was wondering if Tessa planned to leave me sitting there, she returned.

"Oh, how silly. I forgot to put the flowers in water." She pressed both hands to her mouth and giggled girlishly.

"Mrs. Warren, I didn't introduce myself." I gave her my card.

"Maggie Sullivan." She tried to appear attentive and failed. Plenty of men had probably fallen for it, though. "What a pretty card."

It was several miles off the reactions most people had when they read *Private Investigator*. Taking a seat across from me, she arranged her head in its decorous tilt.

"What was it you said you came about?"

"You lived in a house just behind Warren's menswear shop before the big flood."

As briefly as a firefly's blink her focus sharpened.

"Somewhere over there, yes."

"You told a policeman you saw men put a mannequin out in the alley the day the buildings caught fire there."

"I..."

"Actually, you called it a store dolly. Your mother explained to him that you meant a clothing dummy."

Her hands, which had lain decorously in her lap, moved toward each other. She didn't know the policeman in question was dead. Nor could she be certain that Cy hadn't already given me some song and dance about the mannequin story. Suddenly she giggled again.

"I was such a silly little thing. Always imagining. Mama said I just dreamed it, because I'd lost all my own dollies. Cy says so too.... What does this have to do with his campaign?"

I knew mad people bobbled around sometimes, rational one minute and not the next. Tessa's question about the campaign confirmed my suspicion she kept track of things just fine. She wore her ethereal aura like other women wore perfume, but she wasn't mad. She knew exactly what she'd seen that day.

"In your, ah, *dream,* was your husband one of the men who carried the clothes dummy?"

The tip of a small pink tongue darted into view as she moistened her lips. Once more, she couldn't be certain what — if anything — Cy had told me.

"I - I don't remember—"

"When you got older, you realized they were carrying out a body, didn't you?"

She stood up, pressing a hand to her temple. "Oh, dear. I'm getting a headache. You need to leave."

"The body of a man named John Vanhorn."

"It was a dream, I tell you!" The woman actually stamped her foot. Her voice had grown shrill.

"Your husband knows you know the truth. He wants to get elected, and he'll get rid of anyone who could cost him that. He's already killed the other man who was there that day. Your life isn't worth a plug nickel if you stick around."

The front door banged open in anger. No need to guess what prince was charging to the rescue of the damsel. I got to my feet.

"You need to get out," I told the woman staring at me. "Go to your sister. A friend. Take a trip."

I wasn't sure she'd heard.

"What the hell are you doing here?" Cy strode in. "How dare you bother my wife!"

Serenity back in place, Tessa fluttered to his side. Leaning against him, she rested a hand on his chest and gazed up.

"Oh, Cy! She keeps asking about that dream I had — about the flood. I told her it was only a dream. I'll bet lots of little girls had terrible dreams afterward, don't you?"

She gave him such an adoring look I thought I might lose my lunch.

He missed the adoration. He was too busy glaring at me.

"Of course they did," he said shortly.

For all intents there were only the two of us in the room. Tessa had become another decorative item like the vase of water waiting for flowers.

"Keeping tabs on your wife, are you Cy? What is it, that car parked down the way? Or did you buy one of the houses around here so you could keep track of comings and goings?"

It was the only way I could figure he'd gotten here so fast. The likelihood of her calling him was something I'd anticipated, but I'd kept track of time, expecting to be gone before he arrived.

"Don't be ridiculous."

Deprived of anticipated attention, Tessa thrust her lip out. Cy patted her absently.

"You're agitated, sweetheart. Go upstairs and lie down. Take one of your tablets."

Still pouting, she took her leave. My ears strained, trying to determine if Cy had brought some of his men with him. I moved so the low table wasn't blocking me, crossing my arms and surveying the room as I did so.

"Your wife has better taste in decorating than she does in men, Cy. This room's as beautiful as I've ever seen."

"I couldn't find a more perfect wife."

He closed the gap between us, watching to see if I'd retreat. I didn't.

"Handy, too, since spouses can't testify against each other in court," I observed.

"Pity that the policeman she told her ridiculous tale to is long dead, isn't it? Being a devoted husband I naturally looked for anything that could put her mind at rest when she first told me her dream."

Watching my every move, he took a cigar from his pocket and brought out a silver lighter to start it. In private he didn't need the folksy touch of matches. The lighter lid clicked open and closed, open and closed, with no attempt to summon a flame. Open and closed. Its sound was a challenge as we watched each other like two cats waiting to spring

"If you even attempt to contact my wife again, I'll destroy you," he said.

"I don't need your wife, Cy. I've got you for Alf Maguire's murder. Two witnesses."

The clicking stopped.

"You're bluffing," he said after a pause. "You're good at bluffing."

At last he snapped a flame to life and lit his cigar.

"Want to dig into my past?" He chuckled softly. "Go right ahead. I dare you. But you won't find anything, and some of my over-zealous supporters might get carried away. Without my knowledge, of course. They might do worse than that."

He indicated my face by leaning forward and blowing a stream of smoke directly into it.

I nearly coughed, but managed not to. When several seconds had passed and the air was marginally clearer, I took a breath. His eyes were hard, trumpeting his superiority.

"Don't dare a dame, Cy. One may call your bluff."

Plucking the cigar from his startled lips, I dropped it into the vase full of water and brushed past him out of the room.

THIRTY-NINE

Because of my work I'd seen more than my share of the ugliness that hid in life's corners. Nonetheless, the Warren's marital arrangement made my skin crawl. A woman married to a man who'd kill her to silence her. A man who, knowing what she'd seen and aware of her unstable behavior, paraded her on his arm. Wherever the match had been made, it wasn't in heaven.

Jesus.

The whole thing was unnatural.

I tried to make sense of it over a pint at Finn's, and then over a second one. I let Billy cluck over me while Seamus shot me an occasional look of commiseration. I jawed at Wee Willie. Somewhere after I settled myself at a table, Connelly joined me without my objecting. I could hardly say no, considering how he'd come to my aid a week ago at the hospital. It led to my telling him about Cy and Tessa.

"Maybe Mrs. Warren's one of those women who knows she's got looks enough to land a husband, and doesn't much care who he is as long as he's got money," he said.

"Voice of experience?"

"The ones that were eager to land me didn't have money." He flashed a grin.

"But it just happening to be Cy...."

"Yeah. That smells bad. Any chance she was shaking him down?"

I gave a short laugh.

"Tessa? Threatening to spill the beans if he didn't marry her? First, I can't see her figuring out it was him she saw on the day of the fire. She was seven years old. He was in his twenties. Besides, as much as she's honed her talent for making a man feel important, I can't see her managing something that took so much planning."

"And even if she did, given how respectable Cy's become and his connections, why would he even blink at what some kid prattled about a quarter-century ago?"

"There is the fact he's running for office. But yeah, I thought of that too."

"Even with you roiling the waters."

"Even that."

I thought how smug Cy had been that afternoon, blowing smoke in my face. It reminded me I was facing what could prove to be a long evening with Heebs.

"Got to go," I said pushing the rest of my Guinness aside and standing. "We must've set some kind of record though, sitting here without squabbling."

Connelly studied me beneath lowered lids.

"Maybe I'm losing interest."

I paused a fraction as I turned my coat collar up. The crackle of whatever existed between us had just surfaced, strong as ever.

"Or maybe you're changing tactics," I said.

His touch as light as a feather, he laid a finger on my hand, detaining me.

"Mark your calendar for Saturday, though, will you? Rose served notice when she was drawing my beer a week or so back that I'd be in bad favor unless I got our scruffy little group to play some tunes in the big room here."

His eyes held mine. I saw goodness there, and more.

"I wouldn't miss it for the world," I promised.

***

At half past eight I picked up Heebs. Ten minutes later I was parked in front of a bar on a seedy strip along the river. Using the list I'd drawn up with Seamus and Connelly, I'd come up with a plan to look for Neal while conserving my energy, which still wasn't a hundred percent up to snuff, and which I'd need if I found him. While I sat in the car where I could keep an eye out for trouble, Heebs went in and showed the photograph of Neal and asked if he'd been in.

"Piece of cake, Sis," he reported swaggering out of the first one. "Showed 'em the picture and said he'd skipped out on my stepmom and me, and the little ones were getting awfully hungry."

"Had they seen him?"

"No."

I started the engine. I needed something concrete on Cy, and if Tessa wouldn't talk to me — which I still hoped I could persuade her to do — Neal was my best bet. There had to be some reason why he'd run.

Eight places later, we still hadn't had any luck. I'd had to double-park twice in narrow streets, waving out-of-sorts drivers around me while I waited for Heebs. He came out of the ninth place with his hands filled with peanuts.

"Want one?" he offered cracking the shell.

"Not sure my mouth could manage it yet, but thanks."

"They hadn't seen Neal, but the guy serving beer said a dry cleaning place had called hunting him too. Gave me a wink and said Neal had left some money in pants he dropped off — like he was telling me to go get it." He finished the peanuts. "All the yakking I've done tonight made me thirsty. Okay if I get a beer while I'm in the next place?"

He made it sound as casual as he could. I gave the little hustler a sideways look.

"Nice try, Heebs, but there's Coke in that sack if you're thirsty."

Unruffled, he took out a bottle and pawed through the sack for the metal opener that was my only claim to kitchen equipment. He pried off the cap of the bottle and sipped in silence.

"What happens if you don't find this guy, Sis?"

"I don't know," I admitted. "But here's another place to try."

Heebs set his bottle of pop down carefully on the floor of the DeSoto. I sat waiting, listening to the mournful wail and clatter of a freight train as it passed. The streets we'd been traversing had a weary feel. Just across the river were colored neighborhoods, some nice and some not so nice. West Fifth and other streets there had clubs and theaters that brought in fine entertainment. My photographer friend Matt Jenkins and his wife and I had gone over once to hear jazz. There'd only been one table left, at the back of the room, and ours had been almost the only white faces.

Heebs returned to report no more success than he'd had elsewhere. It was past ten. Only four places were left on my list. By the spring in his step when he came out of the third one, I knew he'd learned something.

"Old Neal's been coming in regular," he said bouncing into the car. "Last week he got such a snootful that two of the regulars had to drag him home. Tonight he came in about five. Left just when they were thinking they'd have to do it again."

"Sweet Mary. Tell me you got an address."

He rattled it off.

"It's a fleabag hotel called The St. George. Cheap rates if you rent by the week. As drunk as he is, the two of us could take him easy."

"As drunk as he is, I'm not likely to get any answers from him. I'll wait till tomorrow," I said.

But I was lying.

FORTY

The St. George Hotel fell somewhere between the Ritz and a roach farm. It inclined toward the latter. After I'd dropped Heebs off, I came back and located it and circled the block several times to get the lay of the place. Twice as I passed I saw ladies who didn't appear at all matronly enter the hotel accompanied by men unlikely to be their husbands.

One hint the establishment wasn't the classiest came from its neon sign. Sputtering in the front window, it proclaimed ST. GEORGE HOT, the final EL having burned out. As I pushed through the swinging door into its small lobby, one of the girls I'd seen was cozying up to her guest of the evening as they climbed the stairs.

Half a dozen steps beyond where I'd entered, a desk clerk with a sharp nose and sharper eyes looked up from behind a counter. There were pigeonholes in the wall behind him and a phone and register book on the counter. By the way his eyes flickered I knew he noticed my face.

"Need a room?" he asked sliding the register toward me.

"What I need is to talk to Neal Vanhorn."

His expression told me nothing. The bilious hue of his necktie made me glad I hadn't eaten much supper.

"Came in drunk as a skunk a couple hours back," I prompted in case Neal was using some other name. "What room is he in?"

"We don't give out information on guests."

I put four bits on the counter.

"Good policy."

His fingers moved an inch and stopped.

"He do that to you?" He gestured with his chin.

"No. I just need to talk to him."

"Room 22. Two up, right."

The four bits clinked as he transferred them to his pocket. I made a quick inventory of the inside. To the right of the counter an archway opened into a small bar. The plant at the entrance was bigger than mine, but almost as dead. The bar looked empty.

"Neal have any other visitors?" I asked.

The clerk shook his head. Hard to say whether he was telling the truth.

"I need to borrow a bucket to take up."

He stared uneasily.

"The janitor locks his up when he leaves for the day."

"Don't you have a key?"

"No. Look, honey, I don't want any trouble—"

"Then give me a bucket. Tell you what, I'll settle for that champagne bucket."

I could tell he meant to deny they had one until he realized I was looking into the bar where one sat in plain view. Empty.

"It's the only one we have. We might need it."

I wondered what he thought I meant to do with it, not that I cared. Reaching under my jacket I brought out my .38. With my other hand I caught his ugly yellow tie and jerked his face close to mine.

"See this?" I tapped my cheek with the tip of the gun to make sure he got a good look at the ends of stiff black thread which poked out of my skin like barbed wire now that the swelling was gone. "The guy who did it won't be walking for quite a while. I'm disagreeable when I get peeved. So unless you want me to put a hole in that champagne bucket — and maybe a couple of other things — I suggest you march in there and bring it to me." I released his tie. "Feel free to call the police. I'm sure they'd be interested in those girls you have doing business upstairs."

His face turned three shades of red.

"I don't have anything to do — they just rent rooms!"

He scuttled backwards, wrenching his eyes from the gun long enough to make sure he didn't run into the door, and returned with the champagne bucket.

"Thanks," I said, and headed upstairs.

I heard voices behind one of the doors that I passed, snoring from behind another. No sound at all emanated from Room 22. I knocked softly but got no response. I upped the volume with no better results.

The door wasn't locked. I eased it open a couple of inches and listened. There was the sound of even breathing. Neal sleeping one off, or someone calm and confident lying in wait. No guarantee I wouldn't encounter both when I went in. It wasn't the use I'd had in mind for the champagne bucket, but that didn't stop me from tossing it in. Better it got shot at than me. It clattered to the floor untouched.

I slammed the door full open in case anyone was hiding behind it. They weren't. I locked it behind me and went to look at Neal sprawled face up on the bed. He'd managed to shed his shoes and his jacket. One toe poked through a hole in his sock.

Odds were he was passed out rather than sleeping. I lifted my foot and nudged his leg. A gargle of protest escaped him, but he didn't rouse.

The room reeked, mostly of sweat and booze. In addition to the iron bed, it held a chest of drawers, a ladder-back chair and a lamp. A mostly empty bottle on the chest of drawers suggested Neal supplemented his visits to beer joints with home cooking. I tried to open the window to let in some fresh air. The wood had swelled.

"Hey, Neal." I shook his shoulder. He didn't respond any more than he had when I'd used my foot. Time to use the champagne bucket I'd borrowed.

I went into a tile-floored bathroom. It didn't have a bathtub, just the toilet and sink and a shower the size of my file cabinet. A tub would have made things easier, but the shower would do. I ran the water to make sure it was nice and cold, then held the bucket close to the shower head to fill it. Returning to the bedroom, and not without a certain enjoyment, I threw the contents directly at Neal's face and shoulders.

He yelped and flailed in an attempt to sit. I missed the entertainment since I'd left the water running and lost no time in filling the bucket again and repeating the dousing. This time he swore and managed to push himself up on his elbows. He looked around blearily, hunting the source of his torment. After wheeling unsteadily, his gaze picked me out. A little more effort and he finally focused.

"You!" he said thickly. He looked as though he might have had more to say, but suddenly he collapsed, hanging his head off the bed just in time to vomit.

When I saw the heaves were diminishing, I returned to the bathroom and filled the bucket again. This time I turned the shower off. Neal rested unsteadily on one arm, his head still over the side of the bed. As he became aware of me, he looked up long enough for a baleful glare.

It was also long enough to register what I had in my hands. He would have dodged if he'd been able to. This time I delivered the water with less force.

"That'll make you feel better, Neal. Honest. Cleaner at least."

He sputtered.

"Who sent you?" he gasped weakly.

"Nobody sent me, Neal. I've been hunting your miserable carcass for almost two weeks. Why your sisters care about you, I can't understand, but they've been worried sick since they learned you were missing. Now. Start talking. Who did you think sent me?"

He started to shake his head, but fell back with a groan. I saw his chest heave and wondered if he might get sick again. He didn't.

"I can't," he moaned holding his head in both hands.

Checking the ladder-back chair to make sure it was reasonably clean, I sat down.

"Neal, listen to me," I said patiently. "If I could find you, so can whoever else is looking."

I was vain enough to think it was a lie. He moaned again.

"Oh, God! I can't!"

I tapped the bucket.

"Don't make this hard on yourself, Neal. Let me help you. Here's what I already know."

He was sobering up some, but was still too soused to realize most of what I laid out was speculation rather than fact. With luck he'd confirm it and be scared enough he'd tell me the rest.

"You ran because a man was waiting for you outside where you work the day after Alf's funeral. He knew you'd been at Alf's house the night he was murdered."

"No! That's not—"

"They saw you there, Neal. So did one of the neighbors."

"I don't — I wasn't there!"

"You even told George that someone had killed his father."

"I told George—?"

His eyes had been closed, hoping that if he couldn't see me I'd disappear. They flew open.

"Yep. You did. The night after Alf's funeral. Now you better start talking fast if you want me to help you. The people looking for you don't know how much you saw. They're not going to take chances."

He started to blubber.

"Oh, Jesus! How did I get in this mess? Jesus, what am I going to do?"

FORTY-ONE

I let him bawl like a baby for five or ten minutes. Snot dribbled from his nose and his eyes got red and puffy. When I'd had enough, I went into the bathroom and found the glass tumbler provided by the hotel. I rinsed it a couple of times before putting an inch of water in it and carrying it out to the man on the bed.

He cringed when he realized I had more water.

"Rinse your mouth out," I ordered. "You might as well spit on the floor. It's not going to matter much, considering what's already there."

He shrank back from the glass I offered him like he expected me to jab a knife in his chest. At least he complied, which suggested progress.

"What kind of mess?" I asked when he finished.

"Huh?"

"A few minutes back you said, 'How did I get in this mess?'"

He sighed and scooted up on his pillow a little.

"That first time I met you, at the house. I'd called my sisters the night before to say I was coming over the next day to get Alf's things. Corrine told me I couldn't, that someone was coming to discuss 'personal matters'. She had that superior sound that she gets. It made me sore, and I ranted about it to Alf. He thought maybe they were up to something — maybe fixing to sue him the way he'd done them. I guess ... I guess maybe he went over and sneaked in to listen, only he knocked something over and made a racket and had to run."

"You guess that's what he did, or you know?"

He looked at his nails and pushed at a cuticle.

"I know. He told me. He didn't say what he'd heard that upset him, but I know something had."

"So he's the one who killed the dog."

He twisted his shirttail, which was hanging out, avoiding my eyes.

"He didn't need to do that," he mumbled. "There must have been some other way."

"What's that got to do with the people you're running from?"

A whine I recognized crept back into his voice.

"I never expected him to go over there!"

"Neal."

"It wasn't my fault." He started to snivel.

"I don't care whose fault it was. Just answer my question."

"My head hurts."

"It'll hurt more if I smack it." I went to the side of the bed without a puddle and used his shirtfront to haul him to a more or less sitting position. He groaned. Yanking him forward, I turned his single pillow longwise and shoved him back against it.

"What did Alf's eavesdropping have to do with his murder?"

"I don't know! Please. Give me some of that whiskey... an aspirin... something."

"I'll get you some water." I brought him an inch. "Now answer my questions. Don't make me use this." I wagged the champagne bucket.

"Yeah, okay," he said sullenly.

"Why were you at Alf's house the night he was killed?"

"He called me. Right after I got home from work. I'd never heard him so worked up. That's when I found out he'd listened to whatever you and Corrie and Isobel talked about. So see, you know more about—"

"Finish your story, Neal."

He might have attempted a glare, but maybe he was just squinting. His face was the blue-white of skimmed milk.

"He said he had to see me that night — that it couldn't wait — and not to tell George. He said come around eleven, that he had to go see somebody else first."

"Any idea who?"

"No."

"Then what?"

"I went over around eleven, like he'd said. I rang the bell, but nobody answered, so I waited ten minutes and left. I came back around midnight and tried again, but there was still no answer. Then I noticed there was a light in the kitchen."

"Was it there before?"

"I don't know. But I thought maybe Alf was back there or was in the crapper or something and hadn't heard me ring. Anyway, I went around the side of the house, thinking I'd try the back door. Knock and then go in and yell it was me, you know?"

It was how I'd done at Kate and Billy's when I was a kid, and at Wee Willie's, too. I nodded.

"There's a window there on the side. The shade hangs up about an inch from the bottom unless you notice and fiddle with it. One time George and I peeked under and saw Alf and his girlfriend—"

He broke off at my expression.

"Yeah. So. It was starting to feel funny, Alf making such a big deal over needing to see me and then not being there. I looked through that gap and saw Alf at the kitchen table, passed out with a bottle beside him."

"Was he already dead?"

"I - I don't know." He looked so miserable I almost felt sorry for him. "I didn't go in. I thought, well, maybe he was just a little bit drunk, or maybe sleepy. I went on to the back door, still meaning to knock. But just as I was starting to..." He swallowed with effort. "I heard somebody moving inside. And I... oh, God... I don't know what I thought.... Just that something wasn't right, and I'd better clear out, and that's what I did. I figured the people in the other side of the duplex would be asleep and wouldn't see me, so I went that way."

"But somebody did see you."

"Yeah."

"Somebody who knows Alf was murdered and thinks you saw the killer."

"All I saw was what I've told you!"

"And cars."

"Cars?"

"Maybe they think you recognized cars."

Neal looked blank. Maybe he made connections better when he was sober. I doubted it. I switched directions.

"Who's got you scared, Neal? Who came to see you that day at work? Was it one of Cy Warren's men?"

"Cy Warren?" he repeated stupidly.

"He and Cy were thick when they were young."

"I know who he is. You think I'm dumb?" Irritation pushed color into his face. "He's running for something. Statehouse, maybe. Of course it wasn't anybody he sent!"

"How can you be so certain?"

"Because ... because it was somebody from the other bunch."

"The other party, you mean?"

He wet his lips. His eyes darted nervously from the door to the window.

"No. His own. The ones who paid me to dig up dirt on him."

***

I leaned against the wall of the shabby hotel room and let the import of what he'd just told me sink in. That was why so much in this case hadn't made sense. Why someone already was snatching Corrine at the very moment my presence first alerted Cy Warren to the fact I'd made a connection between him and Alf. Why a car tailing me bore a license plate that didn't appear on the list Heebs compiled. Why there'd always seemed to be an extra element that didn't fit.

There *was* an extra element. It had nothing to do with Percy Street or the Vanhorns. It had to do with politics. Not money — at least not as far as I could see — but power. Or maybe prestige.

"Jesus, Mary and Joseph," I muttered to myself. "They're as bad as gangsters."

Neal was holding his head in his hands, as miserable at what he'd done as from the bender now hammering him with its effects. I went into the bathroom and got him half a glass of water. This time I added a miserly splash of whiskey from the bottle on the dresser before I gave it to him.

"Who are these men? What did they want you to find out?"

It was late, and my patience was strained. Apparently Neal could tell.

"I-I don't know any names. The one who hired me, he's some bigwig. In the party, I mean. Not anybody who's been elected. But he's there sometimes, at headquarters."

"Cy's headquarters?"

"No — the party's. Alf's kind of — was kind of — keen on politics. I'd tag along sometimes. Pretend I was too, because...."

"Because you wanted to butter him up."

"I guess. George said all their blather was boring. I thought so too, but I went now and then. That's how I knew about Alf and Cy being pals. Alf always made it a point to go over and talk to Cy, though to tell you the truth, they didn't really talk. More like Cy pasted on a smile and said 'Good to see you, Alf.' Like I say, this other guy, the bigwig, was around. I never paid him much attention. I think he runs people's campaigns or something like that."

"What's he look like?"

"Fair. Real fair. Kind of blocky." He shrugged. "I only talked to him once."

"When he hired you to spy on Alf?"

He looked down guiltily and swallowed some water.

"Yeah. I guess. But I never spied. I was... I'd just get him to talk about Cy, about what they did in the old days. Then I'd tell a guy who worked for the bigwig."

"What were they trying to find out?"

"They never said. The important guy came up to me at a meeting. He slipped me five bucks and said if I wanted to make five more, be down at the corner in ten minutes. I wasn't to tell Alf or anyone else.

"So I went and a guy of his met me. He said they'd pay me a fin a week to pump Alf about anything stupid Cy had done. I couldn't see it would hurt Alf any, so I said sure. Every week I'd meet the same guy somewhere and tell him anything I'd learned, but it never was anything important. Just pranks they'd played, stuff like that. Then Alf died and the guy I'd been reporting to turned up—"

"Outside where you worked."

"Yeah. He called me names. Said they knew I'd been sneaking around at Alf's the night he died.

He said unless I told what I'd seen — who I'd seen — they'd pin it on me!"

He sank back, hands shaking as he used both to raise the glass to his lips.

To pressure him, they'd terrorized Corrine. What they didn't know then was that Neal already was in the process of running. Even now, he probably had no inkling what had befallen his sister. Meanwhile, unaware of a second faction, I'd erroneously assumed her abduction was intended to scare me — or the sisters — into dropping the case.

Thinking of how much trouble was stirred up by people who 'never meant to' do any harm disgusted me as much as the smell of the room. I'd had all I could take for one day.

"You've got two minutes to get out of those clothes and into the shower to clean yourself up," I said. "Get moving or I'll do it for you."

FORTY-TWO

The doc who'd embroidered my lip had said the stitches should stay in at least a week. One week and thirteen hours later I tried to hold him to taking them out. He argued waiting two more days would be better, so we finally compromised. He'd take them out if I promised not to use lipstick for another week.

As soon as I got to my car I got out my lipstick. Then I had second thoughts. Tiny holes remained where the silk or catgut or whatever it was had been pulled out, and there was a line where skin was still growing together. Feeling uncommonly virtuous, I put the lipstick away, had breakfast, and bought some fresh Vaseline, which at least gave me some shine. Then I headed over to check on Neal.

"Franklin's already been by. Brought some groceries and a paper and that. Big bottle of aspirin." He grimaced. Avoiding my eyes, he rubbed his hands together awkwardly. "I don't know why he's being so nice, the way I used to sniff at him."

The night before, once Neal got out of the shower and into the more-or-less-clean clothes I'd found for him, I'd offered a choice: I could take him back to where he lived with George, or to Franklin's currently empty apartment. I wasn't going to risk his sisters' safety sending him there. He was smart enough, and sober enough by then, to realize he'd be safest at Franklin's. I'd used the phone in the St. George lobby to call Franklin and make arrangements.

Finding him up and around in fresh clothes that clearly belonged to his stepbrother was a nice surprise. He didn't add anything new when I asked him the same questions I'd asked the previous night, but at least he wasn't surly this time around.

"Don't worry, I'm not going to take off, and I'm not going to pull anything stupid," he said fervently.

With one less thing to worry about, I went to my office — where things began to go downhill.

Amid my mail was an envelope with no stamp. It probably had been dropped through the slot of the building's phone booth- sized mail room. It bore my name and office address in impeccable penmanship. The writing looked vaguely familiar, but I couldn't think where I'd seen it. Tearing open the envelope, I unfolded a sheet of typing paper.

Miss Maggie, it began. My eyes jumped to the signature for confirmation. Yes, it was from the two Negro girls who cleaned in the building.

Miss Maggie,

Sophia and me thought you should know someone was snooping around in your office last night. We'd just come in and it was our night to do third floor first, and right as we started down the hall, Sophia saw a little bitty light go off in your place.

Her brother Zekiel was with us so he could visit while we worked, cause he doesn't get up to see her much. He's a mighty big man, and when we whispered it wasn't right, somebody being in there, but that no account night watchman wouldn't get up from his card game even if we told him, Zekiel slipped into the mop closet and grabbed a handle that had broke off. He marched into your office, and told those hoodlums to get, that he'd already called the police. Guess they thought he was the watchman, cause they took off running. There was two.

Gilead

P. S.

We thought it would be safer to poke a letter through the slot downstairs than leave it on your desk in case those men came back, so we used one of those extra envelopes you keep in your basket.

Despite the bad news, it tickled me picturing the incident. When I worked late enough that Sophia and Gilead were around, I yakked at them and they kidded me. At Christmas I gave them each a couple of bucks, and sometimes during the year a peck of apples or beans that looked especially good at the market. They were hard working women trying to hold their own in the world, just like me. As I sat considering the ramifications of someone searching my office the telephone rang.

"Hey, this is Donnie. How are you?" said a voice when I answered.

My eyes jumped toward the clock. It was well past the time he'd start work at the factory, and much too early for lunch.

"Good," I said curiously. How about you?"

"Okay, and I've got news. Not where Neal is, but something I'm pretty sure you'll want to know."

He didn't need to tell me he was in a hurry. It came through in his quick delivery. Either he was on a break or had sneaked out to phone.

"Shoot."

"That place we had the beers together? I was in there last night. One of the bartenders called me over. Said a guy had come in Monday night hunting Neal. The bartender told him he hadn't seen Neal, and that somebody else was hunting him too. The guy asking wanted to know if that somebody else was a woman. That chucklehead at the bar said Yes, trying to be helpful."

Every nerve in my body snapped to alertness, humming with certainty.

"Did the bartender give a description?" I asked.

"Brown hair. Nothing to notice, he said."

I suppressed a sigh.

"Thanks, Donnie. I really appreciate it. Keep this to yourself, but Neal's okay. I found him last night."

"Yeah?" He sounded pleased. His short pause held equally brief hopefulness. "Well. I better go."

I hung up and swiveled my chair and thought. Night One, someone on Neal's trail learns a woman is also hunting him. Night Two, someone breaks into my office. My earlier surge of certainty told me one led to the other. What it neglected to mention was the identity those involved, or what team they played for. Most likely it was the same men who'd scared Neal into running. Still, Cy Warren could have gotten wind of Neal's presence on the night of the murder, and be worried enough to try and learn what there was in my files.

I decided it was late enough I could call Tessa Warren even if she was the sort to sleep late and have breakfast in bed.

"Is Mrs. Warren in?" I asked the maid. "This is Margaret."

Tessa was bound to know a Margaret or two, and it *was* my name.

Several minutes passed. The breathy voice that sounded like the end of a sigh came on.

"Hello?"

"Mrs. Warren, I meant what I told you before your husband walked in on us yesterday. Your life is in danger. Even though you can't testify against him, you can still tell people you saw him carry that body out—"

"My husband would never hurt me! He wouldn't," she said petulantly. "And you don't know what I saw that day. Nobody knows but me!"

"What you saw? I thought it was a dream."

There was silence.

"Don't be a fool, Mrs. Warren. Please. Can we talk? Will you meet me—"

"You're jealous. You're jealous of me. That's why you're doing this." God help her, she sounded victorious. "Don't bother me again or I'll call the police!"

She hung up.

I went to the window and rested my forehead against the cool glass. There was one other person who'd been where Tessa was the day of the fire. Someone who might have seen the same thing.

It was a long shot.

Playing basketball in school had taught me sometimes you have to take those.

***

Tailors and dressmakers can tell you things they don't even know they're telling about their customers. The trick is to get them talking without arousing suspicion.

"Oh, my, yes. I used to do all the sewing for Tessa and Jane and their mother," this one bragged. "Lovely people, all of them. They were all such *ladies*."

She was fiercely girdled, her plump form decorated by a measuring tape around her neck and a pincushion on her wrist. I'd told her I'd heard she was the magic behind Tessa Warren's fine wardrobe. It seemed smarter than saying I'd picked up her name while knocking on doors in their old neighborhood.

"Tessa looked like an angel in everything I ever made for her," she enthused. "An absolute *angel*. And taste — my stars. Sometimes she drove her poor mother crazy putting her foot down, insisting on a different material than what we were planning."

The dressmaker had been on her knees, chalking the hem of a garment under construction, when I entered the shop. Now the customer having a fitting was gone, and a woman who seemed to be an assistant had disappeared through a curtain at the back of the shop. We were sitting across from each other, the dressmaker on an upholstered bench and me on a slipper chair.

"It always looked just perfect on her though. Of course it would, with those looks. Poor Jane was on the plain side, I'm afraid."

I seized my opportunity.

"You know, all the way over here I was trying to think of Jane's husband's name, and for the life of me I couldn't, or her husband's either."

"Mosley," she said. "I don't recall his given name, but I ran into her one day and she joked that he's the last one in the phone book." She lowered her voice even though the assistant I'd noticed would be well out of range. "She didn't marry as well as her sister. I think he's a teacher. Has to do her own sewing now, I expect."

She frowned, remembering why I'd come.

"Now, you said when you came in that you're hunting a dressmaker. I can't take you personally — my eyes aren't what they used to be, I'm afraid, or knees either. But my niece started working with me when she was in grammar school. She does lovely work and is starting to get her own customers. If you wanted me to call her in to take your measurements...."

I heard the sound of a door in back, and supposed the niece had just returned from some task. I stood up, gathering my purse.

"Oh, I'm afraid I'm meeting someone."

We had some more polite back-and-forth, I said I'd have to call, and I took my leave. To my surprise, the assistant I'd thought I'd heard returning stood just out of sight of the shop window, lighting a cigarette. She'd gone out instead.

"Don't believe the sainthood stories," she said to me.

"What?"

"Saint Tessa. I guess you're a friend of hers, but she treated my aunt like dirt when they came here. I went to school with Tessa, sang in a choir with her. I know what she's like. All that gushing turned my stomach."

Her head went back defiantly, waiting for my reaction. I fished a card from my pocket and handed it to her.

"I didn't come here hunting a dressmaker. I needed to find out her sister's last name."

The assistant chuckled and swept a fleck of tobacco off the tip of her tongue with a fingertip.

"You're good." She had chestnut hair and a wryness which she probably had to hide a lot. "I take it Tessa wouldn't tell you?"

"Tessa didn't seem to like me much when I tried to talk to her."

"She doesn't like anyone other than Tessa. I suppose I sound jealous. Maybe I am. But she's been a snot her whole life. That wonderful fashion sense my aunt was going on about, and how Tessa would pick different fabrics? If she couldn't get her way by turning all big-eyed and crying, she'd make herself faint."

"Actually faint?"

"It sure looked genuine. They even called a doctor once. I think she held her breath or something. Of course she had that fairy princess act down to a T."

"Is she looney?"

The assistant shrugged.

"She liked to say things that set her apart," she said thoughtfully. "She knew it would get attention. It was very... clever, in a childish sort of way. Made her fascinating even when we didn't believe her. Once she said the art teacher had asked her to take off her clothes so he could paint her. Another time she said she knew a man with lots of money who'd marry her in a flash because she'd seen him do something naughty."

I tried not to show particular interest.

"Did you believe her?"

Her cigarette was almost done. She crushed it under her foot.

"Tessa may have believed it. The rest of us didn't. I've got to get back."

FORTY-THREE

Jane Mosley had told the dressmaker they were the last Mosley in the phone book. The one in my office listed a Z.W. Mosley, but no one answered there. On the off chance the book had changed since the two women talked, I tried the listing above it, but the woman who identified herself as that Mrs. Mosley wasn't named Jane.

Twice more that afternoon I tried Z.W. Mosley. I checked on Neal. I checked on Corrine. I fidgeted. I took a walk to clear my head. When I got back from the walk I sat down and typed a note to Gilead and Sophia.

Every floor in the building had a utility closet, but those small spaces held only a sink for filling scrub buckets and a trash can on wheels for emptying wastebaskets from the various offices. The buckets and mops and such that the women used every night all stayed in a janitor's closet downstairs. It was the same closet with the obsolete door opening into the gap between buildings. I didn't want to use the door just then, but the room itself seemed like the best place to leave a note where the women would see it and no one else would. I found what I surmised were clean rags since they weren't stiff as boards, spread one across a bucket, and put the envelope I'd addressed to them on the top.

I needed a favor.

***

Nobody answered my knock at the address I was guessing belonged to Jane Mosley. It worried me. I decided to ask a next door neighbor if they'd gone somewhere.

"Why no," she said. "Jane's usually home in the afternoon. Perhaps she went shopping. Or maybe she's at her book club, except I think that's on Tuesdays. Shall I tell her who stopped?"

"My name wouldn't mean anything," I said genially. "We have a mutual friend."

I was starting to feel uneasy.

***

Whoever had been monkeying around in my office was likely to try again. I'd learned enough to make them sweat, so chances were even they'd try again tonight. This time, though, they'd be smart enough to wait until the cleaning women finished up.

Most offices in the building closed at half-past five, but the podiatrist on the second floor stayed open until seven most weeknights. Sophia and Gilead came to work at seven thirty. They generally finished somewhere between midnight and one in the morning. Knowing that schedule allowed me to have a nice long nap at Mrs. Z's.

At half-past eleven I took a slow pass down Patterson in front of my building. There were only two cars on the street, and neither looked occupied. Our building's service entrance as well as its main both opened on this side. Since there was no discernible door at the rear, there'd be no reason to station a lookout in the alley. I checked anyway.

To kill time I went to an all-night diner. When I got back to Patterson, there was a different car parked across from my place. I saw a shape on the driver's side as I passed.

I wasn't worried about being spotted. My car tonight was a jalopy borrowed from the young assistant at Wheeler's Garage and I had my hair tucked up under a man's cap. I rounded the corner, doused my lights, and did a U-turn, pulling to the curb. I got out and hugged the shadows back to where I could watch the guy in the car. He made no move to get out. I counted to sixty in case he was slow, then drove into the alley.

It was pitch black. Roof overhangs blocked moon and stars. There were no outside lights. As soon as my eyes had adjusted, I got out and, with my .38 at my side, walked the alley's length. Satisfied no one was watching, I made my way through the narrow passage to the old door.

As I'd requested in my note, it was wedged open slightly. Getting in was harder than getting out, and I had to squeeze some, but I managed. Then I stood amid the damp smell of recently used mops and rags, waiting for my breath to slow.

Before leaving Mrs. Z's I'd changed into gum-soled shoes. My steps were soundless as I made my way along the back hall. Through a half-open door I could see the night watchman playing cards with pals, as he did most nights. When I heard them laying their cards down and figured eyes were intent on the table and who had the winning hand, I crept by.

Next it was a matter of up one flight of stairs and listen; up another flight and listen. I was on my own floor now. Ducking through the door from the stairwell to avoid weak light from a single bulb above it, I stood watching and listening. The only other night illumination came from an equally feeble bulb at the far end next to the elevator. After several minutes my eyes caught a splinter of yellow leaking beneath the door to my office.

Shifting my weight from heel to toe with each step, I moved without noise. My pulse had accelerated, but I moved with confidence on my home turf. As I neared my door, I bent low to keep from being seen through the frosted glass panel on top. I was holding my breath.

Now I was in position. I watched for a minute. Sure enough, I caught sight of a shape moving inside. Then came a whispered spurt of speech, followed at once by another. Like last night, there were two of them, though right now I couldn't see either. Then one bobbed up from rifling my desk drawers. His chum was probably keeping lookout where the opening door would give cover if someone came through it.

I took a breath.

"Guns down, hands up!" I ordered slamming the door back hard as I switched on lights.

The door banged into the wall, and I knew I'd been wrong about where the second guy was. He stepped out of the corner next to the window, hands empty, while the figure in front of me dropped a gun on the desk. I snagged the weapon with my free hand while the intruders were still half blind. Finally I took a look at the one closest to me.

Skinny and ratlike. Lank hair.

"Oats Ripley," I said through my teeth. "You lying s.o.b., I ought to put a bullet in you just for the aggravation you've caused me."

He tried to make a run for it, but I tripped him, following up with a shove that sent his top half sprawling onto my desk. Stuffing the semi-automatic he'd relinquished into my pocket I ground the nose of my .38 against the back of his head.

"Whoa, whoa, honey. Wait. You got this all wrong," said the one by the window.

For the first time, I spared him more than a glance... and tried not to stare. I'd never seen a live person who was that pale. His hair was white even though he looked like he hadn't hit fifty. His skin was equally void of color. Pink rimmed his squinting eyes. If he wasn't a true albino, he was close.

Albino. The association dropped faster than a hooker's drawers.

Albino.

Eskimo.

They sounded vaguely similar. Rare and exotic. To someone who seldom used either word they'd be easily confused.

"No, I've got it just about right," I said slowly. "You hire an ex-con who's threatened me all over town to break into my office. You come with him because you want to know what I've dug up on Cy Warren. And because you hope something in my files will lead you to Neal Vanhorn so you can threaten him some more and maybe kill him—"

"We only wanted to talk—"

"Save your breath. He didn't see anything. But there's another witness who'll put you there."

"Warren? He's a lying bastard. I saw him go inside."

"Be sure and tell the cops."

Oats was inching his spread arms toward his body, waiting for my attention to lapse so he could launch himself back from the desk. I tapped his skull to get his attention.

"Lock your hands together behind your head, Oats. Now stand up."

Once you've done the first, the second isn't as easy as usual. It kept him from making any fast moves. My voice was hard enough, and we had history enough, for him to think twice rather than cross me.

"Now spread your legs. Wider. Wider!"

Whitey had let his hands sag to shoulder level. He was looking worried.

"Okay, I went about this wrong. You've got dirt on Warren. I'll pay you for it. Two hundred dollars. Simple as that."

"So some boy you've picked gets elected instead and you get the spoils?"

He shrugged.

"Good a reason as any. What do you say?"

"I don't take bribes. Or do business with people who hire goons to split my face open—"

"Hey! That wasn't me! It was Warren—"

"Or to rough up a blind woman."

He didn't have an answer for that one.

"Move over there." I gestured to a spot closer to Oats where I could keep an eye on them both. I took the gun Oats had been carrying out of my pocket. "Now get down on your knees."

Whitey stayed calmer than most men would. He shook his head.

"Listen, honey, you do anything to me and you'll be in a peck of trouble."

"Call me 'honey' again and you'll go out that window head first. Get down."

Whitey complied. Making sure there was a round in the chamber, I popped the magazine from the semi. The eyes of both men followed my every move. I put the gun on the desk and marched Oats over where he could reach it.

"Now, Oats, unclasp your hands and pick up the gun. See if you can put one in the wall beside my door."

"What?" He croaked like he thought I'd taken leave of my senses.

"You heard me."

He picked the weapon up uncertainly. My .38 pressed his head to discourage creativity. The needles prickling the hand he'd been clasping behind his head probably would have deterred it in any case. He fired at the wall. Plaster flew. Before he could think about making trouble, I hit the back of his head with the Smith & Wesson and knocked him cold.

As I reached for the phone, Whitey saw what I meant to do next. He got to his feet.

"You've got plenty of piss and vinegar," he said mildly. "You ought to see the futility of keeping me here. It's your word against mine. I've got the right friends. The kind that come with getting people elected. I wouldn't spend fifteen minutes in the police station — and I'd get an apology."

"The cops in this town aren't crooked."

He smiled.

"Police are small potatoes, honey."

He tossed a business card onto my desk.

"If you change your mind about filling me in on Warren, my offer's still good."

He strolled out.

FORTY-FOUR

Jane Mosley's house radiated cheer and contentment, starting with its bright blue color. The trim and picket fence were white. Pink and white impatiens overflowed a flowerbed under the front windows. It was half the size of her sister's house, and more modest than the one she'd grown up in, but there was a swing on the front porch and what looked like a nice size yard in back.

I'd been considerably relieved when Jane answered her phone this morning. She'd agreed to see me at two, and I was a little bit early, so I sat for a minute, enjoying the view and the sense that good people lived here. It reduced the bad taste lingering in my mouth from watching the albino walk out of my office last night.

Galling as it was, I'd recognized truth when he said it would be his word against mine. So I'd called the cops, and when they came I said I'd seen two men, but one had gone out the window when Oats shot at me. The lateness of the hour and the bullet hole next to the door had prompted the police to say I could come in this morning to make a formal statement, which I had.

Given the widely known threats Oats had made against me, as well as his lengthy rap sheet, he was facing a charge of attempted murder. As might be expected, he'd turned himself inside out insisting I'd held a gun at his head and forced him to shoot at the wall. It had been met with snickers. A slick lawyer wasn't likely to get him off this time. Oats was going to enjoy a long vacation behind bars.

That part put a spring in my step as I went up the walk to the blue house and rang the bell.

"Oh, hello," smiled a brown haired woman with a friendly face and a sprinkle of freckles across the nose. "You must be Miss Sullivan. Come in."

The living room was sunny, with ruffled curtains at the windows and books piled everywhere. Two rocking chairs with footstools shared a floor lamp. A comfortable looking sofa was covered in chintz.

"Goodness, it looks like you took a tumble," said Jane as we sat down. "I hope it wasn't that nasty hump in the sidewalk down from where we used to live. It sent me sprawling more than a few times."

I laughed. "No, they've fixed that. Your old postman pointed it out to me when we were walking around."

I'd told her on the phone than I was collecting information about the neighborhood where she'd lived before the flood. She might have gotten the idea I was working on some kind of history.

"I hope you don't mind lemonade," she said, offering a glass. "I've been canning for two days, yesterday at a friend's house and today over here. I'm still a bit overheated.

"You know, I think I remember that postman. He was always so jovial. He'd ask what mischief we were up to if my sister and I were playing out on the porch — which we didn't do often. I'm afraid my mother had rather odd ideas about what well-brought-up girls should do." She made a face.

"What kind of ideas?" I wanted to steer the conversation right to Tessa, but I knew I'd do better if I put her at ease first.

"Oh, you know ... too much fresh air spoils your skin, gives you a ruddy complexion, makes your hair frizzy. That kind of thing. Now I have a little patch of garden in back. Not much, just peas, tomatoes, string beans, lettuce. Puttering in it is absolute heaven.

"Goodness. I'm rattling. I should let you ask questions."

"Hey, I like to hear about gardens. And the lemonade's great. What I wanted to ask about your old neighborhood, though, was the flood — the day of the fire."

She nodded, more serious now.

"I remember, of course. I was quite frightened. My father kept saying we had to leave, but my mother was afraid to get in the boat."

"Could you see the stores behind you? The ones that burned?"

"Oh yes. They were just across the alley from our back yard. Tessa and I shared a bedroom, and we could see the backs of half a dozen shops from our windows. It was wonderful entertainment. Arguments. A man who liked to come out and sneak a drink from his hip flask. A prissy clerk who got in a hair-pulling match with another woman."

"I'm interested in what your sister saw that afternoon. About a clothing dummy. I'm trying to find out what became of a man who disappeared at the drugstore that day."

She looked startled.

"Then it's Tessa you need to be talking to, isn't it?"

"I did, yesterday, but her husband came home. He didn't like it."

"I don't suppose he would. He has political ambitions. I've never been able to fathom why he married her, given the way—"

She broke off.

"The way what?"

She shook her head.

"Mrs. Mosley. Your sister claims now that what she told about seeing — the mannequin carried out — was just a bad dream. I think her husband has pushed her into believing that. Half believing it anyway. Is that possible?"

"I... don't know. Look, she's my sister. I don't want to tell tales out of school. I'd only sound jealous. I suppose I am — not of her house or her husband's importance. My husband's a principal. He cares about people because that's how he is, not because of what they can do for him. But I *am* jealous because they have a wonderful little girl. Hannah. And they don't even *care*. We'd give anything to have a child, but I haven't been able to...."

She fished out a handkerchief and dabbed at her eyes.

"The missing man's daughters have wondered about him for years," I said softly. "Learning what happened would give them some kind of peace."

The handkerchief pressed her mouth. After a moment she sighed.

"Yes. I see how awful it would be, not knowing. Still...."

"Did your sister really see what she told that policeman she'd seen? What she told your family?"

"I - I'm not sure. I think she might have. I'd stepped away from the window just then."

Ice water thrown on me couldn't have felt any worse. I'd been counting on Jane to substantiate things.

"Things were awfully chaotic by then," she was saying. "Most of our neighbors had already evacuated. Mama called for me to come to our bedroom door. She said we had to go, and not to alarm Tessa. She never understood that Tessa didn't *get* scared, only excited.

"I went back to take Tessa's arm — we had to do that sometimes, just steer her away from something she was interested in, or she'd pitch a fit. Tessa was pointing and chattering about men putting out a big dolly."

She took a breath. She drank some lemonade. Her hand was shaking.

"I wasn't paying attention. I knew we had to get out — not miss the next boats that were coming around to rescue people. Tessa wouldn't budge.

She was pointing, screaming that she wanted to go get the dolly so she could play with it."

The account was so gripping I was afraid to stem the flow by asking a question. She paused, though, and by the look in her eyes, I knew she was reliving the incident.

"Did you look?" I prompted.

She blinked.

"Yes. I was so frustrated... Yes."

"What did you see?"

"Behind a garbage can — wedged up tight against the drugstore — I saw a leg sticking out. Trousers and a shoe. It could have been a mannequin that washed up there and got stuck. All kinds of things were bobbling past. But I was old enough to know people drowned in floods. I thought that's what we were seeing. Some poor soul...."

Her voice trailed off.

"And the part about two men?"

Jane chose her words carefully.

"Tessa finds ordinary things quite tedious. She might watch the same thing you and I did, but if it didn't suit her, she'd see it differently. It's not lying, really. I think she convinces herself that's how it is. Only...."

When she didn't say any more, I nudged things a little.

"You saw something too?"

"A rowboat. A small one. A man dragged it out of a lean-to behind the drugstore. He yelled back into the store and another man came running out — of the drugstore, that is. He knelt and reached back inside as if he was doing something. Then he jumped in the boat and the two of them took off, paddling like mad, whooping and laughing as if they were having the time of their lives.

"I had to smack Tessa to make her let go of the window. We'd barely gotten out of our room when there was an explosion. Across at the buildings we'd been watching. It shook things so we stumbled. I knew we had to get out, and I dragged Tessa, and we got downstairs just as a boat already full of other people was pulling up. We all got in and I heard somebody yell 'Fire!' and all I remember after that is Tessa and me and our parents hanging onto each other for dear life, and getting soaked by the rain, and people crying."

Jane looked drained. I felt bad about putting her through it.

"How did your sister meet her husband?" I asked.

The change of direction surprised her.

"She went to work for his realty firm. It stunned us, actually, her taking a job. Some girls did of course, until they married. But we didn't need to support ourselves, and Tessa was hardly a suffragist. Still, she's always gloried in things that set her apart."

"But you knew Cy from the neighborhood where you lived before the flood. You both did."

"Well, yes, but he was a good deal older than us. Already grown."

"You both knew him by sight, though."

"Yes, of course. His father had the menswear store. He'd be out and about sometimes when we went for groceries, or to get shoes repaired. Why?"

"Could Cy have been one of the men you saw in the rowboat?"

Jane grew very still. She got up and went to the window, her back toward me. Her finger traced the curtain ruffle as if for reassurance.

"It — looked enough like him that it occurred to me a time or two before they were married. But it can't have been. It's - it's too outlandish." She turned suddenly to face me again. "If that's what you came here for, to make trouble, I think you should leave."

FORTY-FIVE

When I got back to my office I called the Ford Street station, and thanked my lucky stars that Seamus was working the desk.

"A woman I met today may have some people come around looking to hurt her," I said. "Next time the patrol in her area checks in, could you ask them to keep an eye out? I'll fill you in later." I could hear his pencil scraping as he took down the address.

"And say, Mick got told to stop and talk to Lieutenant Freeze on his way off shift. Could be they're going to have a look at him after all."

"I'll keep my fingers crossed," I said. It was the closest anything had come to good news all day.

Since I hadn't finished my lemonade at Jane's house, I made myself a gin and tonic and carried it over while I stood at the window. For the umpteenth time I wondered whether I should have warned her she could be in danger. I thought the chances were slim it would even occur to Cy that she'd seen anything. Even Tessa might never have realized it, self-absorbed as she appeared to be. Mostly, though, I'd concluded Jane wouldn't believe what her sister had pulled or how ruthless Cy was.

By calling Seamus, I'd done all I could to ensure the safety of a nice woman content with her cozy home and her garden. I leaned my forehead against the window.

Too many decent people were at risk in this case. Jane and Tessa, and I'd even stretch the decent part to include Neal. I hoped the Vanhorn sisters and the nice old dime store clerk Theda were in the clear now that I'd unearthed the one witness Cy had to fear. I couldn't be sure. I was starting to see that men like Cy and the albino had no more regard for those who stood in their way than for a wad of gum on their shoes. From now on I'd stick to cases I understood. Ones with crooks and killers and blackmailers. Not family matters that led in directions never anticipated by those who hired me.

Then I realized this whole case had begun with a killer. The Vanhorn sisters had hired me to look into what they believed was a murder. They'd been right. But between that crime and now, a quarter century of people living their lives had intruded.

"Hey, Sis, if you're thinking of jumping, you need to open the window first."

I chuckled and turned to see Heebs strolling in.

"Hey, why aren't you selling papers?"

The clock on my wall said five till five. Prime time for peddling the evening edition.

"One of the guys lost a bet to me," he said with a grin. "Has to sell all my papers before he sells his own."

"What if he doesn't cough up the money for yours?"

"Some of the guys heard him bet me. They'll see he makes good. You're looking a hundred percent again, Sis. Since I don't have to work my corner, I thought maybe you'd need some errands run."

I returned to my desk and put down the half-empty glass. Heebs was in my visitor's chair, legs stretched out and hands clasped behind his head like Connelly did.

"Sorry, Heebs. I wish I could give you odd jobs on some kind of regular basis, but most months I do well to pay my expenses, and some months not even that."

Guilt nipped me at the thought my expenses included meals and a nice place to sleep. Heebs' bed was a doorway somewhere most nights.

"See, that's why you need an assistant," he said sitting eagerly forward. "You could get sheets of paper made up advertising your services. 'Discreet, confidential, experienced'. Something like that. Then when things were slow, I'd take some around to places. Drum up business."

I already was laughing and shaking my head. The devil of it was, it had some appeal.

"There'd be the cost of the printing for starters. That doesn't come cheap."

"Okay, then, I could type 'em up, get six or eight on a page."

"Can you type?"

"I learn fast — and I spell real good."

His pitch was interrupted by the ringing phone.

"You were right!" gasped a whispering voice. "I should have listened!"

"Tessa?"

"He's - he's after me! Help me. Help me please! I've got to hide—"

Her voice rose on the last, and there was the sound of a phone being dropped.

"Tessa!"

I couldn't tell if she'd dropped the phone voluntarily or it had been knocked from her hand. I might already be too late to help, but I had to try. And getting anyone else but me there was going to be tricky.

My eye fell on my wastebasket, mostly unused today. I grabbed out the card the albino had tossed on my desk. I dialed the number on it while Heebs watched with quickening excitement.

"You want dirt on Cy Warren?" I said to whoever answered. "Get to his house — fast!"

With my left hand I banged down the phone. With my right, I scribbled Warren's name and another number in big letters. I grabbed my .38 from the pocket under my chair, giving orders to Heebs as I made for the door.

"There's the number for Market House. Tell them you're calling from my office. Tell them to get to former councilman Cy Warren's house. His wife is about to kill him."

***

When I got back from Jane's, I'd parked a few doors down from my building. I took off at record speed, hoping someone among us got there in time. Telling the cops the truth, that Tessa was the one at risk, might have caused them to waste time walking on egg shells because of Cy's status. The albino or whoever he sent — if he acted at all — might be useless once he got there.

Second thoughts over my own audacity gnawed at me as I raced north over the river. If I was wrong about Tessa being in danger — if she'd been turning a molehill into a mountain in one of her little fantasies when she called — the police would put a black mark by my name that didn't erase.

My pulse was pounding by the time I turned onto the curving boulevard where Cy lived. Men had started to come home from work. There were cars in driveways. Would Cy be crazy enough to risk murder at this time of day, with neighbors around?

Why not? He'd committed one in the midst of a flood.

Whooping and laughing as if they were having the time of their lives....

I tried to shake off the image from Jane's account as I pulled up in front of Cy's house and took a couple of breaths before going in. Several cars were parked on the street. Maybe one belonged to the albino. Maybe not. There weren't any squad cars, and my straining ears detected no hint of a siren. I couldn't delay.

At the front door I slid the .38 out of its holster and rang the bell. I stepped to the side where I'd be out of view when it opened. If the maid came to answer, I'd feel foolish. There were worse things.

No one answered. I tried the door. It was locked. Keeping down, out of sight of the windows, I ran to the back.

The kitchen door had four concrete steps leading up to it, and a pane of glass maybe a foot square. Ducking down again, I approached it and peeked inside.

Due to the miserly size of the glass, I couldn't see much. To my right, toward the center, I could see one end of a plain looking kitchen table. Almost directly in front of me, a door to what looked like it might be a pantry stood ajar. My eyes came to rest on it and my breath caught. Just outside it lay a high-heeled shoe that assuredly hadn't been worn by the maid with bad knees. Beyond that a silver teapot lay on its side. Peeping out of the pantry door, on the floor, was a slender leg in a dove gray stocking.

If the maid was anywhere in the house, she'd be beyond helping anybody. I listened and heard only silence and knew it could be the sound of someone waiting for me. Maybe Tessa was still alive. Maybe Cy was still there and I could hold him at bay until someone else arrived to witness him red handed. Balancing my Smith & Wesson, I eased the door open and stepped in.

My eyes swept right and I stopped in confusion. It was the same instant the barrel of a gun pressed the back of my head.

FORTY-SIX

"I don't like you," said Tessa's voice. Its cloud of gauziness had fallen away. It was the voice of a vexed child.

"Put your gun on the table right now or I'll shoot you," she said. "I will. I know how. One of my sister Jane's beaus taught me. I stole him from Jane." She giggled.

"Okay. Sure," I agreed. "I'm too far away, though."

I was staring at the opposite end of the table, the one I hadn't been able to see through the small window. Cy sat slumped in a chair, his head on the table, his eyes unfocused. I could feel Tessa nudging me forward. I put my gun down.

"Did you shoot him?" I asked nodding at Cy. I knew he wasn't dead. I could see him breathing.

"Oh, no," she said serenely. "I just gave him some of my pills. The ones he's always pushing at me. I don't take them often. Just when I'll have to sit through one of those dreadfully dull affairs where everybody makes speeches. I had to keep him until you got here so I could shoot you both."

She'd stepped around me now. We could see each other. I wouldn't bet on her aim, but her hand was remarkably steady as it held a small revolver.

"Everyone's going to feel so sorry for me," she said with a delighted sigh. "You pushed your way into our home and shot him — right in front of me. You'd have shot me, too, so I had to kill you." She smiled dreamily. "I'll make such a pretty widow. Good political wives are hard to find, ones who sit through speeches and smile and remember names. I'll be snapped up."

I'd faced stone-cold killers who hadn't unsettled me half as much as this woman standing dreamy eyed with a gun in her hand.

"You... bitch," mumbled a thick voice.

Cy was coming around. I wasn't sure which one of us he meant. I still didn't hear the sound of a siren, or even a car rushing up.

"Tessa, listen," I said. "If you tell that you saw Cy dragging that body out when you were a kid, he'll go to prison. I know who the dead man was. Once you tell the police, and say Cy discovered you'd seen him, you'll be safe."

"Are you stupid?" She actually stamped her foot. "If he's not important, I'm not important! I'd be disgraced. With him dead, I'll do just fine."

"Sweetheart... we can work this out...."

Cy had managed to push up on his arms enough to raise his head. Funny how the prospect of immediate death can clear your mind.

"I don't trust you, Cy." Tessa's gun, which had been favoring me, shifted toward her husband.

"She spoiled it. She spoiled everything. Before that, you wouldn't have hurt me. You thought I believed that nonsense you fed me about what I saw all being a dream."

Cy's breathing was odd, deep and labored. His muscles tensed and slackened, tensed and slackened. I darted a glance at the gun I'd put on the table, but he'd be a fool to try for it. So would I. Was he heading into some kind of seizure?

"Sweetheart...." he said hoarsely.

"But then *she* found out," Tessa went on as if she hadn't heard him. "She found out about me and came to the house and - and after that, I knew I couldn't trust you. You'd kill me so she didn't have proof."

"Tessa! Think. Kill her... 's no danger to... either of us. Two dead... make them suspicious."

A flicker in her eyes told me she was considering it. I thought I heard something outside.

"No," she decided, her tone becoming that of a peevish child. "I like my plan."

"Fine. 'Long as she gets what's coming to her," he said harshly.

"Like Alf got his when you killed him?" If I could keep the two of them arguing someone might get here.

"Sure I got rid of Alf. Just like I did that poor sap who walked in on us as we were pushing the shelves down on old man Dillon. Alf had ideas — he's the one who when word came of fires downtown ran over and said he knew how to get what we wanted — how to be more than clerks all our lives."

He gave an ugly laugh. Anger was making him lucid. "What he didn't have was guts. He panicked when he heard those biddies tell you what they'd heard when they were kids. Called me and said we had to do something. So I did."

His eyes glittered hatred at me. He tried a new approach with his wife.

"I'd have gotten rid of this meddler too, not you, you little fool. But go ahead — try to explain two bodies. You'll rot in jail."

Tessa looked uncertain, wary of his sudden smugness. I played into it.

"Shooting him would be self defense, Tessa. I'd swear that's what it was. You'd be safe then."

"No. You - you'd tell lies about me."

"Suppose I did?" I said. "It's you they'd believe. You're the pretty one."

Her attention wavered between Cy and me. She was losing confidence.

"Tessa...." Cy broke off, giving a gasp and clutching his chest. "What was in — what did you give me?" He staggered to his feet, leaning heavily on the table and gripping its edge. "Poison — I'm having... a heart attack."

Tessa wore a puzzled look. I saw his fingers shift. I realized what he intended, but before I could decide whose side to be on, he shoved the table.

It slammed into Tessa with brutal force, knocking her backward. Desperation gave him strength. As he released the table he heaved upward, sending it over on top of her as she fell.

By design or accident, the edge of the table caught my shoulder as I tried to dodge. I stumbled, going down on one knee. As I tried to recover my footing and spot my gun that had slid from the table, Cy went past, shoving me flat. Tessa had already wiggled and kicked herself free of the weight on top of her. She fired wildly. I grabbed for her skirt and yanked her toward me, trying to catch her arm to get her gun. My fingers closed on her sleeve. Tessa swung at me with her free hand, bucking and twisting like a rabid cat.

Behind me metal screeched and groaned. I heard a faint hissing. My nostrils caught an odor. Gas. Jesus.

"'Limpie?" called a frightened little voice from the depths of the house. "'Limpie? Where are you?"

I froze. *Their kid.*

Tessa used my lapse of attention to pull free. She brought the gun up, aimed at something beyond me.

"Tessa, no! Gas!"

I slugged her as hard as I could and dazed her enough that she dropped the gun. A door slammed behind us. Acutely aware how this struggle was using up what little strength I'd regained in the past week, I slugged her again. This time I knocked her out cold.

A key rattled in a lock. My blood ran cold at the sound.

"*Limpie!*" the child called again.

Stumbling to my feet, I ran to the kitchen door in time to see Cy disappearing. He'd locked the door from the outside. I pounded it with my palms.

"Damn you, Cy, your kid's in here!"

Frantically my eyes swept the door frame, the nearby wall. There was an empty peg for a key. The gas line hung drunkenly where Cy had yanked it loose at the stove. I paused just long enough to kick the revolver Tessa had dropped away from her reach. Then I ran for the stairs.

The little girl huddled fearfully at the top.

A pretty mite of about three, she had her mother's hair, but the terror in her eyes told me the child lived firmly in reality. At sight of me, she bolted and ran.

"Wait!"

Halfway up the stairs, I began to feel lightheaded. This time I knew it wasn't because my ribs were taped — and that I didn't have much time. Breathing as little as possible, I climbed on. What was the kid's name? Her aunt had told me just hours ago. Annna? Hannah.

"Hannah?" I called as I neared the top. "Hannah? I'm your Aunt Jane's friend. She wants me to bring you to her. Where are you?"

There was no answer. Then a small voice said, "Aunt Jane?"

I spotted her peeking uncertainly from the last door on the left end of the hall.

"That's right. Aunt Jane has lemonade. I'll bet she'd read you a story, too."

Everything was fine now. Everything was lovely.

No! I was succumbing to the gas. It seemed worse on the stairs. Worse up here. I moved toward Hannah as briskly as I was able.

"Try not to breathe the stinky air, okay? It'll make you sick."

Her eyes were already drooping as I eased her fingers away from the doorjamb and lifted her. She was tiny, so the gas was affecting her more.

"Hold tight to my neck," I said. My legs weren't feeling too steady.

"No! Stringy! Don't leave Stringy!" She began to scream, arching and thrashing so she almost toppled me. Her hand reached frantically back.

I retraced a few precious steps and looked into the room.

"Your rag doll?" It sat on a shelf.

She nodded.

Still more squandered steps and she had it. Fighting an urge to close my eyes, I carried the child and the doll she clutched down the stairs. At the bottom I had to stop and rest against the newel post a minute. My legs felt wobbly... not connected to me....

My eyes snapped open. The door. I had to reach the front door. I started forward again and staggered.

Sweet Mary, I don't deserve any favors, but let this innocent little girl get out.

The pale blue carpet I'd thought so pretty the first time I saw it dragged at me like quicksand. I nearly fell as we reached the door. Hannah's head rested against my chest. Her eyes were closed. But she was breathing.

Breathing poison.

I shook her, rousing her a little.

"Hannah," I said thickly. "I have to put you down for a minute."

I propped her against the wall as if she were a doll herself. My fingers fumbled, turned the doorknob hard, then shook it in frustration. Locked. Thoughts floating now, I looked vaguely about. On the other side of the door from where I'd put Hannah, there was a pretty little table with a footed silver bowl. I veered over and peered in the bowl. Inside were a pair of gloves.

And a key.

It took three tries to fit it in the lock. It turned. Opening the door half a dozen inches brought me to my knees. I reached and pulled it wide in time to see a cop's puttees. They ran past my head and I felt hands preparing to lift me.

"No. Get the kid out." I pointed. "I'll be along. I just need a minute."

FORTY-SEVEN

I crawled outside and sat gulping air and saying some thank-yous. As soon as my legs would let me, I stood and rested my back on the door frame. More breathing cleared my head enough for me to see there was only a single patrol car parked at the curb. No sign of Cy Warren being arrested. His car was gone. He could be halfway to his political hangout by now, soon to have an excuse with his lackeys all swearing he'd been back for an hour. If I told how he'd tried to kill me and his wife and his daughter, he'd deny it all.

But Tessa might be mad enough that she'd tell on him now. About John Vanhorn, and about today. She was vain and childish and she'd tried to kill me, but Cy Warren didn't deserve to get away with yet another murder. If I was alive, chances were she was too.

I saw more cruisers arriving, one already pulling up with others behind it. There'd be help soon. Drawing a final breath of sweet, clean air, I went back inside.

Before I'd gone three steps, I knew I'd made a bad decision. The air was so thick I choked. A hundred miles away, at the kitchen door, I saw movement. An arm came up, and my blurring vision made out a gun.

"Tessa, no!" I croaked. "The spark—"

I turned and tried to run. Instead, I felt myself falling.

The fall accelerated. Everything around me spun upside down. Long seconds swirled past before my sputtering consciousness registered that strong arms had scooped me up.

Connelly. My body sensed it. Maybe it was a dream. Maybe the gas had already gotten to me. But I heard a fiercely pounding heart where my head pressed his chest.

I saw light. The dwindling of a fall day. Outside. We cleared the front steps and Connelly broke into a run. The patrol cars had gone, parked up the street in front of a different house.

Behind us something went *whump*. Connelly pulled me parallel to him and fell on top of me, covering my body with his and tucking the top of my head down under his chin.

"Don't breathe!" he shouted.

Searing heat blistered over us, wave after wave. After an eternity I felt Connelly's form lift a fraction. He turned his head to the side and coughed.

"You okay?" he asked hoarsely.

I nodded and coughed and gasped some air and coughed again.

"Yeah. Thanks." Once before he'd tried to save me. This time he had.

"What kind of fool woman runs back into a house filled with gas?"

"What kind of fool man runs in after her?"

His whole face hardened. Then he smiled.

"Sure you're okay, then?" He pushed up on his forearms, his eyes taking inventory.

"When my head clears, I will be. I was never as glad to see anyone in my life as I was you, Connelly." He flinched as I have him an awkward pat. "Shite, Mick! The back of your neck's burned."

"Worth it," he said with a wink.

A pair of cops thundered up. One knelt.

"Shall we make a stretcher for her? Sally's on the way."

"I'm okay," I rasped. Over Connelly's shoulder I could see flames shooting skyward. Sally, the City's only ambulance, operated by the police, couldn't help anyone now.

"The little girl. She's crying for her aunt. Do you know who that is?"

I told him. He and his partner trotted off shouting.

Connelly looked down at me

"I've dreamed of being with you like this more than a few times. Can't say it ever included a crowd."

Becoming aware of other voices, activity all around us, and sirens coming, I started to laugh. Connelly's rich, full chuckle resonated in my bones as well as my ears. His hand moved into my hair. Then, as he was maybe fixing to kiss me, Boike ran up.

"You two okay?"

I felt a faint disappointment. Connelly cleared his throat.

"Just need to catch our breath for a minute. That gas we breathed made us both pretty wobbly."

"Don't take too long, or you're gonna get trampled. Fire trucks are just turning into the street." He leaned around Connelly, speaking to me. "Freeze wants to see you, soon as you're able. Some muckety-muck claims he happened by to talk to Warren about a political matter and overheard him confess to two murders."

So I had heard someone outside.

"Make it three," I said. "Warren's wife was in there."

Boike went quiet. After a moment he rallied, pointing a finger at Connelly.

"And you — you're in Dutch, telling him you'd swipe a car if he didn't bring you too."

"Does this mean he won't want my help with that field demonstration he was starting to tell me about?" Connelly asked wryly.

Shaking his head, Boike left.

Connelly rolled off me and onto his elbow.

"Guess we better not get knocked about by fire hoses," he said.

He helped me up and we sat there awhile, shoulder to shoulder, leaning against each other.

FORTY-EIGHT

It was Saturday night, and I was celebrating. Cy Warren was in jail and would probably sit in Old Sparky. The Vanhorn sisters had cried some when I'd told them every detail I knew of their father's fate, but they'd thanked me a dozen times. So tonight I'd thrown caution to the wind and put on lipstick.

I stepped into Finn's and stopped in surprise. The place was packed.

Some tables had been moved out to clear space for a motley group of musicians. They were playing at breakneck speed and their faces glowed with joy. A rosy-cheeked girl sat next to my old concertina teacher, both pumping the little squeeze boxes on their knees while their fingers flew. Finn and a woman I didn't know were playing fiddles. There was a man with a long-necked mandolin of some sort, and another with the right kind of flute.

Sitting at the center of them, with one foot tapping, was Connelly with his whistle. His whole being radiated happiness.

As if drawn by a signal, he looked up and saw me. His eyes cut to the other players. Without missing a beat, they swung full tilt into a centuries old reel.

My throat closed over with emotions so intense I couldn't move.

The name of the tune was *Over the Moor to Maggie*.

ABOUT THE AUTHOR

Private Eye Writers of America named M. Ruth Myers a 2014 Shamus Award finalist for this book. Her novels have been translated into several languages, optioned for film and condensed for magazine publication. She has also written under the name Mary Ruth Myers.

A native of Missouri, Myers spent most of her growing up years in Wyoming. She returned to Missouri where she earned a Bachelor of Journalism degree from the University of Missouri. She worked as a reporter and feature writer on daily papers in Saginaw, Michigan, and Dayton, Ohio.

A fan of Irish traditional music, Myers plays (or attempts to play) concertina, button accordion and harp. She and her husband live in Ohio as domestic staff to an over-empowered cat. They have a grown daughter.

Www.mruthmyers.com

Facebook * Twitter * Pinterest

CPSIA information can be obtained
at www.ICGtesting.com
Printed in the USA
LVHW021420130620
657889LV00015B/2184

9 780615 965079